CHARLIE'S
TRUTH

Alistair Rainey

**Grosvenor House
Publishing Limited**

This book is published by
Grosvenor House Publishing Ltd
Link House
140 The Broadway, Tolworth, Surrey, KT6 7HT.
www.grosvenorhousepublishing.co.uk

This book is a work of fiction. Any resemblance to
people or events, past or present, is purely coincidental.

A CIP record for this book
is available from the British Library

ISBN 978-1-80381-092-8
eBook ISBN 978-1-80381-093-5

For

Nate and Travis

PREFACE

I've always been fascinated by Roman Britain since reading Rosemary Sutcliffe's novels as a child. In a long career as a primary teacher, I loved telling the stories of Boudicca's exploits or asking classes to form *testudo* with plastic shields and swords and advance on the enemy but never could I find the time to write my own story to embrace them. Now retired and living in Norfolk with my wife, Pam, and our black Labrador Flo, I have been able to indulge that writing desire.

On visiting the ancient site of *Venta Icenorum*, a Roman settlement just south of Norwich, I wondered how it would be to find oneself suddenly sucked back into that time. What wonders or dangers would a child of today find? How would they cope? With a sprinkling of Latin thrown in for a touch of authenticity, **Charlie's Truth** was written.

This is the children's first adventure but not their last together. Alfie's tale is in development and no doubt Saima's will follow too - look out for them soon. I hope that you enjoy the book and perhaps you might even recognise a bit of Charlie, Saima or Alfie in yourself. I'm sure there's a little bit of them all in each of us. What do you think?

PERSONAE

Charlie Hipkiss (Caius)
Saima Noor (Sabia)
Alfie Madely
Miss Nina Parton (Teacher)
Mrs Vearn (Classroom Assistant)
Miss Isadora Dean (Librarian and Museum Curator)
Adil Noor (Saima's Dad, Chair of the Council and Convenience Store Owner)
Mrs Noor (Saima's Mum)
Mr Tisbury (Councillor)
Mrs Knapp (Councillor)
Vitus (Soldier)
Faris (Leather Worker)
Drusus (Soldier and Contubernium Leader, Member of the 3rd Century)
Orcus (Clerk to Publicanus Lucius)
Publicanus Lucius (Senior Official at the fort)
Ruus (Metallus's Son)
Metallus (Metalworker, Smith)
Centurion (In command of the 3rd Century)
Mr Blewin (Property Developer)
Sergeant Mace (Policeman)
Headmaster (Wicton Primary and Nursery School)

(Other characters who play a small role are unnamed here. All names and persons described are purely fictional)

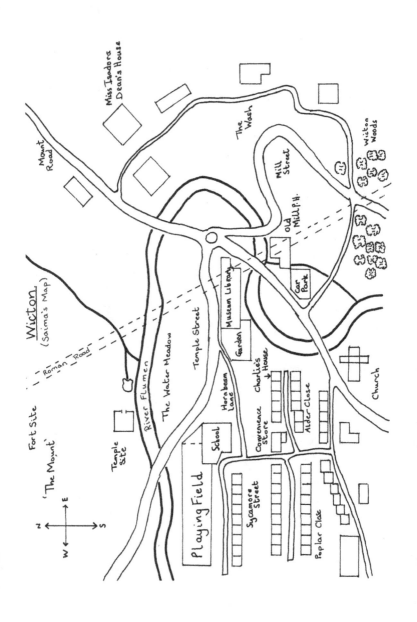

Wicton
(Saima's Map)

PROLOGUE

Big lies, little lies, fibs, porkies or whoppers – what's the difference? Nothing, of course; they're all lies! But *little lies* aren't that bad, are they? I expect you've heard about *little lies*.

Bet Mum or Dad has said…

"Come away from that screen, you'll get square eyes."

But you won't, so why do they say it?

It's all about someone's feelings or concerns. That's why someone tells a little lie. It's a *good* lie really, isn't it? It can keep everyone safe and happy and no relationship is harmed. All is well, and the lie is so small it hardly causes a ripple in the lake of truth.

Do you lie? You do, you know. We all do, but who taught you how to do it? Oh yeah, probably Mum or Dad or even both.

"Nearly there," they say when you're still fifty miles away from somewhere. So, it's OK to lie, isn't it? Adults do it all the time.

Imagine a slope with you on it, a bit like a slide. Truth is at the top; big lies are at the bottom, and in-between are all the little fibs and half-truths. Where are you on that oily slide? Slipping down? Can you climb up? Of course you could, but will you? You could dig in your nails and climb. It's steep, it's hard. Are you hiding something we should know? Hiding something can't be a lie, can it? Of course not. You're slipping…

Charlie *always* lied. Big lies, little lies – always lies! He lied about school, homework, breaking things, even stealing. You name it, he would lie about it. Lying got him into big trouble: he'd lie to get out of it. Lying was his saviour.

Saima always told the truth.

CHAPTER I

Charlie wasn't that keen on listening. Paying attention was hard when the grass outside the window was calling, and the class football in his eyeline seemed to glint and beckon him to play. The ball knew Charlie, mainly because Charlie used to play with it most playtimes. They'd won the FA Cup together, been selected for England together, gone to play at the World Cup in Brazil together... all on that grass beyond the classroom window.

It was 9.38am. Assembly had finished eight minutes ago, and it was another hour and two minutes until he could play in the first round of the European Cup. He fidgeted and scraped his chair, which irked Saima whose chair backed onto Charlie's. She turned, put her index finger to her lips and made a shushing sound. Charlie didn't know how to keep quiet. Just like his football pitch heroes, he'd whine at whoever would listen to any injustice done to him. On this occasion, Saima was the cause. Saima the truthful, attentive and hard-working; Charlie the liar, hating whatever lesson was coming, unless it was PE. He would do anything to delay the start and bring playtime closer. Here was an opportunity. Clutching his face, Charlie tumbled from his chair to the classroom floor. Saima had definitely hit him, hadn't she?

He lay there writhing, but when absolutely no notice was taken of his play-acting, he sat up, legs outstretched and bleated, "Awgh, Ref. Ref, did you see that?" Then remembering where he was... "Miss, Miss, Saima elbowed me off my chair for nothing."

Saima didn't look shocked, nor did Miss Parton; both rolled their eyes.

Charlie had blonde hair and striped eyebrows that he had gone on about having till his mum had given in; anything for a quiet life. His off-white polo shirt hung out the back of his mud-streaked, dark grey trousers caused by making a superb sliding tackle on the field before school. He now looked a rather small, forlorn figure who sat pleading for justice.

"Charlie, Charlie," said Miss Parton in a tender but resigned tone, "go with Mrs Vearn. She'll help, I'm sure, and I'll speak with the class about behaviour."

Both teacher and teaching assistant had a mass of experience when dealing with 'Charlies', and one good way was to keep calm and remove them for a short time to 'chill'. The class all watched as he left, heads turning towards the door. As they reached it, Miss Parton called out, "We've a special guest arriving at 10 o'clock, so not too long please, Mrs Vearn."

Barely satisfied but happy to escape the classroom even for a moment, Charlie hobbled out, forgetting his face, which was miraculously cured. He was now limping and was clutching his knee instead. As he left, Miss Parton gave a soothing wink in Saima's direction. Saima creased a gentle smile. Miss Parton knew Saima well, her best student and a good listener.

The door squealed its own complaint as it closed the last few centimetres.

"Right," she said after they'd gone. All heads swivelled back to look at their teacher. "This morning, we are going back in time, back two thousand years."

Alfie, whose tree wasn't overladen with conkers of wisdom, blurted, "Dinosaurs, Miss?"

At least a third of the class thought the same, but when three or four others laughed out loud, they kept their eyes down and said not a word.

"You're a few years out, Alfie, but I'm glad you're keen to learn and contribute."

Alfie had nearly crumpled with embarrassment when the laughter rang out, but his teacher's kind words lifted his spirits. Nina Parton, Miss, was like that. A young, enthusiastic teacher with a sense of all children having worth and, in turn, they felt valued. It was the reason she hadn't bawled at Charlie. He was Charlie; that was the way he was. Every teacher from Reception upwards had tried to leave their mark and effect change but never had the leopard, lightning centre-forward of Miss Parton's Year 5 changed his spots.

CHAPTER II

At 10 o'clock precisely, the classroom door squeaked open once more. The visitor, Miss Isadora Dean, gave it a stern glance. Upon her long, thin face was a nose like an eagle's beak, and nesting there were half-moon spectacles. They had a knobbly, gold and black chain that drooped from behind her ears and swayed on each side of her long and scrawny neck. These were the sort of glasses you could peer over and scowl at loud, unruly children, not that any of Miss Parton's class were loud or unruly when in Miss Dean's presence. Her aura spread through the room. She projected an invisible cloud of respect and, for some, fear. The latter hit Charlie. It made his insides shrivel like a wizened walnut. He made himself as small as possible as he sat in his chair that had been strategically placed beside that of Mrs Vearn.

Isadora Dean, who the children believed to be the 'Witch of Wicton', was chief librarian and curator of the village museum. She had served in both roles for forty or more years, and no one would ever have the nerve to suggest she might like to retire her voluntary services. On Mondays, Tuesdays and Wednesdays, she would leave her house, cross the bridge over the Flumen on Mount Road, then using the crossing by the mini roundabout on Temple Street, arrive at the library at ten sharp. On Thursdays, Fridays and Saturdays, she made the same journey but opened the museum next door, which was accessed through the library. On Sundays, children were sure she must stir her cauldron.

Charlie's fear was borne out of an incident in which he had visited the library with his school some time ago in February. He'd been hungry and decided to visit the convenience store at the end of his road, Alder Close. Saima's dad owned the shop and was busy that particular morning helping a customer find, of all things, parsley sauce. Near the till was the usual array of sweets and other goodies. With a swift glance to see if the coast was clear, he palmed a small chocolate bar and pushed it into his trouser pocket. Mr Noor looked up a moment too late.

"Morning, Charlie," he said.

Mr Noor knew most people on the estate and, in particular, the children as the school was so close. Mums would bring their babies in, of course, and he would see them grow and eventually go to the village school, Wicton Primary and Nursery.

"Can I help you?"

Charlie stuttered a little, thinking of a reasonable excuse to be in a shop when he had no money and should be on his way to school.

"Er... I called in to see if Saima was about. I... um... wanted to ask her about last night's homework," he lied.

"No, she left for school a quarter of an hour ago. You better hurry or you'll be late."

"OK, sorry, thanks," replied Charlie as he sidled out the door. He knew that Saima would have gone early as she helped sharpen pencils and pencil crayons for

Miss Parton before school. She was trusted with the old desktop sharpener. Charlie had taken it apart once when it had a broken lead stuck in it. Saima was horrified when he dismantled it but rather pleased when it worked better than before after he'd reassembled it.

On Wednesdays, Year 5 went to the library. It was a short walk down Hornbeam Lane, past the museum garden wall that curved elegantly to form a junction with Temple Street. Charlie was in the middle of the crocodile of pairs that walked that morning. His partner was Alfie. He managed to persuade Alfie to be on the outside of his pair nearest the road; this was so that he was in the best position not to be noticed. Remembering his chocolate, he fished it out from his pocket. The bar was no longer solid; it was limp. As Charlie started to unwrap it, Alfie's eyes lit up.

"Wow, give us some!" he exclaimed.

"Hush up," hissed Charlie through clenched teeth.

Charlie tore off the top rectangle. It was more squidgy than he imagined. He gave it to Alfie, who pushed it against the roof of his mouth with his tongue. It oozed and melted, glueing up his teeth and tonsils. Charlie ate several himself and put the open wrapper with the remainder of the chocolate back in his pocket. At the library, Miss Dean greeted the class at the door.

"Have they washed?" she asked as the children spread out inside.

"Yes, of course," said Miss Parton. The same question each week, come hell or high water, followed by the same answer because Mrs Vearn was tasked with ensuring it.

Charlie went straight to Children's Non-Fiction. His favourite sections were 608: Inventions and 670-690:

Technology. He dragged out a book and sat on a beanbag sagging in a corner near the window. It had no pictures at all on the cover. It must be in the wrong place. Dipping his hand in his pocket, he reached for the chocolate, unfortunately the pieces that were left had melted totally and while he sat, they had been squeezed out from the wrapping foil into the lining of his pocket. As he withdrew his hand, he could see his fingers and palm had a covering of sweet, sticky brownness. The beanbag had engulfed him and made it hard to stand. He rolled, trying to at least get his knees to the floor without touching anything. He tucked his elbows in, and holding his palms upwards with fingers extended towards the ceiling, he managed a kneeling position. The book was in front of him on the beanbag with its front cover open, and it looked as if he was praying to it.

Miss Dean was on the prowl and rounded the shelving. Her nose sniffing like a bloodhound, she was no doubt after Charlie's blood. Quickly hiding his chocolatey hand inside the book, he closed the cover on top and pretended he was reading the title. She hovered around him; the aroma was strong. He was for it now. She bent closer and sniffed again, strong it was and very close. Her face arrived next to Charlie's, cheek beside cheek. If it wasn't for the tacky aroma of chocolate, he'd have noticed the scent of rosewater and mothballs.

"Great book." Charlie smiled, hiding his hand even further inside the cover.

"What's that smell, young man? Sweets? You've been eating sweets, haven't you?"

Her voice was a whisper of menace in a silent space.

"Oh," he countered, "you can probably smell the Coco Pops I had for breakfast. Lovely, aren't they?"

As she sniffed once more, her green eyes flicked and seemed to cloud like a snake's, then she withdrew her head and left on her flat, silent shoes. Charlie was reminded of the velociraptors in the film *Jurassic Park*. She was probably a cast member.

It was at time to leave, however, when his ingenious lie had come apart. He was in line with the others and presented his book to be stamped. The system was as old as Miss Dean herself. The title cards were removed from a sleeve in the book's cover and placed in another sleeve bearing the child's name. Then the library book was stamped with a return date, and the book could be taken.

"Name?"

"Charlie."

"Yes, child... Charlie what?"

Charlie, being cheeky and full of his cleverness at getting away with the earlier problem, said, "No, Miss, Charlie Hipkiss not Charlie Watt."

Alfie, who thought he'd be clever too, burbled, "We ain't got a Charlie Watt in our school, Miss."

Miss Dean's reaction was wholly predatory. She put one hand on the book's spine, and the other gripped the cover and slowly pulled it away across the old oak desk. She opened it and gasped. Fingerprints were spread on the inside from top to bottom. A dog's paw prints in a Hug Rug advert could not have been clearer. Her face changed from puce to deathly white in the space of a millisecond.

"My precious book, ruined," she spat.

The books all seemed to belong to her, whether they did or not.

"You, your parents or your school will pay. I will not have a single, grimy book on my shelves. Take it, remove it from my sight and expect a letter to your head teacher by this afternoon."

CHAPTER III

So, the thought running through Charlie's head was that Wednesday was library day. Miss Dean should be at the library checking hands, stamping books, sneaking up on chatterers. She was, however, here in his classroom. What on earth could she be doing here? Miss Dean, tall and thin as a tent pole, was wearing a scarf that hid her neck and drifted from just under her chin down to the collar and lapels of her green tweed jacket. She was carrying a shiny leather bag, the sort doctors might have used years ago. She placed it on a desk at the front. The children's eyes flicked between the bag and Miss Dean and back again.

Then Miss Parton spoke.

"I know that we usually go to the library, but today is different. Miss Dean has come to us."

Nina smiled in her direction and got a nod of recognition.

"She has come to talk to us about Wicton and especially its Roman past as part of a project for 'Our Village' week. So listen carefully and think what questions you would ask to help you and me find out more. I will now hand over to Miss Dean. Miss Dean."

Miss Isadora Dean placed the tip of a long, bony finger into a brass ring that was attached to a similar brass plate on the bag. Charlie's eyes watched intently;

he loved mechanisms. Then he remembered his library encounter with the 'lock' book from a couple of months before and bunched down into his chair. Mrs Vearn nudged him, and reluctantly he sat up. The finger moved the ring down, and a catch on a leather tongue sprung open. She eased the top halves of the bag apart. Her hand disappeared inside, then a quarter of her sleeve. Charlie imagined her as an evil Mary Poppins, not searching for a hatstand but instead a bottle full of snot-green poison. He couldn't stifle a chuckle. Miss Dean immediately looked up. Who dared to interrupt? Mrs Vearn and Miss Parton both glared at him as Miss Dean returned to her task and pulled an object out of her bag.

It was… a brick.

The disappointment from almost everyone was profound. Lifting it in front of her chin with two hands, she peered out at the class over the top of her glasses.

"This," she said with her cold love, "was found several years ago in a corner of an outside wall at our 'Temple' site at the bottom of the 'Mount'."

In a voice of deep reverence, she explained the story,

"The 'Temple' is no longer there, but some walls and a strange, raised square mound is. Archaeology students discovered differences in the soil and those revealed inner walls in a square around half a metre down in the ground. The ruined walls on the outside still partly stand. 'A Temple,' they said. Just think, our village has its very own Roman temple."

Charlie thought he detected a tear in the corner of her left eye. Then, Saima's hand went up. "Please, Miss, why is it a cube shape? Bricks are cuboid."

You could tell that Saima was no ordinary pupil. She was observant and wanted to learn all she could.

"A good point, well spotted, young lady. Roman walls were sometimes built with square bricks; in other places, they used thin rectangular ones. It was a matter of choice, I suppose. If you look at our walls, they have a special pattern, but that is for your teacher to show you."

Alfie shoved his hand up. "My dad built a barbeque with bricks in our garden. They weren't square, though. It worked well 'cos he cooked burgers on it and everything."

Miss Parton quickly intervened before the sniggers around her became full-blown belly laughs.

"Thanks, Alfie. Yes, bricks are useful for building all sorts of things. Now are there any more questions?"

Charlie had been studying the brick quite closely. He didn't want to draw attention to himself but couldn't resist.

"Excuse me, Miss," he said in his politest voice, "I can make out some marks; what are they?"

Miss Dean turned to face the voice as the hand shrank back down. She knew the face but couldn't place why or where. Miss Parton examined the brick and turned to the board where she drew the marks so that all could see clearly.

"Well, we are told those are maker's marks. Brickmakers and stonemasons always seem to leave their signature mark somewhere. On some clay bricks, there is the stamp of a legion. We think that is what they must be, but we'll never know, will we?"

"Well, class, that's a rather intriguing introduction to our week. Can we please show our appreciation in our usual way?" Miss Parton chimed.

The class gave a polite round of applause apart from Alfie, who thought it best to whistle. Mrs Vearn gave him a severe look from her position across the desk. He stopped and drooped his head, not realising what was wrong with his form of appreciation. Miss Dean had placed the brick back in her bag, and the tag made a satisfying click in the lock. Miss Parton had some final words.

"On Friday morning, we will be visiting the temple and the museum to look at more artefacts. A letter will be sent home this evening for your parents to sign and give their consent. Once again, thank you, Miss Dean. I will come with you to the door. Mrs Vearn, can you find out what, if anything, the children might know about Romans? I'll be back in a jiffy."

With that, the door was pulled open by Miss Dean, and its creak sounded to Charlie as though she might have had too many prunes for breakfast. The edges of his mouth turned up.

"Oh," said Mrs Vearn, seeing the smile emerge, "I can see you enjoyed that lesson."

The smile grew wider.

CHAPTER IV

The blood oozed from the middle of the soldier's chest, his tunic reddened and wet. A drip fell from the arrow shaft and dropped onto the roadway creating a small dark spatter. Drusus yelled, and immediately the rest of the scouting party – a *contubernium* of eight soldiers, bonded by living together, eating together, fighting together and trusting each other – muscled their shields into a wall and faced the direction from which they believed the arrow had come. Silence... another yelled command and swords grated from scabbards and were thrust through the narrow gaps, created for the purpose, between the shields. Silence...

... Broken by a crow cawing in an oak tree close by. It was eying up the tasty looking meal lying dead on the road.

"*Contubernium... Procedite!*"

As one solid unit, the tent party of now only seven soldiers advanced ten paces.

"*Consiste!*"

They halted... waited... silence...

Nothing stirred other than the same crow rearranging its wing feathers for the short glide to lunch that hadn't moved. The blood had already started to congeal and formed a short, fine string with a small globule at the end. As it got longer, it got thinner and thinner. Eyes, though, were staring ahead, watching and waiting. Drusus smiled to himself. He knew. He knew the lies; he told the lies, and he carried out the lies. He dared to look above the wall of shields. He knew he was safe because he had created the lie. Did the others guess? No. Drusus was renowned for bravery, especially when in tight battle situations. That was what he was relying on. He surveyed the scene cautiously; the others awaited the outcome. The archer was gone, his job done. Drusus stood tall, and the group relaxed a little. This road was usually safe.

"*Animum attendite. Procedite – Gradum Servate*!"

"Pay attention. Forward march – Keep in step!" he bellowed. "No point in us all getting killed."

No one wanted to leave a fallen comrade, but they knew that their survival today may depend on it. As one, their shields unlinked, swords sheathed, they advanced at double pace and left the dead man lying where he fell.

That thinnest wire of the soldier's blood had been stretched by gravity, and as the globule contacted the ground, the wire snapped, leaving the tiniest, dark-red yolk in the middle of the drying spatter from moments before.

As the group rounded a bend, so the dead soldier's right eyelid slowly lifted, and his gimlet eye moved in its socket, scanning, seeking, searching. The crow waited its chance and, launching from its branch, outstretched its wings and tilted its beak skywards, deftly landing on two feet beside the body on the roadway. Its momentum made it bounce and come to a standstill like a gymnast after a vault. It folded its wings and strutted purposefully towards the eye. That was as good a place to start as any. Soft, tender, tasty. Black beak, long and sleek, shining with dampness, having wiped both sides across its tree perch. It stretched its neck and, with clawed, short steps, moved towards the tasty jelly. Jumping, it landed expertly on the uppermost cheek of the soldier's face. It blinked, made a final check, then bent its head downwards, ready to peck the eye.

Vitus, for that was the soldier's name, kept stone still. He exhaled through lips that formed the smallest 'o', rapid and silent, with fingers still wrapped around the short handle of his military dagger from the time he fell. His elbow bent, and he impaled the crow where it perched. Its dark right eye stared in astonishment and so it remained. Certain now no one was in sight, Vitus rolled onto his back. Extracting a muddied claw from the edge of his nostril, he tucked the bird under his armpit and pulled out the *pugio*. He wiped it across his tunic and sat up, letting his right arm release the dead bird, which dropped to the ground.

The arrow jutted from his chest. He smirked and stood up gingerly. He felt bruised and sore, but other than that none the worse for wear. He would need to buy the archer a good measure of wine for his accuracy. They would both be well paid. His legionary life was over; he would be able to retire with a new name, buy some small estate and live off tales of his merchant exploits. A harmless story if not strictly true. A little lie. He pulled his tunic above his head, and from the front he jiggled it over the projecting arrow through the square hole it had made, letting it fall to the floor. He winced. Beneath lay a quartered quilt of calf skin. Each quarter had been filled with blood, and the hems made of elastic stomach lining; it had been sealed with precise stitching. Behind this, it was reinforced by a good many layers of hardened leather, which had been bound to the pouches and in turn tied by straps around his waist, chest and over his shoulders to ensure it remained in its exact position. The arrow had pierced the upper-right pouch from which the blood had exited. It had been prevented from killing him by the layers of hardened leather behind. He peeled it away. Unfortunately, the arrow had not been stopped entirely, and a nasty puncture wound had been created. He was lucky. It would heal in time, and he supposed it was no worse than he had received by spear thrusts and sword cuts while on campaign. Picking up his stained tunic and the 'lifesaver', he kicked the crow into the ditch before jumping over it and striding directly away along a fox path. A time and place had been set. He would go to the clearing and wait. Wait for the archer, Faris. The road was clear apart from the blood that had been spilled, now being washed away by a persistent drizzle.

Crouching in the trees, face white with shock, lay Ruus. He'd seen... he'd witnessed. He could still smell the stale sweat that was ever-present on soldiers under duress. He could still hear the thud of the arrow as it found its mark. He slithered on taut belly into the roadside ditch. No sound did he make. He listened and watched the route Vitus chose. The metalworker's son waited barely a minute, then stalked that same path.

CHAPTER V

Drusus knew that some of the group were bitter at having left Vitus lying on the road. It was unheard of to question a superior's order, but Drusus could feel the swell of discontent and knew he would soon have to quieten it down. He had, however, let just such a feeling grow on purpose. He called a halt.

"I've been thinking."

He needed to make them feel as though he was even more concerned about the body than they were.

"It is only your safety I'm thinking of. Of course, you rely on me for that but…"

This was where he would turn the tables. This is where he would make them believe they were the chickens that fled from danger.

"Vitus was a mate. How can it be that just for your safety, I leave him lying cold in a rain-soaked wheel rut? In little more than half an hour, we'll be back eating our fill while out there a brother in arms has our need. We'll be branded cowards, and I know you are aware of the consequences of that. What must be done, I cannot ask of you all; the risk is too great. You must return and report what happened here. I will go back. I am responsible. I will not let one of my own be lost."

He scanned their faces. He had them in his grasp, so he continued, "It will be obvious to you I cannot carry him on my own. I need just one who will come back with me. One who has courage, heart and love for his fellow man, as I do. Who will then shoulder his shield with me and carry our brother home?"

The group stood stock still, stunned to think that it was they who had let Drusus down. It was they who had abandoned the very soul of the *contubernium* – their solidarity, their togetherness. Near the back of the rank, a soldier lowered the bottom edge of his shield to the ground, holding it firmly in place with his left hand. He clenched his right fist and slapped it across his chest.

"For my brother!" he shouted, "I will go with you."

His action was immediately followed by the man next to him, and the rest followed suit. Drusus had convinced them. His desire to do the right thing shone through. Their belief in him had wavered but not now. He was the sword in their fist, the shield on their arm. He cared, he protected. He was their brother and best friend, although that was only half the truth.

CHAPTER VI

The band of brothers had gone back up the road to the exact spot where they had been attacked.

Drusus had warned them, "Stick close; those half-naked heathens daubed in blue would like nothing better than to stick your heads on their spears."

But they needn't have worried. There were no attacks of screaming tribesmen, and the body was gone; even the blood had seeped away in the drenching drizzle. Where had it gone? There could only be one answer. Vitus must have been carried away. His head would at this very moment be strung by its hair at a roundhouse door, a trophy for the village to admire; a trophy that would perhaps have brought a youth the status of a man – a 'warrior'.

The report that Drusus made was supported wholeheartedly by his companions. The *Optio*, second in command of the century to which Drusus belonged, had been instructed to question Drusus, then separately the remaining members of the *contubernium* who were with him on patrol. All gave the same account. They had ensured that their small unit was safe but had not abandoned the scene and, with bravery, had sought to bring Vitus home. It was most important that their fearlessness was not called into question. As punishment, any one of them could have been beaten to death by the rest of his tent mates if there was even a hint of cowardice. Nonetheless, Drusus and his men were subject to lesser punishments as a warning to others. They would eat nothing but barley and water and would clean the camp latrines for three days, but this was a reasonable price to pay in light of what might have been.

CHAPTER VII

At a thousand paces from the road, the path branched. Trees overhung it to the left. The smell of damp and decaying leaves from the previous autumn rose from the ground, an earthy, encompassing smell that enveloped the senses. Vitus carefully pushed aside branches which, laden with raindrops, drooped their heavy boughs. The path widened onto a glade, then into a circular clearing. Vitus approached cautiously. These places teemed with spirits, and he had no wish to disturb them. Keeping to the shelter of the trees and shrubs at the perimeter, he edged round. Not far away, just a few paces from the middle, he noticed a blackened tree stump. This would be a good place to rest and wait. The rain fell harder now that he was clear of the tree canopies above him. The heavy mizzle from a soulless, grey sky gave no comfort and blurred his sight. The quicker they met, the quicker away from here they'd be.

The stump moved! So taken aback was Vitus that he tumbled and began to scrabble away. What manner of magic could make dead trees come to life? Rising, the black stump lifted from the ground. It swayed and wafted. Now it sprouted dark, deathly wings that unfolded from its heart and spread to enwrap him. An arrow in the chest was one thing, but this was far more terrifying. His fate was sealed. Here he would die, splayed open in the grimmest image of his legion's eagle by a spirit demon of Druidic Britannia. Rain was now streaming into his eyes. He screamed as a face emerged from the gloom, cowled in shadowy folds.

The scream had warned Ruus. He'd left the path that swept through the glade and was making his way as best he could through bramble and thicket. The steady patter of rain, bouncing from the leaves above him, muffled his approach. He squatted down and watched.

Unable to face his fate, Vitus pulled his arm across his face. Shivering now from exhaustion and fear, he had no fight left in him. His arm was grasped tightly by a strong hand, surely a devil's grip.

"Get up, comrade," came a rough but calming voice. "You must get up and change quickly. We must not remain here long."

Faris, the archer, had covered himself and crouched down low in his oiled, black woollen cloak to keep dry. Hearing Vitus approach, he had stood, and the cloak had given Faris his ghoulish appearance. Vitus's wound was oozing blood, and he seemed weakened.

"We must stop that bleeding. Get dressed and I'll find some herbs to help it heal."

Vitus was given a leather bag, which held dry clothes very unlike his army uniform. These would help disguise him back in the *vicus,* a group of houses, workshops, and bars where food and wine would be served. The *vicus* lay outside the main fort but lined the road that led in from the south-east with buildings of wood, straw and mud spilling randomly on each side two or three deep. Faris, meanwhile, examined the ground and occasionally pulled off small, leathery, veined leaves from weeds growing among the thin grass.

A dull tick from a damp branch interrupted him. That wasn't normal. The sound aggravated his senses, and he was immediately aware of someone or something close by. He shouted across to Vitus.

"Search. Search your side. I'll look over here."

Both men headed to the boundary of the clearing. Faris pushed outwards and round to the left. Who was there? It was vital they found whoever it was and despatched them before they could tell what they'd seen. Vitus, *pugio* in hand, roamed round to his left from the far side where the ground rose and the undergrowth was less dense. They would complete the circle between them and catch the culprit. Ruus scrambled down a shallow bank between a beech tree and a tall oak. He could hear Vitus no more than twenty-five metres away coming up the bank from the far side. There was no bush or undergrowth to hide behind. In a matter of seconds, he'd be face to face with Vitus and have a dagger across his throat. Crouching low, he slid backwards further down the bank, keeping his eyes on the crest of the rise. He grabbed a root and pulled himself tight to the oak tree's trunk. Vitus breasted the mound and looking right and left, started to descend. Ruus was desperate. Nowhere to go! The hunter Vitus and his prey Ruus – *Venator et Praedandum*.

Ruus had only one option. He had to swing on the root and pull himself over and behind it and hope he wouldn't be seen. The root was as wide as his arm, and the muddy slope had not improved his grip, but with as much stealth as possible, he rolled to the safer side. Simultaneously, Vitus looked in that very direction as Ruus disappeared. The root he had clung to was part of a network. A badger had burrowed between them and created a kind of cave. The tree was above, and the roots were a huge spider's web into and between which he had fallen. The fly was trapped but unseen from the side or above. Vitus began to scan for any trace, Ruus hunched up inside the wooden web, still and cocooned. Faris had grabbed a stick and was beating bushes on the far side. As he did so, another dull crack was heard, and a fox sprang out in front of him and dashed for safety. Faris at once relaxed and straightened, content that it must have been that animal he had heard.

He called, "Come on, we're wasting time."

Vitus was at the base of the oak tree right beside the clinging root as the shout came. He turned, pleased to be called back. He was tired and feverish. Ruus did not stir for a good fifteen minutes even though his toes, arms and fingers tingled painfully with pins and needles.

He, too, was going back to the *vicus*.

CHAPTER VIII

Mr Noor, Saima's father, kissed his wife and smiled at Saima, who was reading a screen on her iPad and writing in her notebook at the kitchen table. Her 'extra homework' she had called it. Inspired by the brick, which had been the subject of questions, she had decided to find out more about it before the museum and temple visit with her class on Friday.

Adil Noor had become a respected member of the Village Council for over three and a half years. During that time, there had been some tough decisions made. However, at tonight's meeting, he was going to make his hardest decision ever. He was pretty sure what other committee members would say, what the right course of action should be, the best way forward for the village and its survival, and in a way he had to agree.

He watched Saima and teased, "What are you writing? You finished your homework before dinner. We can't have my clever girl getting square eyes and writer's fingers, can we?"

His daughter looked up with that same gentle smile she'd used on Wednesday in class. Her father crouched down, and with arms spread he invited a cuddle. Mothers and sons are very close, but the love for this father's daughter was everything to him. He started to read her notes, one hand and elbow resting on the table as he crouched beside her chair.

"Bricks? You are writing about bricks? What has my girl become? Don't tell me you want to be an architect now? Always such grand plans you have."

"No, of course not. I still want to be a train driver."

The joke made them burst out laughing, and Saima's mum raised her eyebrows at the pair of them and then turned back to watching the local news.

Saima explained, "We saw a brick yesterday in school. But, instead of it being rectangular like the ones we have today, it was square. It was Roman. It seems they had all sorts of bricks, some even like ours but flatter. I was finding out how they built with them. Look."

She pointed to her iPad and then her notebook, where she'd made a sketch of the wall that was on the screen.

"I think the temple was built like this. See, the bricks are set on their corners, not on their edges. The wall looks like it's been made with stone diamonds. I bet that's what Miss Dean was going to tell us but stopped short so we could discover it. I've never really thought about looking that closely. I just thought it was a jumble of old crumbly walls."

Saima started to flick to the next screen page, and perhaps she would write more notes. Adil could see she was fully engaged in her investigation and loving the discoveries she was making. He had been unnerved, however, by the mention of Miss Dean. It was she who ran the museum and had done so for such a long time. It was through her that generations of children had borrowed books or learnt how Victorians would have dressed at 'the big house'. In the antiquated library and museum building, the village's past lived through her and her alone. Tonight that could come to an end. He rose, and his knees creaked.

"Old man," Saima jested.

"I must go; the meeting starts in fifteen minutes. I mustn't be late."

Saima and her mum both understood what was at stake this evening. Adil had promised that he would do the right thing. He was chairman, after all; a respected businessman of the local community. He would see that things went the right way. Permissions had been refused before.

CHAPTER IX

The major issue on the agenda this evening was a planning application for a new housing development. This, in itself wasn't really a problem. The village would certainly benefit. Adil's business would have extra trade, so would the Old Mill Pub squeezed in a triangle of land with the Flumen to the front and The Wash road a couple of hundred metres behind. The school had fewer pupils than when he started his business here eleven years ago. Classes would be full again. The developers had even said they could build new classrooms along the north side of Hornbeam Lane to accommodate the growth, which would be fantastic.

No, the problem was the proposed site for the building of the houses. It even made perfect sense too. New houses on the south side of the lane, down to the mini roundabout on Temple Street. That meant the museum and library would have to go. Not wholly knocked down but converted into exclusive apartments with gated parking, and they might expand the cellar and build a state-of-the-art swimming pool. Of course, such residences as these would have colossal price tags. That money would then be used to ensure affordable housing for other families with a major 'help to buy scheme'. How wonderful it would be. People would flock to buy and give the village a new vibrancy, a real lift.

Adil believed that what made the village unique and such a great place to live were the very things that would be lost; the quaint library and the museum with its dusty relics of ancient times. How could he vote to destroy that? How could he take away such a resource that had served the village and its children so well for so many years? Perhaps he wouldn't have to. Others would see it his way too, yet his doubts remained.

At the school, the site manager had set up the tables in the school hall by the curtains at the back. Behind those, if you weren't scared to look into that dark grotto, was a trolley with mini cones for ball skills and spilling from a hook were hoops of various sizes and colours. In one corner was an old vaulting box that had once trapped Alfie inside for half an hour during a wet lunch playtime when Charlie had explained about the 'Wooden Horse' war film he'd seen. He told the story with such enthusiasm that they'd all wanted to play, and Alfie had volunteered to be the tunneller under the 'box'. Trouble was they'd got too loud and were told to sit down. This left Alfie in a webby, wooden chest with just the handle slots for light and air. He was eventually rescued by the midday supervisor and the cook, who helped lift off the heavy leather top. Ever since then, the box had remained quarantined behind agility mats.

Chairs had been optimistically arranged in four rows of ten and faced the table at which the committee would meet. As Adil arrived, he passed through the double doors to the hall and approached the table down the right-hand side. He could see that just one chair was occupied. Dressed as usual in her tweeds and also this evening garbed in a waxed jacket and wide-brimmed, crushable bushman's hat, Miss Dean sat with arms folded and legs crossed, waiting for the meeting to start.

There were strict rules, of course. Only the Village Council committee members were allowed to speak and would present the arguments for and against any proposals. The public had been consulted weeks before, but now the decision would be made. Isadora Dean could listen but could not put forward any extra arguments or reasoning. After all, that's what a committee was for, to make decisions. No point in having one at all if everyone wanted to chip in; they'd be there till doomsday.

Adil Noor called the meeting to order. First, there were any Apologies for Absence, but the whole of the council were there, so that was skipped over quickly. Then there were Matters Arising from the last meeting. There were two items. First, the seat in the bus shelter that had been vandalised had been replaced. Secondly, Mr Peters, the pub landlord, had requested that his application for a barbeque, marquee and licence extension be granted for the Midsummer Celebration night. This had been passed to the local police and was awaiting their judgement, although the council were happy for it to be granted.

So, they finally came to the main item and, in fact, the only item left on the agenda apart from Any Other Business, the decision regarding the Oaks Housing Development.

"Item four," Adil stated clearly. "The proposal to build houses on Temple Street and other items included within that proposal."

"Chair," said Mr Tisbury pompously, "there is no doubt the proposal is hugely beneficial to our community. I move we agree the proposal, further discussion is unnecessary."

"Whoa!" countered Mrs Knapp, a stable owner who lived on the edge of the village, sitting at the far end of the table, "You can't just gallop this through. Rein back, sir. Hold your horses. There's a great deal to be lost here too."

The arguments ran back and forth for three-quarters of an hour. Some were clearly against, but some were most certainly for the new development. The clerk who was taking the minutes and who sat next to Adil said confidentially, "Mr Noor, having heard the arguments, it may be advisable to move to a vote."

Adil nodded in agreement.

"Thank you for your most important comments," he said, aiming his words carefully to each person at the table, "We will move to a vote as I believe everything needed to be said, has been said."

There were nods of agreement.

"The proposal is that the Oak Housing Development be allowed to proceed. All those in favour, please raise your hand."

Three hands went into the air.

"Those against the proposal, please raise your hand."

Three hands went in the air.

The clerk turned to Adil and said solemnly, "The vote is tied three apiece. You, Mr Noor, you have the casting vote. Your vote will decide."

Adil had never imagined it would come to this. The committee were split, and he must make the decision on his own. He paused and rubbed a hand across his forehead. The room was silent; there wasn't a jot of movement. You could have heard a pin drop. He felt cold and sweaty all at the same time. His head thumped as the arguments beat against his skull. This was so important, and now only he would decide the fate of the village's heart and the life of the school. Saima's faith in him scorched his soul. The time had come, and this decision, his decision had to be the best for the village, whatever anyone else believed. He stood and, turning to his left and right, he addressed the committee and the one member of the audience, who had sat in stony silence throughout.

"Ladies and gentlemen, fellow committee members and villagers; I am torn between head and heart, but I have come to a conclusion and…"

The room seemed to become smaller, crowding and bowing inwards upon his every word.

"I have decided…" He paused. "That based solely upon the arguments for and against—"

He was interrupted.

"Get on with it, man," grumbled Mr Tisbury.

Adil stumbled a few more words then said, "I feel that it is my duty, for the sake and future of the village, to vote… in favour of the proposal. The Oaks Housing Development will be constructed."

The room exhaled and exploded wider than it had ever been. Some members threw their agenda papers in the air; others sat in utter shock. Tisbury knocked back his glass of water and rushed to Adil's side, grasping his hand and shaking it up and down as if it was an old water pump handle. His group came and slapped him on the back.

"Excellent decision, Chairman."

"Well said, sir," chirped another.

All Adil could think about was how he should tell Saima. What could he say?

The clerk made a swift announcement. "We still must deal with Any Other Business."

This was always the last item on the agenda. They all agreed there was none and that the next meeting would be a month from tonight. The meeting ended at 9.17pm.

It was then that Miss Dean rose and walked back towards the hall doors. On reaching them, she turned and, with green eyes ablaze, stared up the length of the hall. The group tidying their papers and having conversations were suddenly frozen.

"Mark my words closely. Your decision will set an ageless force in motion. There is no turning back."

A long, bony index finger sprung from her right fist and raked the members of the top table with ill-disguised menace.

"Whatever dangers befall, the die has been cast and only by cunning and strength of character will those involved survive the ordeal."

Although low in tone, the threat in her speech carried to each and every person in the room. Adil shivered, and in an instant, she was gone.

CHAPTER X

Saima was at breakfast, and while she was spreading apricot jam on her toast, she spoke, "How did the meeting go? Where's Dad this morning?"

Her mum was just squeezing a tea bag on the side of her mug. Her spoon slipped and it slopped some tea onto the table. She could feel her whole stomach heave. Adil had been so ashamed at letting down his daughter that this was the one morning he wasn't listening to the news on the radio and spooning his cereal from his bowl. This was a morning he didn't sidle round the table and pretend to take her last toasty triangle. No, he had decided this was a morning to go early to the warehouse in his van. A morning to avoid relating the outcome of the meeting he knew would cut Saima to the quick. Her mum knew and she lied, just a little.

"He had to go out early; you know, busy days Fridays. He said he wanted to tell you himself later. 'Don't tell her,' he said, so you'll have to wait till this evening."

She smiled, giving the impression that all was well, when of course all was far from well. She had told a *little* lie to save her daughter from upset and her husband from his shame. Her lie, though, was much bigger than that. Adil had left with not a word. She had to find a way to cover. She was hiding from telling the truth too. Saima swung from her chair, grabbing her bag from where it hung full of notes from her clever detective work. She skipped to the top of the stairs and shouted a carefree, "Bye, Mum."

Then she ran down and trotted out into the sunshine smiling at the thought of her many museum visits to come.

CHAPTER XI

Mrs Vearn had her tote bag over her left shoulder. She'd been through the permission slips and all were in order, even Alfie's. Her bag contained the important items that would cover all eventualities. She had tissues, water, first-aid kit, pencils and, of course, Olivia's EpiPen as well as several children's asthma pumps. The children carried clipboards holding blank sheets of paper. Each had taken a pencil from their table pots. Mrs Vearn had also had the forethought to bring a couple of sharpeners. She stood at the front of the class line waiting at the school gate by the bend on Sycamore Street. Miss Parton joined her at the front, and the class set off. Turning left out of the gate, Mrs Vearn waited on the kerb as they turned the bend into Hornbeam Lane. She then joined the back of the line of children. They would first go to the temple. The pairs came to the bridge on Temple Street, and they formed a single file line facing the road. Mrs Vearn gave a thumbs-up, and with Miss Parton at the other end, having checked there was no traffic, they shouted, "Together, cross."

On the other side, they formed back into their pairs. A wooden fence and small, latched gate near the bridge provided access to the temple site and the river. The class passed through and then formed a semi-circle as the two adults, with their backs to one of the ancient outer walls, stood in front of them.

"I am going to ask you to explore," explained Miss Parton. "You must look carefully and find out how the walls might have been made. Look for the brick pattern. Go inside the walls and imagine where the main temple building would have been. We'll learn more about that when we meet back here in twenty minutes."

Olivia was concerned. "I haven't got a watch, Miss."

Miss Parton smoothly explained, "Don't worry, I will blow a whistle, and that will be the time for you to come back. A few safety rules: One – don't let me see anyone attempting to climb any walls, they're unsafe and we want them to remain standing for a good few years yet. Two – the river is low but the banks are high. Stay away. No one is to go near the far wall where the ditch and river meet. Clear?"

There were a few nods, but already six or seven had broken away and were examining the square bricks. Others had gone up the hill a little and were lying on their stomachs, drawing the most intact walls and the square, central mound where the temple once stood.

Saima was in her element; drawing, investigating, learning, and all outdoors on a sunny day. Nothing could stop her from explaining to all who would listen about Roman cement and how it was made or how some bricks were clay but others were carved stone and took much more skill to make. She even estimated the height of the walls. All noted on her clipboard to be transferred to her notebook later. Alfie clung to Charlie. He wasn't sure, but he wanted to believe Charlie was a mate. After all, he let him go in goal at playtimes. Alfie couldn't save the shots that Charlie hit because they were too hard, but he liked playing and kicking the ball back for Charlie's next go. He didn't much like the fact that they didn't have nets and the ball would fly past the jumper goalposts, though. Charlie had seen where everyone else was and decided that if his teacher had said explore, that's what he'd do. So the two boys ran past the figures lying on the ground and went to the wall furthest from where they had come in. The ditch was a good way off, although they could easily see where the wall ended by the river. Alfie went up to a wall and touched the bricks. Some were quite smooth, but all were almost the same size squares.

"Clever, those Romans," he said.

Charlie came and looked too. He was actually quite impressed and agreed with him.

"C'mon, let's go further down. You can go in the gap and have a look inside like Miss said."

"Um… we're not supposed to go too far down there, we'll get told off."

Alfie didn't like breaking rules; they kept him safe like the rule in school for walking not running. That was a good rule. Safe. They walked down to the gap.

"OK, you stay here and have a look, but I'm going to the end," said Charlie without looking back.

Saima had eased her way slowly along the top side and had just reached the corner. Charlie, meanwhile, had made his way to the end of the eastern wall and was by the river where it turned a right angle and another wall ran away parallel to the bank. He might have slipped a couple of times, but he'd found some helpful handholds at around waist height. The handholds were gaps where a couple of bricks were missing from the corner of the wall. Three of his fingers seemed to melt into the stone, and that was enough for him to lean and peer round the corner. Along the wall on that bankside were nettles and some flag iris leaves, not much more. Time passed as his eyes searched the far bank.

The whistle went.

Charlie ignored it; it was an unnecessary distraction. Then his attention was drawn to events on the far side of the river. He watched two moorhens, one had a red and yellow beak and some white feathers on its side, and the other was smaller and brownish. He rightly guessed that it must be a young one. He watched for a while as they strutted on the sloped, muddy bank, youngster following Mum. Then without warning, they scampered into some straw-coloured reeds. Why?

Bang! A hand dropped heavily on Charlie's shoulder. Mrs Vearn had come looking when he and Alfie hadn't turned up. Alfie was standing next to Saima, looking worried at the top corner of the wall. He had been told to wait with her. Mrs Vearn escorted them back to the class, who were seated and ready to listen.

"I will speak with you, Charlie Hipkiss, as soon as we finish here. For the moment, sit and listen," said Miss Parton sternly.

Alfie sat very quietly next to Mrs Vearn. She was safe.

CHAPTER XII

Faris had to half-carry Vitus back to the settlement outside the fort. He was shivery and weak and needed support. The ordeal had taken more out of him than he would ever have imagined. He was sore, wet and hungry. Keeping to the smaller alleys between the houses and with a woollen cloak wrapped around his head and face so as not to be recognised, Vitus was gently urged through a workshop and into some living quarters beyond. Charred wood was smouldering in a hearth near the centre of the single room. It had a comforting, homely smell. The roof above his head was made of straw and reeds. It was blackened from where the smoke had risen and tried to escape leaving behind years of sooty deposits. Around the edge were some shelves of rough timber holding a variety of bowls, a mattress of hay and a crumpled, woollen blanket.

Faris led him there and sat him down, then he fetched some dried kindling wood and two larger logs. The fire had nearly burnt out and would need coaxing back into life. He blew softly. Ash rose into the air but the charred wood started to glow. First one piece then another, the glow turned from a dark orange to a vibrant yellow and as he stopped blowing, a lick of flame emerged and wrapped around the wood above it. He blew again, and this time as he stopped the flame was stronger, more intense and set a piece of kindling ablaze. Other pieces of the thin, dry wood caught hold. Faris placed some larger pieces on top, and satisfied that they had caught the flames too, he positioned the two large logs on top. Within five minutes, warmth and a little more light filled the space. There was no time to lose, however; he must ensure Vitus was fit for their future task. The job was not complete.

He took a small wooden bowl and two others from a shelf and poured in a little sour wine and olive oil from two earthenware pots. Then he pulled from his pouch the plantain leaves he had picked back in the clearing. He found a wooden spoon and started to mash the leaves in the liquid until a greeny, purple paste emerged. At once, he instructed Vitus to remove his tunic and smeared the potion across the wound. It was sticky and clung. Next, he went out into the workshop. He pushed himself in and under a bench and started to collect. Then he stretched up to the rafters. Here was a much larger offering where a spider the size of a small pebble had been sucking dry the carcass of a fly. It shot up into the joint. Faris smiled.

"If I was that spider, I know what words I'd be saying right now."

The web that Faris had taken was added to the others clinging to his left hand. He went back through from the workshop and immediately felt the fire's warmth. He placed his left hand on the edge of the puncture wound, then ensuring they stuck to Vitus and not himself, he pulled and pressed the webs across the balm. It acted like a sticking plaster; the blood would soon scab over and seal the wound. Vitus seemed much enlivened by the warmth and could smell something tasty in the large cooking pot that hung from the tripod over the fire. He was hungry and ready to eat.

CHAPTER XIII

The children following Miss Parton arrived in front of the old oak library desk, at which stood the imposing figure of Miss Isadora Dean. She took the lead as twenty-seven children filed smoothly through the library and into a room that had rows of glass cabinets. Some were tall and stood on four dark, spindly legs. They had double doors, and the exhibits were arranged on three or four glass shelves. Each exhibit had a card that stood up beside it giving a description of the object to which it belonged. There, in one of those cabinets, were the bricks safely preserved.

Saima gushed, "Miss Dean, I saw how the bricks were set in the wall at the temple. They're on edge like diamonds, and I think I—"

She was cut short as Miss Dean had recognised who had spoken. She sharply interrupted her. "I have no desire to hear from you what you know or think!"

Saima was bewildered. Why would Miss Dean speak to her in such a way when just two days before she had been so nice? Miss Parton started to intervene as politely as she could, but she was rather offended that one of her children should be spoken to in such a harsh manner.

"I think Saima is very enthusiastic and is keen to share her discoveries with you," she said.

The reply cut her off too, and she would have no answer to it.

"It is a shame her father does not share her enthusiasm."

Saima dived in, showing great courage to argue with an adult, which was totally out of her character.

"My father loves the museum; everyone knows that."

"Oh really, then explain to me how it is that at the council meeting last night, he stopped loving the museum and voted FOR the new housing development."

"That's a lie! He'd never do that. He told me before he went that he'd do the right thing."

"Well, his right thing and your right thing don't seem to match. He had the chance to save it. He had the final vote, and it was he that condemned our library and museum to death in just a few short weeks from now."

Miss Parton could see the horror on Saima's face. Her father had lied, a huge lie. Now she had to face the truth of it and it stung. All the trust she had in him leaked and trickled away in the tears that started to flow freely down her cheeks. This was the worst day of her life. Her whole world had been turned on its head. If she couldn't believe her dad who was her world, her happiness, her life, who could she ever believe again? Mrs Vearn intervened by putting a consoling arm around her shoulders and leading her to a seat at a table in the library next door. Miss Parton was also knocked sideways by the revelation. The visit was not going at all as planned. She needed time to talk to Charlie and see that Saima would be okay. Miss Dean, realising that she had perhaps overstepped the bounds of acceptability, offered to open some cabinets for children to handle the artefacts. This was unheard of.

"Well," she said haughtily but with a little more humility, "If we are to close, there's no reason to preserve them. The children can draw and touch as many as they like, I suppose. Perhaps Saima might like to draw one from my cabinet of special and rather strange objects."

The class morale lifted, and almost all were eager to get started. That would at least give Miss Parton some time to deal with the most urgent issues. She asked the class to find an artefact that interested them, make a careful 'observational drawing' then label it. She then followed Miss Dean to a small cabinet that had no glass to view through. It had solid oak doors and a curious brass lock attached securely to the front left side. On the right-hand door was another smaller box of brass that received the bolt. Both parts of the lock were etched with trees whose branches seemed to wind around each other in an intricate knot. Even stranger was the fact there was no visible keyhole. Standing directly in front, she placed the fingers of her right hand precisely on various branch endings, and a series of clicks came from the lock's innards and the right-hand door pushed itself ajar. Miss Dean slipped her sinuous arm into the gap.

When she withdrew it, she said to Miss Parton, "An intriguing and ancient object, I'm sure they'll enjoy this."

Her eyes gleamed a bright green, and Nina Parton heard not a word she spoke nor did she see her go. However, when she looked down, there was now an object in her hand and a laminated piece of card which she knew she had to give to Saima.

She shook her head to clear it and walked back to the short hallway that separated the library from the museum, collecting Charlie en route.

"I am prepared to forgive many things, Mr Hipkiss."

That was new. She hadn't called him by his surname before.

"This time, I can't forgive that easily. You placed yourself in danger and you could have endangered others."

Charlie couldn't see the logic.

"Alfie didn't come with me; he said he didn't want to."

"You didn't know that when you asked him, though. Either you or he could have fallen. There's no telling what could have happened. To make matters worse, Mrs Vearn was placed in danger. She had to come and find you. What if she had slipped? Then there's the class. Why do you think there are two adults with the group? Don't speak because I know you know. I'm left with twenty-seven children to care for out of a safe school environment. What would we do if another decided to wander off or go out onto the road or climb the walls or feed the sheep up on The Mount?"

The last comment was her pure frustration at not feeling in total control anymore. Her favourite pupil was in tears, her lesson ruined, and a child in her care had made a chancy error.

"You will go to Mrs Vearn in the library. You will apologise, and then you will sit and make the best observational drawing you have ever made. If it's rushed, careless, slapdash or untidy, you will spend your time back in school at playtimes and lunchtimes drawing it again and again until I am satisfied. I have had enough, Charlie Hipkiss, enough!"

She broke away, saying he must find Mrs Vearn. He watched her turn into the museum, a hanky pulled from her blouse sleeve dabbing her eyes. He turned in the opposite direction, suitably reprimanded and feeling as low as his teacher.

The light in the library was bright compared with that in the small space between the two rooms. He saw Saima sitting on the far side of a table on the right. Mrs Vearn wasn't in sight. He chose to sit on the table that was past hers on the left. He didn't need to be near a weeping girl, that's for sure. As he ambled past, a voice called,

"Next to me, Charlie, not down there."

Mrs Vearn was at the same table as Saima. She had been unseen because of a bookcase near her back. He raised his eyebrows, turned and smiled at her though he wasn't feeling very jolly.

"Sit here next to me, Charlie," she said.

Mrs Vearn squeezed her ample bottom onto the next chair down, and Charlie sat on the one she had been on opposite Saima. At least she'd warmed it up for him, he thought impishly.

Mrs Vearn looked straight at him. "And?" she said expectantly.

"I'm sorry, Mrs Vearn. I didn't mean to cause so much trouble."

"Very good, Charlie, now apologise to Saima."

"What? What for?"

Saima's chin was on her chest. She didn't want any apology. What was Mrs Vearn thinking?

"She is a classmate, and you placed her and the class in danger too. Apologise to her, please."

"Er... sorry, Saima. I didn't mean to—"

Saima stopped him, "That's OK, Charlie, I know. You were just exploring, doing your own thing as usual. I get it. Thanks."

She looked up into his truly repentant face. He smiled, as did she.

Nina Parton had replaced her hanky and wondered why she was holding an artefact and card in her hand, then she remembered she was going to give it to Saima. She had no idea how she came to have it, but she supposed that didn't really matter and set off for the library.

"Has all been said?"

"Yes," replied Mrs Vearn.

Miss Parton asked Saima if she was okay and if she minded sitting with Charlie to draw. She said it wasn't a problem, and at that, Mrs Vearn stood and, squeezing from her chair, popped out from behind Charlie's into the main aisle. Both ladies wandered back towards the museum.

Charlie looked up from his blank sheet of paper to see Saima looking at the object in front of them. It had a light green, mossy tinge. It obviously couldn't have been cleaned properly. The strangest thing was that it was just a head. No, not strictly true. It was two heads joined together as if one. It had two faces, one on each side. Charlie turned it to look. One face had a beard and longer hair at the sides and back; the other had no facial hair and short, tight curls that stopped above the ears on its half of the head.

"What the heck's this all about?" said Charlie, not really expecting a response.

"It's a bust."

"Looks like it's not just bust; it's bloomin' wrecked. Where's his body?"

He put the sculptured head down between them. Saima tutted. She pulled the small, laminated sheet that had been left with it towards her and read out loud, taking hold of the head in both hands, elbows on the table in front of her, looking down at the notes.

"This is Janus, one of the oldest and most important Roman Gods."

"Never heard of him."

Saima ignored him and continued in full teacher mode, "He is the God that looks backwards and forwards. January is thought to be the month named after him. He is sometimes thought to be the God of Opposites. He was the ancient God of Doorways, Entrances and Exits, Right and Wrong. Even some believed he was the God of Truth and Lies."

Charlie let out a gust of breath and leaned over to hold the head to take a better look. Saima wouldn't let go. His hands encircled Saima's, his fingers wrapping around the backs of her hands. He was surprised at the strength of her grasp. Her fingertips covered the eyes, nose and lips of the bearded side of the statue. She was being forced to let go but couldn't, nor did she feel she wanted to. Her face peered directly at Charlie, her chin right over her hands and his. Charlie stared right back.

His hands were stuck to hers, which he found embarrassing, so to cover this awkwardness, he spoke, "I guess that's where the expression two-faced comes from."

As soon as he said it, he knew what he'd done. He hadn't meant it to refer to her dad, but of course it did, and it cut deep. Saima's nose wrinkled first, then her lips pulled wide and thin, and tears welled under her eyes; heavy, salty tears. Of course, her dad had lied to her. He had said the museum and library were safe with him, but he'd lied. He *was* two-faced. Saima's tears started to flow silently down her smooth cheeks. A flood, a torrent, as the memory of Miss Dean's revelation kept repeating over and over in her head. The tears tumbled onto the table, the laminated card and onto Charlie's warm hands still wrapped around Saima's own and the 'bust' beneath them.

Charlie watched them trickle over his knuckles and through between his fingers. He wanted to pull them away, but they were stuck fast as if their hands had been superglued together. Down the drops fell. Deeper. Weedling their way through to Saima's and on they went. A moment in time; two faces staring outwards beneath clasping hands and two real-life heads drawn in together, peering at each other. The first droplet, the tiniest microscopic drip of misery, fell from one of Saima's fingers and slipped into the bearded God's eye. That drip changed their world.

CHAPTER XIV

There was no flash, no rushing lights like in *Doctor Who*, no roaring sounds that pounded their ears. Everything just dissolved, a kind of melting away. Saima could feel the bust vaporise under her fingers. Charlie could feel Saima's hands evaporate. Saima saw Charlie's hands disappear, as did her own. The process continued up their arms across their bodies until there were just their necks and heads suspended in the library. The space above the table was disappearing too. Now it was their necks and on up past their chins and mouths. Strangely, the tops of their heads were fading downwards until all that was left of the two children were pairs of eyes opposite each other, surrounded by a sombre, olive-green glow. The eyes gawped; white spheres with discs of blue in one and brown in the other. No explanation, nothing.

Then they were gone.

CHAPTER XV

The rain hadn't stopped, and in the ditches to either side of the road, small puddles joined others and would flow by nightfall. The road had been well constructed. This one, like so many others throughout the Empire, had been created by toiling soldiers. The surface of the road was curved from the middle to edge, cambered so that water ran off and the ditches at the edges collected it.

The first to appear was the last to have gone; eyes of brown and blue materialised, then foreheads, hair, noses, mouths, chins, feet, legs, bodies, arms and finally hands still clasped together holding... nothing. For a split second, they seemed to be hovering in a sitting position with no chairs and then, squelch; they plomped into the bottom of a soaking ditch. Their hands had parted, but they were still looking at each other in utter disbelief.

"What did you do, Charlie?"

"Me? This is nothing to do with me!"

"Hold on," said Saima. "What did you just say?"

I said, "This is nothing to do with me."

"No you didn't; you said *hoc nihil* something or other."

"Now you come to mention it, you're not speaking English either. I can understand you, but it's not English. Oh blimey!"

"What now?"

"Look at you, look… at… you; your clothes, they're all different."

He looked at himself.

"Mine too."

"Charlie, this is no dream. It can't be. How could we have the same one at the same time? That's impossible."

A not-too-distant sound filtered down the bank and stopped their conversation. It was getting closer. Until they had a clearer idea of what was happening, it would be best to remain out of sight. They hunkered down in the sopping ditch by the bank closest to the road as the sound of crunching feet closed on their position. They squeezed themselves into the grass and cow parsley stalks. The scraping and crunching passed right by their heads, then moved on and passed them by. After waiting a few seconds more, their heads surfaced like submarine periscopes looking in the direction of the diminishing sound.

"They're soldiers."

"Roman soldiers," added Saima.

"Now we've got bloomin' Roman soldiers as well as weird clothes."

They scrabbled up to the road and stood watching the century disappear.

"We need to find out where we are and what's happening to us."

Charlie wasn't so sure that he meant it, but they couldn't just stand in the middle of a Roman road like a pair of dummies.

"*Abeamus*," he said, beginning to walk in the opposite direction to the soldiers.

"Yes, let's go," said Saima copying Charlie's Latin.

CHAPTER XVI

They walked by the ditch in case they happened upon another patrol. The road had been raised because the land to either side seemed boggier than where they had just come from. There were clumps of spiky marsh grass to either side, and up ahead was another bridge crossing a river. The bridge was wide enough for a large cart. It had been made of sturdy timbers which were a silvery grey. No one could be seen on the road ahead or on the bridge. The ground on the far side climbed a hill. On the ridge were mounded earthworks, on top of which was a tall, palisaded fence made of stout logs and two large wooden towers that stood either side of a massive double gateway, the entrance to a Roman fort. Stretching back down the road towards them was the *vicus*.

"Well, if we're going to find out anything, that looks like a good place to start."

Saima brushed past Charlie and headed off up the road.

"Hey, wait for me."

He ran to catch her up, and together they walked up into the lower edge of the straggle of dwellings and trading places.

They may have been wearing the right clothes for the period, but they certainly didn't feel as though they fitted properly or even that they themselves fitted in. The whole idea of being thrust back into history and having to survive did not amuse Charlie at all. Saima, however, was in her element. She could cope with this. She'd read a few bits about Romans, and she knew that Britain had accepted Roman ways. She just wasn't sure if those ways had been accepted at the moment of time in which she found herself.

They continued on up the main street. Near the top, on their left, was a blacksmith working at his forge, and opposite was a lean-to structure. Underneath it were some shelves with rows of cups and pottery bowls. They could smell food being cooked, its aroma wafting over from the rear of what must be a pottery and kitchen. The pair stood gawping at the sparks flying from the smith's hammer as it hit the searing glow of the iron being bent to the smith's will. Suddenly, there was a gush of steam as he quenched the hot metal in a leather bucket full of water. This was fascinating, and totally out of any experience they had ever met before. Saima wanted to move on and, without looking, turned and abruptly barged into a large belly bulging from beneath a shining ornamental breastplate. She bounced off and fell at the feet of an enormous man towering over her. He was flanked by three other soldiers, each carrying a *pilum*, a wooden-handled spear topped by a narrow metal shaft that ended in a wicked square-coned point.

"What is this?"

Saima shifted backwards and looked up. The soldiers stepped to the front and pointed their *pila*, so their points hovered barely a centimetre from her startled face. Drusus waited for a command to strike. When none came, he pulled back his spear and thrust out his leg.

His foot struck her left shoulder leaving a perfect pattern of stud marks from his hobnailed, military sandal.

"Move."

Charlie, without thinking, rushed to Saima's side.

"Sorry, sir, this is my sister. She's a bit simple, sir. That is, she isn't that bright, sir. We keep her locked indoors most of the time and only let her out for a little exercise and fresh air now and again, sir."

He got Saima to her feet, and they stood awaiting judgement. The blacksmith had been watching and moved to the front of his workshop by the road. He didn't know Drusus but he knew the fat one. Orcus was his name. Full of self-importance and would think nothing of ordering the pair stabbed to death where they stood; a cruel, heartless beast of a man. Charlie was like a rabbit stuck in the headlights. He couldn't move. His feet rooted him to the spot right in the middle of the road.

"Get the wretches out of my way," seethed Orcus. "Despatch them."

"Yes, sir."

Drusus began to withdraw his gladius from its scabbard, ready to follow orders.

"Stop, sir. Please. These are my slaves. They mean no harm."

The smith had stepped quickly between Drusus and the children. He still held his hammer and the piece of forged iron in his hands. He was marginally smaller in height than the soldier but his face showed genuine care and determination. Drusus sheathed his sword. The fat man, Orcus, switched his attention to the blacksmith.

"Oh, they're yours, are they? Well, there's a price for interrupting the Imperial tax collector in carrying out his duties."

Orcus was just a middle-ranking clerk in the office of the local *Publicanus*, the person responsible for collection of taxes. However, he had proved himself so effective in scraping every last '*denarius*' from the locals that he had become the man to whom the *Publicanus* turned when taxes had to be collected. It wasn't for the *Publicanus* to worry how they were collected, just that they were and on time. Orcus had bullied and battered many families and businesses over the years. He had a reputation for savagery and cruel ways of punishment if his demands weren't met on time. Today was his 'Reminder Day'. He made sure everyone knew what was expected and when while he grew fatter on the proceeds. Rome did not receive its full dues; some went astray straight into Orcus's *bursa*. He had designs on becoming the *Publicanus* and had made several visits to the temple priest in his secretive quest. This had had no effect so far, and he was becoming more annoyed with each passing day and visit. Prayers and sacrifices were one thing, but they hadn't worked and he needed something stronger. He had the answer; there would be no sacrifice this time other than the money he would have to lay out. He'd visit the priest this afternoon.

As the smith stood barring the route, a boy darted out from the shop. He was just a little older than Saima and Charlie by perhaps a year. He ushered them to the side of the road and in under the forge roof. Orcus stirred from his thoughts.

"That's very touching, but it doesn't solve my problem."

Orcus stepped through and past his bodyguard. An evil sneer came to his lips and continued to break across his whole face as he continued, "You see, I've been held up. Tax reminders must be given by the end of the day, and I'm now behind schedule because I'm having this little chinwag with you," he said. "Let me be honest, this is a severe offence. You should be duly punished, perhaps branded with your own irons, but I am a reasonable man. I'll turn a blind eye; I'll show mercy. You could say it's a kindness. Now how much did you say your slaves were worth?"

"I didn't."

The smith stood his ground, staring straight into Orcus's mean and yellow-tinged eyes. He wasn't easily frightened, but this man was able to be sickeningly brutal.

"Hmm, I reckon they are worth about ten *denarii* each, that's not very much, is it? But then they don't look like they are worth much." He had noticed their soiled hands and clothes. "That'll be twenty; I'll collect on *Calends*, the day after tomorrow. Have the money ready or tell your slaves they'll be sold to the highest bidder at the market. Now it's been nice chatting but I must get on."

Orcus started forward, and the smith stood aside to let him pass. Beneath that enormous belly, Orcus's legs wobbled, and as he walked, his feet turned out at forty-five degrees. He took short, little steps that moved his body from side-to-side with his arms stuck close in. In truth, he resembled an overstuffed duck.

CHAPTER XVII

The smith returned to the workshop. He had overstepped himself. Twenty *denarii* was almost a soldier's pay for a month. He hadn't any chance of finding that much in two days. Still, he couldn't leave those young children to be murdered in the middle of the street, could he? The three children were standing in the warmth given off from the furnace. There were tendrils of ditch-water steam rising from their clothes into the blackened thatch. The two huddled, wondering whatever was going to happen next. Slaves, he called them. Were they now to become his slaves?

"Ruus, fetch some wine and food."

They were sure that wasn't how slaves would be treated, but they waited uneasily. Ruus went and was back in less than three minutes with two bowls of something hot and steaming. He fetched two more, and then after bringing four cups of wine, he beckoned Saima and Charlie to sit next to him and his father. For the next ten minutes, not a word was said as they ate, but neither Saima nor Charlie touched their cups of wine.

"So, who are you and why are you here?"

Metallus was the first to speak. That what everyone called the blacksmith. It was an obvious nickname, not his real one. People had called his father

Metallus, and when it became time for Ruus to take up the reins of the business, no doubt he would be called Metallus too. He hardly remembered his real name, but that didn't worry him; one name was as good as another.

"We've come from a long way away," said Saima.

This wasn't true, though Saima had no idea where she was.

"Yes, it's taken us *ages* to get here."

Charlie winked at Saima, and she shook her head, wondering how he could joke at such a time.

"I'm Caius and this is Sabia."

The names that left his mouth were not the ones he had formed within his head. His tongue and lips had mutinied. Ignoring his brain, they had become independent beings with a life of their own. Just like their clothes and speech, it seemed that even their names had changed too. He'd not remember them; hopefully his mouth would.

"Why are you so far from home then?"

This was a question that hadn't had a chance to enter their heads. Charlie needed time to think. He reached for the cup of wine and drank. It tasted foul. He all but drained the cup in one gulp. He'd seen a film once where someone had done the same. Unfortunately, it caused him to choke, and he started a hacking cough that made his eyes water and bent him double. Metallus and Ruus thought this hilarious and burst out laughing. Saima, meanwhile, was banging him on the back with the flat of her hand. Neither helped Charlie to recover. However, as he sawed in his breath, he thought of a very good reason why they had come. He wiped his mouth on the rough, woven sleeves of his tunic and peeked around to see if anyone else would overhear him. He was acting the part well, for Metallus and Ruus leaned forward to listen expectantly. He began to speak but kept up the pretence by occasionally glancing to either side to check if all was still clear,

"We have been on a long journey in search of an object stolen from our village. We are the 'Chosen Ones'."

He paused to let the importance of being 'chosen' sink in.

"They sent us because we wouldn't be noticed; children get everywhere and can go anywhere. Well, until today, we hadn't been noticed. Since the theft, our village has suffered such dreadful problems. The crops are failing, and we have been raided more times in one month than in the whole of last year. We believe it is because the Gods have abandoned us. They demand we have a most sacred object returned."

Saima, realising that Charlie's story was a good one but would very soon start to get out of control as his lies grew, said, "We must find a statue, our statue and bring him home."

"The heavens are easily disturbed. The Gods hold us in the palms of their hands, it is true. They move us as they will for their sport," said Metallus. "I am surprised that *you* were sent on such an important mission."

Charlie was now fully warmed up and had all the answers as usual.

"You're right, it is strange, but you don't know what it's like where we live. Here you seem settled and calm. I expect that's because of the soldiers. Where we come from, our village is attacked by other local tribes, so they couldn't let a single fighting man or woman leave.

We were the oldest of the children left. I have three years till I come of age. I wanted to fight but they wouldn't let me. They said if we went together, that would be more natural."

Again, Saima interrupted his flow, "If only we could find Janus and return him, our troubles might be at an end."

It was only after making that statement that they both looked at each other and realised that was exactly what they needed to do. That was probably their only way back. They had to find the bust. That was what they had both been holding in the library. If they found that, perhaps they could reverse whatever magic had befallen them and return home.

"Janus, you say? Well, there's a strange coincidence. The *Publicanus* commissioned the building of a temple down by the river. This temple is to be dedicated in two days' time on the *Calends*. There will be a special sacrifice, of course. I don't know all the arrangements, but there will be a great deal of celebrating afterwards, no doubt."

Ruus took up his father's tale.

"There will be a procession, and we are all supposed to give an offering. Orcus, the fat man, will stand with the priest, and he will make note of each donation. Our donation will need to be that twenty *denarii* he demanded for your lives. That is why he mentioned the *Calends*. If we do not have enough, everyone will see. He will use us as an example, and that will bring the most severe punishment upon us, especially my father."

"The point is," Metallus continued, "the temple is to be dedicated to Janus. There will be an effigy to worship. We will all have to bow before it."

Saima and Charlie hadn't got a clue what he was talking about.

"What's an effigy?" they said almost in unison.

"An effigy is a figure, an image, a carving, a statue, anything that resembles the God you are worshipping. They must have an effigy if there is to be a dedication."

"So, that effigy is going to be *Janus,* and it could be the one we are searching for."

Metallus stood. His words echoed his thoughts.

"Well, yes, that's another point too. I usually get asked to do all sorts of plaques and metalwork for the fort. They even bring horses for me to make their sandals."

"Sandals?" questioned Charlie. "Don't you mean shoes, horseshoes?"

"Call them what you like. Here, you can try a pair if you want."

He stood and unhooked some thin iron shoes in the shape of a horse's foot hanging from a beam above his head. They had plates on the bottom, and then they seemed to fold up at the front. These bits were shaped like the front of a horse's hoof. Then there were forged rings with leather straps threaded through them. These would buckle around the horse's legs.

"They're very different to ours."

Metallus hooked them back up while Saima gave Charlie a quick punch on the arm to tell him to shut up. She'd never done that before.

"What he means is, our horses don't have shoes," she said.

"I'm not surprised; they're quite expensive to make. You know an effigy would take weeks of work and be twenty times as much money. I wish I had been asked to do it, but I wasn't, and I've no idea what it looks like or where it will have come from, so I suppose it could indeed be yours."

"We must get to see it somehow. We must check if it is ours," said Saima.

It may have been the smoke from the fire, but Charlie could see that tears were forming in her eyes.

CHAPTER XVIII

Drusus and half his *contubernium* had followed Orcus around all morning and some of the afternoon. This work was easy, but not the sort of task that trained fighters wanted or expected. It was during these expeditions that Drusus had got to know a good many people in the *vicus*. After all, he was the one doing all the threatening at very close quarters if the slightest difficulty with payment reared its head. During such a visit, he had encountered Faris. He was never any trouble and always on time with payments. A Syrian, Faris had grown up among the famed horse archers of the region of his birth. He had also practised bowmanship from an early age, but before his teens he had been apprenticed to a leatherworker. The horse archers became a part of the Roman army yet were unable to become Roman citizens. They formed auxiliary units and were sent all over the Empire to fight. Faris travelled alongside them to Dacia, Parthia, Gaul and now Britannia.

He had become skilled in making footwear and clothing as well as important items such as shields and harnesses for the horses. He never lost his talent as an archer, however, and on occasion competed with the horsemen. He would bet on his ability to beat them, shooting at all sorts of targets at different distances.

He was fond of the moving target challenge where he would say where his arrow would hit. They would bet against him, thinking that a lowly leatherworker would never have a chance against the best in their unit. How wrong they were. Drusus had once watched such a contest. The regular infantry never mixed with the 'foreigners', but he was intrigued and noted Faris's skill. That was when he had hatched his plan and set about putting it into action.

The problem he had to overcome was getting Orcus on board. Drusus knew that Orcus was not a religious man. Oh yes, he bowed before the Gods as any good Roman should, but his supreme God was gold, silver… money. He lived and breathed it and helped himself to the alteration of accounts so he could take for himself without anyone knowing. Drusus suspected but couldn't prove it. He needed something that would force Orcus to cut him in, a plan for which no one would suspect either of them. He needed Orcus's help to get access to the *quaestorium* where the legion's strongboxes were held. Perhaps he should just get him alone and ask him. No, Orcus may be fat but he was not stupid, and he'd laugh in his face at such a suggestion then find a way to make him disappear permanently. He needed to put Orcus on the back foot. He wanted to make him feel as though his world would come crashing down at any moment. Drusus needed some leverage. But how?

CHAPTER XIX

The best way to fix a problem, to sort an argument in your favour, or to make someone die an agonising death was to swear an oath. It was expensive and had been proved to work in at least two out of every hundred cases. If it worked for one person, why, it might work for you too. What was there to lose? A donation to the temple and perhaps payment for a special sacrifice to seal the deal was all it took. Of course, the cost was not to be ignored and could be as much as ten *denarii* each time, but if you had a thing you really wanted sorting out, this was the Roman way to do it.

Drusus had kept careful watch on Orcus, searching for that slip that would give him and his plan the chance it needed. While about his daily tasks, he noticed that Orcus had made several solo outings to the temple over the past month. It was difficult to miss him, round of face and body, sometimes almost rolling down the hill towards the river site, then with a puffed, reddened face stopping to gain breath, bending at the waist and resting his pudgy palms and fingers on his knees but hardly able to reach them on his climb back up to the fort. If it had been just once, Drusus might have accepted that and thought no more of it, but it had become a habit. Drusus was well aware that Orcus wasn't religious, so why all the temple visits he made so regularly? It was his duty to find out why and he was sure this was the opportunity he'd been looking for.

That afternoon, Drusus had been sitting outside his barrack block using sand and water to clean some spots of rust that had started to form on his gladius and chatting with some of his fellow 'tent' mates when he spied Orcus shuffling himself through the *Porta Praetoria*, the West Gate and down the track to the temple at the bottom of the hill. This was too good to miss. So abandoning his soldierly housework, he made an excuse about needing to relieve himself and found his way out of the southern gate. He moved down through the *vicus* and out the other side. He kept to the road and continued till he came to the bridge that crossed the spring stream and ran down the hill to the river near the temple. He could see Orcus still making his way slowly down the worn path from the West Gate. Drusus came off the road on the left side and scrambled down the shallow bank to the stream. He lay on his stomach, feet just above the water but his head at the top of the bank. Parting the grasses, he had a clear view of the river and the *votive* oath pool. Orcus arrived at the entrance formed by a gap in the wall which was on the eastern side of the temple.

From his hiding place, Drusus could see the central building around which was a covered walkway with columns. The inner building, the *cella*, housed the artefacts used in ceremonies and, in particular, the statue of Janus to whom this temple was dedicated. Outside the temple building but inside the surrounding walls, he could make out the altar used in the ceremonies for sacrifices, and standing alongside it were the priest and Orcus who had just arrived. There was a discussion.

Words were spoken but could not be heard at such a distance. What was clear was that Orcus was impatient and angry. He stood with his hands on his hips, chin pressing forward towards the priest, who held out his arms to the sides with palms facing the sky. His shoulders were moving up and down as he shrugged his replies. Orcus, at last, handed him a *bursa* weighted with coins. The priest went inside the building and returned with something small and flat about the size of his palm in one hand and a dove in the other. He handed the flat object to Orcus. Then the priest held the dove firmly upon the altar. He drew a curved knife from his belt and held it aloft. The sun glinted on the blade; its flat, straight, top edge shimmered with a radiance bright enough to dazzle the stars. From the tip of the point, the blade curved out and down as sharp as the finest slither of flint till it turned a right angle back to the narrow, hilted handle. At the end, a lion's head with shaggy mane and fiery eyes stared away from the hand that held it. As he raised his face to the southern sky, indistinct words soared to the sun. Now was the moment of sacrifice.

However, instead of the knife slitting the bird's throat, Orcus shouted something, grabbed the priest's arm and pulled the knife hand away. There were more words exchanged, and the priest returned the knife to its sheath. Orcus raised his arms in a wide 'v'. The priest, taking the dove in two hands, held it directly above his head, then allowed his hands to describe a flower blossoming, and the bird needed no second bidding to break for freedom. Flapping wildly, it clapped its wings as it rose and wheeled away across the river. Both men returned their arms to their sides. Orcus turned and walked towards the pool, towards Drusus.

He was but twenty paces away. Drusus breathed small, shallow breaths as he watched. Orcus held the flat piece of metal, and with a sharp *stylus,* a kind of pen, he scratched into its surface. Drusus then watched him roll up the soft lead into a miniature scroll. He knelt heavily by the edge of the pool. His hands linked, and at arms' length, he lowered them to the water's surface and trickled the '*defixio*' from the tips of his fingers into the crystal clear water. The oath had been made. It glistened as it sank to the bottom of the pool. Without a second glance, Orcus heaved his heavy frame upright and stood. Taking his time, he turned and wheezed his way to the path that led back up towards the fort gate.

Drusus saw the priest disappear back into the *cella.* This was his opportunity, and he could not afford to waste it. Crouching low, he dashed to the very spot where minutes before Orcus had knelt. He could still make out the round depressions where his knees had pressed into the soft grass on the edge. He shielded his eyes and gazed down into the pool. He could see a number of offerings. There was a broken dagger and coins, some of which had been bent into odd shapes, even what looked like a gold brooch. Drusus was not a religious man. He'd seen too many battles and vicious deaths to think that there were any Gods. Might they even care what humans did to each other? Not likely. Did he even imagine there were higher beings that would concern themselves with the daily toings and froings of humans? That was just ridiculous. What he wanted was that rolled *defixio* that Orcus had deposited.

The sun came out from behind a cloud and at once the rays pierced the pool and flickered across the newest, shiniest object. It didn't look far away. He rolled up his sleeve and thrust his arm down towards the scroll. Despite hanging his body over the edge and the water rising up to his shoulder, he couldn't reach it. The pool was deeper than he thought. There was only one way to get it, but he'd have to be quick; someone was bound to notice pretty soon. Kneeling back up, he removed his tunic and poised himself over the edge of the pool. Leading with his right arm and digging his left hand into the soft earth of the bank for grip, he allowed his arm to descend. As his shoulder disappeared, he let his head hang just above the surface. Now he was deep enough. He tried to snatch it up, but his hand missed. He had forgotten that water makes things seem to be in one place, but somehow they're not. He must watch his hand more closely and hover it above the object. He had disturbed the bottom with his first attempt, and a muddy cloud started to cover the *defixio*. He had one last chance.

Lowering himself once more, this time he allowed his head and upper chest to dip beneath the surface. His right hand hovered, then like a kestrel drops on its prey, his hand swooped and gripped it in a tightly closed fist. His hand emerged and he spread his arms wide and pushed against the bank. It was as he shook his head from side-to-side shedding water that he saw the priest coming at a pace out of the eastern opening. He still had the sacrificial knife and was perhaps intent on using it. Drusus had to think fast. Moving both arms and hands towards his trousers, he tucked the *defixio* into the waistband and then, not seeming to notice the approach of the priest, he again spread his arms wide to the bank and lowered his head to the water. Before he could dip his head, he felt the tip of the knife's blade prick the back of his neck. He lifted himself slowly as before, and the priest kept the blade in position as Drusus sat with knees bent and legs tucked beneath him.

The priest spoke his holy-wrapped words, "Oh, Janus, behold the sinner who disturbs your pool. I will make him atone for this misdeed, and it is by your will this base offence will be avenged."

Drusus bent forwards, throwing his arms straight out before him, his chest grazing his knees and his nose touching the grass in front of him. From here, he begged with a voice of deepest aching, "Forgive me, Lord, but I do not steal," he lied. "I come to ask our great Lord Janus to look out for my friend Vitus, who has been so cruelly cut down. I come to ask him to guard, my lord, the steering of his soul across the Styx, the dark River of the Dead."

The priest was taken aback but not convinced.

"You know full well that it is Charon that ferries the dead across the *Acheron*. What nonsense do you speak?"

"My Lord, my friend died in an ambush on the road. We had to leave him, then with bravery we returned to place a small coin in his mouth to pay for the ferryman, but we found that his body had been taken and that the payment could not be made. My *contubernium* are afraid for his wellbeing in the afterlife. As their leader, I felt it was my duty to do what I could to smooth his journey and came to pray for him. Janus, our oldest God, I thought would perhaps know the river better by its Greek name rather than its Roman one."

The lie, so neatly formed, was working, and the priest relaxed and replaced the knife in its sheath.

"Why, if you were so concerned, didn't you come to me? I can perform the rites he needs, and you would be assured of his safe passage."

Drusus returned to a sitting position and looking up at the priest with almost angelic eyes, said in a woeful tone, "My lord, we are poor men, and although we would give generously for your help, we are miserable brothers and wouldn't have enough to pay you. We have gambled and drunk it all away in the taverns. How could I leave dear Vitus to suffer? I had to find a way to help him. This seemed the best chance. I had to make amends, and then I could tell the boys back at camp that all would now be well."

"Well, it's most unusual, but I see you are truly knowledgeable and have faith."

The priest was satisfied and beckoned Drusus to get up. Drusus picked up his tunic and popped it over his head. The priest turned away as Drusus started to stand. The *defixio* slipped from his waistband and toppled off his sandal into the short grass in front of his feet. The priest had a final thought and turned back towards Drusus. It was too late for Drusus to pick it up, and there it lay in full view. Would he see the 'curse' scroll? The priest moved purposefully back towards him. He stood looking into Drusus' eyes, the scroll lying at their feet between them.

"I will pray for him. You have shown me the true spirit of brotherhood. That will be your payment."

Drusus bowed his head and shuffled his foot to cover the scroll.

"Thank you, my lord, we are most grateful."

He raised his head to find the priest already striding across the grass back to the temple. Drusus just hoped that the scroll he'd picked up was the right one. He made his way in the opposite direction back towards the road and unrolled the curse as he went, and smiled as he read it. This was just what he needed. Without delay, he got back to camp and dressed in his uniform before marching straight to the *principia* where Orcus worked.

CHAPTER XX

He was stopped by the guards outside, whose *pila* crossed at his approach. This was the place where the offices were, but also it was here that the fort's riches were kept. Orcus was at a desk in the front office filing his report from the expedition into the vicus earlier in the day.

"I need to speak with my superior officer about this morning," he explained.

Orcus heard and thought he ought to find out what the problem might be.

"Enter!" he shouted, and the guards snapped to attention. Their spears were pulled upright, leaving a gap through which Drusus passed and on into a small office on the left. He stood to attention in front of the desk.

"Yes, Drusus, what is it?"

Orcus regarded the figure in front of him. He was busy and needed to get the false accounts finished.

"I have something important to share with you, sir."

"Do you indeed? That's most interesting, I'm sure; perhaps when I'm less busy. Let's say tomorrow at some time."

Orcus went back to his figures, his fine stylus scratching curls of wax from the surface of a tablet.

"You are dismissed, Drusus."

"No, sir, I rather think it needs sharing now. I believe that a tale I heard from a very grateful dove would benefit us both."

The pen stopped in mid-stroke. Orcus' eyes bulged as his cheeks flushed radish red. He shoved his chair back, hoisting himself upright with a series of pushes and grunts.

"What manner of tale?"

Orcus's tone had become softer, more concerned. If he could have moved quickly, he would have grabbed Drusus by the throat and squeezed the life out of him, but he wasn't at all nimble and never would be. Drusus closed the office door. Then he turned and went back to the desk behind which Orcus had now regained his composure. Drusus had read and learned. How well he played the actor who had just been given his cue. He started his speech, pulled word for word from the *defixio*.

"Orcus, to the most Holy God Janus. I, who am worthy of greatness, would ask your divinity that you suffer..."

Then slowly edging round the desk,

"...*Publicanus* Lucius to fall to sudden illness and failing sight..."

and finally, right beside Orcus' ear he whispered the final words,

"...so that he may expire by your holiness's will. With renewed prayers, I ask that my plea be executed immediately by your divine majesty."

Orcus was stunned, but to give him credit, he tried to bluff his way out of a very tight cul-de-sac.

"You've a vivid imagination, Drusus. Why would you ever think to say such a thing about me? It's pure fantasy. What do you hope to gain, and who would ever believe such a tale from a low-born soldier?"

"I have your *defixio*, sir. It is safely hidden. I'm sure the priest would confirm my story, but we needn't involve anyone else unnecessarily. I have a little plan that will serve you and me very well."

Orcus had beads of sweat forming on his top lip and across his forehead. The light fawn hue of his tunic under his armpits had changed to a dark mushroom colour as cold sweat oozed from every pore. He would need to find a way to get rid of this soldier and the priest as soon as possible, but for now he needed to be careful and decided to play the game.

"I'm always interested in hearing suggestions. Continue with your proposal, and we'll see if it bears examination."

"We both deserve a better fate. You have your desires, and I have mine too. Money will give you great power and influence, a sure way to your goal. Together, we can satisfy all our wants. What is even more important is we can accomplish all of it safely without a hint of anything coming back to haunt us. Shall I continue?"

Orcus was indeed intrigued, and he had no desire to see his *defixio* brought to a higher authority's attention. He sat and planted his elbows on his desk. His forearms created a triangle, and the fingers of each stubby hand steepled together. His wrists rocked his interlocked fingers backwards and forwards till they finally remained pointing at Drusus, indicating he should continue.

Drusus remained polite and respectful as this would gain the best result.

"You work here in the *principia,* and in this building there is the *quaestorium,* the strongroom where coin and other treasure is kept safely. You wear a ring key. Does that unlock the strongboxes?"

Orcus was nervous and twiddled the ring round on his finger, not wishing to allow sight of it. The key now faced his palm, and the ring looked as normal and commonplace as any other.

Drusus was correct. Orcus' finger ring had a short piece of bronze attached to it, and where it turned a right angle, there was a slightly fatter piece with three slots. This was the key. The securest way to keep something locked safe was a ring key. It was always with you unless your hand or finger was cut off and the ring stolen. Orcus nodded.

"How many boxes?"

"Six."

"And you know which ones contain coin?"

"Of course, each chest holds different values."

"How many hold *denarii*?

"Three…but there are two others with *aurei*. Gold is worth far more. Then there's one that holds jewellery, *et cetera*."

"I'm only interested in *denarii*. How much does each *arca* hold?"

"When they are full, six thousand."

"Good. In that case, you must go to the strongroom at some time today. I suggest that you say you are going to check that your accounts are correct if you are asked, although I am sure that someone as important as yourself will not be challenged.'"

Orcus was about to object, but Drusus was well aware of what Orcus was and wasn't allowed to do.

Drusus continued, "Mark two of the boxes that hold *denarii* and leave them unlocked. Perhaps place a piece of straw beside them, but you decide how. Then you will need to take thirty *denarii* from one of the boxes before you leave."

"What are you going to do? How will you get past the guards?"

Drusus had it planned out, and it was best Orcus knew as little as possible other than his understanding that when it was all over, he would be a richer man.

"You needn't concern yourself with how or what or when. All I want you to do is ensure that when you leave here, several people see the ring key firmly on your finger with the key part showing."

Orcus fiddled the ring back so the key was on top.

"You will, of course, be visiting the *Publicanus* to give him your accounts. That will be an ideal time to have it fully in view. Bring me twenty of the coins and the ring in a purse this evening. I will be at the tavern. As regards the other ten, I need you to ask permission from the *Publicanus* to take those as payment for a new key as yours is wearing out. You will not need to spend it, just keep it."

CHAPTER XXI

The night had been spent peacefully enough. Charlie and Saima had dozed off under some warm furs they had been given, the stresses of the day giving way to exhaustion. Saima had lain awake a little longer than Charlie and had pondered about how close she had come to being murdered out on the street that day. Charlie had saved her. He'd actually saved her, and she had so often seen him be totally selfish in school. He never thought of anyone else or of the consequences of his actions. Today, he had thought not of himself but of her. The other thing she couldn't quite get clear in her head was that he and Metallus had lied, and it was lies that had made the difference between her life and death. Until now, she had always held that telling the truth was the right and only thing to do, but if they hadn't lied to the soldiers and said that she was 'simple' or 'stupid' or that she was a slave, then she could now be dead. It was lies that had saved her. Perhaps lies weren't always such a bad thing.

They awoke to the sound of a hammer and a gushing, roaring dragon. Startled, Charlie sprang from the bench, ready to run, only to see Ruus pumping two sides of a large leather bag. He squeezed it in and out, and as it wheezed, it blew air into the fire, heating it till it was white-hot. Sitting in the middle of the fire was a bowl.

At one point, it had been pinched to form a small pouring spout. Inside was a glowing liquid, yellow and orange, which at its surface seemed to have blackened deposits being shifted around by the occasional bubble rising up from below. To one side, Metallus was holding some long tongs with flattened ends and beside him on the earthen floor was a small block mould of hardened sand the colour of bricks. It was supported on each side to stop it from falling over, while at the top was a flared opening. Metallus instructed Ruus to stop pumping the bellows and dipped the open tongs into the blazing fire. The ends pressed together, gripping the bowl and it was lifted out. Metallus swung the tongs carefully so that the bowl's spout was over the mouth of the mould. He slowly tipped the molten bronze, and a scorching stream of gingery fire flowed down into the mould's depths, then as it filled a golden sun rose to the top of the funnel. Metallus stopped pouring and placed the tongs and bowl to one side.

Saima and Charlie watched as the sun's colour mutated to a crimson then purple as it started to cool. Ruus said not a word but directed them to sit and watch while he brought them some thin wine and bread. Over the next half hour, they were mesmerised by the flames from the furnace and skilful hammering. Metallus sat back for a while and had some refreshment before turning back to the cooling mould.

Drusus had visited the evening before. He brought with him the ring key. He said his superior needed it copied as it was worn and may soon break. If Metallus could complete the task by midday the next day, then he would be well paid. Today was when it was to be collected, and the time had come to see if his mould had done its job. Taking a small hammer from the shelf, Metallus tapped the top of the block near the flared funnel. It cracked a little and a small portion of sand fell away from the rim. The metal beneath was still hot but had solidified to a burnt umber. He motioned that they should gather round to watch. Once more he struck, this time to the other side of the mould but still on top. The crack widened and zig-zagged down its right side.

"One or two more should do it," he said loud enough that they all heard.

A sharp tap on the left followed by one to the right and the mould split and toppled open. One half was empty, except it held a perfect imprint of half the ring key. The other held its exact mirror twin filled with solid bronze. Three small prongs attached to a short stalk spur ending with a hollow ring just big enough to fit a fleshy middle finger. A channel of bronze led up from that to a solid cup shape where the bronze had been poured in.

"Is it still hot?" asked Saima.

Ruus replied, "Yes, now it can be worked a little to make it perfect."

"Why don't you stick it in the water to cool it down like that metal bar you worked yesterday?"

Metallus raised his eyes to the roof as if this was the stupidest question ever asked. He waved at Ruus and he explained.

"It's OK to do that with iron, but if you do it with bronze it makes the metal softer than if it cools normally, that would mean the key would break after a very short time. No, it must be left to cool and worked a little to harden it."

"Then I'll polish it with a woollen pad, and it should be ready by the time the sun is at its height. The Gods know how much I need that money right now. This will help, but I'll still be well short come tomorrow," said Metallus.

Ruus looked miserable, and Saima knew that he needed something to take his mind off his father's problem.

"I know," she said, "we could visit the temple and see if we can get a glimpse of the *Janus* effigy."

"Get you with your big words," joked Charlie and the mood was lifted as the three companions set out into the sunshine and headed downhill towards the bottom of the *vicus*.

CHAPTER XXII

The main street was busy that morning. Traders of all kinds had laid out their wares to sell, and the noise of voices and hooves filled the spaces around them. They could see cooking vessels strung by chains above warming fires, and as the wood kindled and smouldered in turn beneath them, curls of delicious aroma-filled smoke drifted on the light breeze across their faces. They were so taken in by it all and by Ruus's explanations that they were surprised when a man loomed in front of them and they had to jink to avoid him. He said not a word but moved on past, turning back briefly with a quizzical glance. They noticed he wore a tanned, leather apron and tied tightly on his wide belt was a *bursa* that hung heavily. Charlie and Saima thought no more of it, but Ruus became very agitated and was keen to put distance between himself and the swarthy-faced figure. He ducked down the nearest gap between a woollen trader and a small fenced enclosure that harboured an ox and in one corner a yoke and simple wooden plough. They followed him, thinking this was some kind of short cut. He was nowhere to be seen. They searched high and low with their eyes, seeking where he might be. Suddenly, a short whistle came from behind them. Ruus had jumped into the ox enclosure and was crouching low behind the woven willow fence that created it.

"That man, go and check if that man is coming back to look for me," Ruus uttered in not much more than a whisper.

"Why? What's wrong?" Saima asked.

"Please just go and see," he pleaded.

Saima marched back up the alley, leaving Charlie behind. She reached the corner and peered round. She could not see anyone like him. Then she heard a rough voice inside a cloth merchant's shop.

"Where is the metalworker's place?"

"Oh, you mean Metallus. Go up the hill and you'll find his workshop near the end just a bit back from the road," was a woman's reply.

There was a grunt of thanks and he pushed his way past a curtain of material that flapped back into Saima's face. He turned left and was engulfed in the bustle. Saima returned to the boys. As she arrived, her nose was assaulted by a most obnoxious, sweet, grassy stink.

"What on earth is that smell?" she gasped, almost unable to breathe through the fumes.

Ruus still hadn't stood up. Saima peered over the hurdle at him and saw exactly where the pong was coming from. Ruus had both of his shoes planted in a sickly, green cowpat. His open-strapped leather sandals had allowed the fragrant ooze to seep in among his toes and up the sides of his ankles.

"Phwoar," exclaimed Charlie. "What a niff; worse than my dog's farts!"

Saima was shocked; she put her hands over her ears and could only say, "Oh Caius, really."

Ruus was less concerned about the smell and more concerned about the man he'd run away from.

"Has he gone?"

"Yes," confirmed Saima, "but he's going to see your dad in his workshop."

Saima explained what she'd heard, and this put Ruus even more on edge. He climbed back over the fence, and despite the smell and his trail of smudgy footprints, they carried on their altered route and exited onto a grassy slope that led down to the temple at the bottom of the hill. Ruus unfastened his sandals and cleaned them as best he could by stroking them through the grass. Then pulling up some more, he continued to wipe between his toes and around his feet. He flung the grass away and jiggled his hands through some of the longer blades and soon was satisfied he was as pure as he could be; then he settled beside the other two who were seated looking down the hill.

"Why were you so worried about that man?" asked Saima.

"It's a long story, but I witnessed a murder."

This time Charlie was the most eager to find out what happened.

"What's that got to do with the man we saw, though?"

"He was the murderer, but the man he killed got up after a while and walked away into the woods."

"That's impossible," pronounced Saima.

"That's what I thought too, but I saw the victim stand up and remove his bloodied clothes and walk away. Even stranger, he met the killer in a clearing in the woods. I followed them and watched as he helped his victim change clothes, but then they heard me and I just escaped by hiding under some tree roots. Fortunately, they gave up and they left together."

"How do you know he was the murderer, though?"

"Well, I don't exactly. I just put the two things together."

"Sounds reasonable to me," said Charlie. "Where did they go?"

"I've no idea, but now the murderer wants to see my father."

"If they didn't find you, then they can't know what you look like or who you are?"

Saima was always the first to see the logic of a situation. Ruus had to agree, but none of them could work out what business such a man could have with Metallus. They agreed to forget it for now as there was very little likelihood any more murders fake or otherwise would take place in the busy *vicus*.

CHAPTER XXIII

The morning was warm, and it was the first time since the museum and library incident that they'd had a chance to relax and just try to take things easy. Saima and Charlie gazed across the meadow. The river, taking its ponderous journey past the temple, shimmered in the brightness. Charlie plucked a blade of grass and, licking his left thumb, stuck the grass on its outside. He brought his right thumb across and trapped the blade in-between. Pushing his lips to the hollow formed by his knuckles, he breathed in and blew into the hole past the blade of grass. A thin, trumpety sound skipped out. Ruus laughed and asked Charlie to do it again. This time the note changed and was a bit deeper; even Saima had to smile. She looked up from making a chain of daisies and buttercups. Ruus by this time was making his own unsuccessful attempts at producing a grassy, reed sound. Saima looked to her left and then once more back down the hill to the temple.

"Caius, doesn't this landscape remind you of somewhere?"

Charlie looked up from making his second musical instrument.

"Not particularly." He was far more interested in Ruus helping him boost the wind section of his rural orchestra.

"Look. There's a temple, a river below it, a ditch that flows down the hill into the river; we're sat on a hill above the temple. Can't you see?"

Saima stood up; she was almost beside herself with the joy of discovery.

"What is it?"

Charlie's attention had been grabbed.

"It's home!" she exclaimed, "We haven't gone anywhere. We've been in Wicton all along."

Charlie was staggered.

"Hold on, you're right. We came from the road over there, not far from the bridge."

"Yes, that's where the library is... er... was... no, will be. Our school would be up there to the right, but it's just grass and a few trees now. So our houses would be..."

Saima put her hands to her face and she began to sniffle. Charlie understood. He went to her side and put a hand on her shoulder,

"It'll be alright, you'll see. We'll find *Janus* and be home in no time."

He had to say something even if he didn't quite believe it himself, but he said it with such confidence that it cheered her up a little and she managed a smile, then wiped her sleeve across her eyes and then her nose.

"URRGGHH! Disgusting," chimed Charlie.

At that precise moment, a fanfare arose from the ground. Ruus had managed to blast his grass trumpet and they all burst out laughing. They approached the temple by meeting the path that turned west off the main road and arrived at the eastern entrance. In front of them was the *cella* and they could see the columns that formed the walkway around it. Inside the outer walls of the complex were other buildings. Ruus explained that this was the *temenos*, although he hadn't been this close before. It had a few small storage buildings and another structure that was the priest's house. They approached the front of the inner temple, where a few steps led up to a large door. It was firmly locked. Charlie was sure he'd seen that lock before somewhere. He'd have to search his memory. As that route inside was blocked, they decided to walk around and look for any other way to get to the interior. They turned right and after a dozen paces turned the corner to walk down the western side of the *ambulatory*. It was in shadow and felt rather gloomy and soulless. Nothing but a blank wall here, so once more they turned and were disappointed that the walls were solid and there was no chance of gaining any access there either.

"This is hopeless; there's no way in other than through the front door," said Ruus as they emerged yet again at the bottom corner of the door wall. Suddenly, there was a shout, and a figure clad in a white gown was striding from the house to intercept them.

"Kneel," Ruus whispered urgently. "It's the priest. Let me do the talking."

They knelt and bowed their heads.

"Children!"

The priest seemed shocked.

"Children in the temple precincts. What sacrilege is this?"

Ruus raised his head and spoke courteously, "My lord, we are so charmed by the wonder of this place; we felt bound to see and experience it for ourselves. We mean no harm, only that you might allow us to share the marvel before our eyes. Our parents told us about it but imagining is not seeing it for ourselves. We had to come here."

The priest surveyed the three of them with a doting smile.

"It is delightful that those so young should wish to share in the mysteries of our divinity. Your parents have taught you well, and despite your trespassing here, I see a passionate fire within you all. I saw you try the door. What did you want within?"

Saima had picked up on the style of politeness required and answered,

"My Lord, we are suppliants at thy feet."

"Blimey," whispered Charlie, "she's off on one again using her big words. What the heck's she talking about."

"Shh… she's got his attention and I think we may be lucky," said Ruus.

Saima continued, raising her head and then her arms to the sky as if in prayer.

"We simply beg to see the one Great Divinity at the heart of his Sanctuary."

Charlie thought he better make a gesture of support for whatever she was saying. He'd never heard Saima speak so many words in one sentence that he didn't understand. He did, however, get that she was trying to wheedle her way inside, so with a massive flourish, he threw himself full length and started to writhe on the floor at the priest's feet.

"What is wrong with him? Do something," stuttered the alarmed priest.

Saima had seen Charlie's antics before and guessed this was his way of showing a kind of religious enthusiasm.

"My Lord, just the mention of His Divinity puts my brother into bouts of fitful dedication."

Sometimes it seemed you did just have to lie. Brother? Charlie being dedicated? No way! If it helped, though, then that had to be alright by her. The priest stepped back further and Charlie started his recovery. To give him his due, he could not have done better on the West End stage because the priest was totally taken in and indicated they should follow him. They stopped at the Great Door. The priest produced a very strange key that Charlie now recognised and stored in his memory. The bolt withdrew smoothly and the door opened. Inside, they faced a smaller opening across an open hallway illuminated by the light from the open door. Here was a room dimly lit by torches held in sconces on each of the four walls. On a plinth in the middle of the room arose a statue. The priest walked forward reverently and lifted the deity from its place. The children still playing their roles all knelt once more. The priest turned to face the children and stepped directly in front of Ruus. Raising the effigy high and speaking soft words of prayer, he brought it down in front of him. Ruus looked and bowed. He moved along the line to Charlie who was next, and with the same actions and words presented it in front of him. Charlie gasped and eyed Saima beside him. This time as the priest performed his rites for her, joy filled her being.

She shouted, "Hallelujah, praise to our *Deus Maximus Ianus*!"

The statue's own four eyes seemed to gleam at those words. The priest was hugely impressed at her reaction. He presumed he had witnessed true devotion. What, in fact, he had seen but could never have understood was that the head of the statue was the exact one the two young travellers had held in the library. The only puzzling thing was that it had a body draped in a flowing tunic with billowing sleeves held in folds at his elbows. His knees and muscled calves were revealed beneath, then came his bare feet standing on their own plinth, all in shining reddish-brown coppery bronze. Inscribed on it were the words Saima had read: '*Deus Maximus Ianus*', The Greatest God of All, Janus.

Perhaps they were wrong. Perhaps this was just another copy of the one they sought. If it was theirs, though, how had its head become detached and what had become of the body? It seemed certain that their head was the very one in front of them. Whatever the answer, they now knew where it was and that to have any chance of getting home, they had to have it. The only question was... how?

CHAPTER XXIV

At the top of the *vicus* nearest the fort, the workshops, houses and alleys in-between ended abruptly. A further one hundred metres on was a defensive *fossa* or ditch studded with sharpened stakes, and then an embankment which rose up beyond that had been raised with all the soil and turf from the digging. Soldiers and goods came and went with regularity. Faris was known in the fort as he manufactured the horse harnesses or mended the sandals when needed. Sometimes wooden shields covered in leather would need repair, and it would be on him they would call. This afternoon, he would rely on the tower guards at the gate remembering him and allowing entry without cause to stop or search.

His first task, however, was to make a call on Metallus. Nearing the end of the main road up to the fort, he turned into a workshop. Metallus came out from the back and regarded the man in front of him.

"It's Faris, isn't it?"

Faris nodded and offered his right arm. Metallus returned the gesture, and both men clasped each other's wrists with their right hands. Metallus knew Faris but they had rarely spoken together. They both visited the fort because of their trades.

After the initial greeting, it was Faris who spoke, "I hoped I'd find you well, but word has it that you have been treated harshly."

Metallus had no idea how Faris would know of his run-in with Orcus, but he supposed that as the *vicus* was a small community and the incident happened in full view of all and sundry, it was only a matter of time before word of it spread. Metallus was unsure how to continue the conversation and wondered why Faris would come to seek him out. He decided to offer just a few words on the subject. It could be dangerous to reveal how he felt.

"It was a pure misunderstanding, an unfortunate set of circumstances and children need protection, that was all."

"I couldn't agree more, but tomorrow your protection will cost you dearly. I'm truly sorry."

Metallus had no desire to stand and chat about his misfortunes and decided the conversation should finish there.

"Thank you for your kind thoughts. If you don't mind, I'm really very busy and must get on."

Faris stood his ground.

"I wondered if I might help you a little."

Metallus turned.

"I'm not sure I need help. I'm only casting and polishing today, and that is a one-man job."

"I think you misunderstand me. The help I'm offering will ensure you can worry a little less about your fine."

"What do you mean?"

"I have a great deal of work to do in the fort, and I wondered if I could hire your cart and your help. I need to transport materials and tools. It would be extremely difficult to traipse back and forth to the fort from my workshop carrying it all by hand. Then, with so much on board, I would need help to pull it back. That's where your services are needed as well. I will pay you, of course. Let's say five *denarii* for the cart and another five for your help."

Metallus was taken aback. Ten *denarii* would provide half of the money he needed, but the amount offered for the cart and his help was overly generous.

"I am extremely grateful for your offer, but I couldn't take so much from you. I'd feel as if I was stealing."

How close to the truth he was. Drusus had provided Faris with ten *denarii* the previous evening. He'd soon owe far more than just twenty *denarii*. However, he kept those reflections to himself and said, "We are tradesmen, you and I. We must support each other when we can. Perhaps someday I may need help, and you might return the favour."

Metallus took a few paces towards Faris with his arm extended. Grasping his wrist as before, he placed his left hand on the leatherworker's shoulder.

"Perhaps I could see the cart, and then I can judge what can and cannot be transported?" Faris asked respectfully.

"Of course, come with me."

They walked around to the back where Faris started to circle the cart and stopped here and there, nodding his approval. The dimensions were as he had hoped. He concluded his tour and pronounced, "This will do nicely."

Metallus felt the need to add his thanks.

"I shall be forever grateful to you; it will be delivered in a couple of hours."

CHAPTER XXV

Feeling at last the fates were on his side, Metallus returned to filing and polishing the ring and its key. A short while later, Drusus appeared. He stepped in from the street and got straight to the point. There was no greeting, no niceties.

"Is it ready?"

Metallus picked up the original ring key and its new sister from behind him on a low shelf. Drusus inspected them. He turned them this way and that, then he walked to the door. Metallus was sure that the promised payment was gone; however, he saw Drusus hold up the key to the sunlight.

"You have done well," he said, moving back inside. "It's perfect."

Drusus withdrew a *bursa* of coins from his belt, paid and left.

Metallus went inside and opened the small bag pouring the coins from it into his hand. Ten *denarii*. He sunk to his knees. With the money for the key and the other ten from Faris, he could pay the fine and all would now be well. The fates were on his side.

CHAPTER XXVI

An hour or so after midday, Metallus went out to the back of the workshop and emptied a few items out of his cart. It had just two largish wheels on a stout, square axle that raised the cart half a metre off the ground. It had been in the family a fair few years and had been a good investment as its wooden boarding was still strong. It may at one time have been intended to be pulled by an ox or a donkey but never had that been the case in the time Metallus had known it. Two wooden arms extended forward, which allowed Metallus and Ruus to stand together to push or pull it. As it had no cargo, it moved easily on wheel hubs that were well greased with animal fat. Metallus manoeuvred the cart out and onto the main street and, standing between the bars, pulled it easily through the thinning afternoon crowds the short distance to Faris's workshop.

Faris had been expecting him and guided Metallus to the rear near a back doorway covered by a hide. They exchanged few words other than agreeing that Metallus would return an hour before sunset to help push the cart up to the fort. Faris disappeared back inside the dark interior and returned with a leather pouch.

"Your payment; I am sure I can trust you, and you will not let me down," he said.

Metallus nodded his thanks. He could find no words that could explain his gratitude further. He thrust the pouch inside his tunic and deep down to where his belt cinched his waist. Here it would be secure. He left, and Faris watched as he turned back onto the main street. Now his preparations must begin.

Inside his workshop, Faris had been busy. He had already constructed a stout narrow plank with wooden slats that had been nailed on at a distance of a *pes* apart, a Roman foot of around thirty centimetres. He called Vitus from his dingy hiding place to listen to his explanation and watch a demonstration of how it was to be used. It was then taken to the cart and placed tightly against one of the sides. Faris gathered together his tools and some hides of varying thicknesses which he readied by the back door, including a long coil of rope and several leather sacks with hide drawstrings. He produced two shields he had repaired and laid those close by. His last act was to provide Vitus with a small frame-saw. Vitus was dressed in a dark tunic and trousers. He took some cold, charred wood from the edge of the cooking fire, which he wrapped in some cloth and tucked into his waistband. After he was given his instructions, he exited the building and nimbly pushed himself between the plank and the far side of the cart. Faris moved to the front of the cart, but with the added weight, it had tipped the wooden, pulling bars skywards. The cart balanced over the axle, and as Faris pulled a bar, so Vitus roughly slid up to the front boarding. He let out a strangled squawk as his head collided with the boards.

"Keep quiet, you fool!" muttered Faris angrily.

There was no reply, but Vitus's livid face told a story.

Faris threw the coil of rope on top of him and then, after loading his few tools, covered Vitus with the hides and finally placed the repaired shields on top. Again, he manoeuvred himself to the back of the cart, ensuring Vitus's crunched body was totally covered and invisible. Vitus arranged himself comfortably. It was merely a quarter-hour later that Metallus arrived and the two men set off for the fort. Metallus made a casual comment about how the cart must be well-laden due to its weight but Faris said nothing. There were few people on the street at this time, so although their progress was slow, it meant they could keep going in a straight line and not waste energy stopping and starting or having to avoid people. They passed Metallus's workshop and soon arrived somewhat breathless outside the fort gates.

A soldier standing on guard above shouted down, "What's your business here?"

"I'm Faris. I bring shields that have been repaired."

The soldier disappeared into the watchtower and a minute later reappeared alongside another who wore a cloak and carried a *vitis,* his vine staff. This signified the rank of *centurion.* He peered down, and recognition stole across his face,

"Yes, that's Faris the leatherworker," he explained to the soldier, then called down, "You are welcome, Faris, but who is that with you?"

"I needed help, sir. This is Metallus the smith, and this is his cart that has helped me bring supplies and repairs."

"Ah yes, now I remember him. Wait there, I'll be down. Draw the bolt!" shouted the *centurion.*

The large, securing timber was slid back, and as the gates swung open, the *centurion* and the soldier appeared. He marched forward and greeted Faris.

"What have you brought us then?"

The cart was piled high, and the shields on top were of immediate interest. He lifted one out over the side of the cart and ran his hand over the new edging that pressed the leather facing to the curved wood behind.

"Nice work," he said, nodding his approval.

He was not so careful in returning it to the cart as he had been removing it. He hoisted it to shoulder height and lobbed it back to its approximate previous position. Its weight as it landed caught Vitus unawares, and he was struck by a corner near his arrow wound. Stopping himself from crying out, he couldn't help his leg from jerking backwards towards the back of the cart. His foot encased in its damp, soft sandal was pushed past the cover of the hides. He couldn't pull it back for fear of the hides being scrunched, revealing his hiding place.

"What's round the back then?"

This *centurion* was being nosy. Faris moved ahead and ambled to the back of the cart. He had to stay calm, but as he lowered the backboard, the shoe and its foot were in plain view. He started to rearrange the hides to cover it, but only succeeded in ensuring no flesh was visible. The *centurion*, who started to move after him, rounded the end of the cart and saw the sole of a sandal sticking out.

"Oh, what's this then?" he enquired.

"That's..."

"Patrol approaching, sir,"

The soldier distracted the *centurion*'s attention. He looked down the road, and indeed a patrol was approaching. Well, they would have to wait. The sandal was his concern, and that would be dealt with first. Faris, seizing the opportunity, pulled the sandal from the foot. He had thought of an excuse during the distraction,

"They are irreparable, sir. I am returning them."

"They? You've only got one here. Where's the other one then?"

"It'll be somewhere underneath, sir," his voice quivered.

Faris thrust his hand beneath the hides and grasped. He caught a leg and rapidly moved his hand down past an ankle and was relieved to find that this was the other sandaled foot. Without taking a breath, he ripped it from the foot on which it sat. The worn leather straps gave way easily, and Faris presented the footwear in front of the *centurion*'s face. He spoke truly, for the sandal was certainly now beyond repair. With a look of utter disgust, the *centurion* brushed his arm aside.

"Don't put that smelly object anywhere near me! Go, Faris, move that cart or my *Optio's* patrol will push it into the ditch."

Faris needed no second telling. Metallus had stayed out of the way and was ready to pull. He had no desire to fall foul of another Roman. At once, Faris and Metallus pulled the cart inside, followed by the *centurion* and then the patrol. They went about their business of greeting and reporting. The cart was hurried up the *Via Principalis* while the gate was bolted once more. They reached the *praetorium*. A narrow road, more like an alley, ran down its left side, then continuing past the end of a workshop, they turned left into another wider street. This led to the stables as it passed a well. On the right were two large granary buildings. Turning left, they halted by the bottom end wall of the workshop.

"You have been a great help, Metallus," said Faris with a smile. "You can help me take it back tomorrow if you would. The quickest way out is through the West Gate, the *Porta Praetoria*. You can skirt round the camp and be back at the *vicus* in no time. I'll just unload a few things, so you carry on and get on your way. Thanks once again."

Metallus and Faris grasped each other's wrists just as you and a friend might shake hands. Metallus walked directly away past the stables and came upon the back of the *praetorium*. Sure enough, to his right, he saw the gate. Passing through with just a brief challenge from the guards, he made his way home.

The sun was setting, and in no more than half an hour it would be dark. Faris fiddled with the hides and tools making himself look busy yet all the time checking to see who might be around. The horses had been fed and tethered in their stalls, so there was no likelihood of being observed by anyone near there. The cart was obscured from view by the guards on the gate as the end of the stables was in the way. The workshop would most certainly not be in use during the evening, and so everything seemed set.

Faris whispered to the mound of leather hides, "Get ready to move."

He lifted those at the back, and Vitus slid himself out and knelt behind the cart, rubbing his legs which had developed pins and needles. Faris pointed in the direction of the workshop on the other side of the alley. He ran in a crouch across the space and then settled low in the shadows under the overhanging roof. Faris could now unload without fear. He was a genuine visitor and would certainly be recognised as one who might readily use the workshop. First, he transported some tools and then the hides. Finally, he pulled out the plank from the side of the cart, tucked it under his arm and strolled across the short space. Faris laid it down inside near the wall where Vitus had now positioned himself. They talked through what must be done in hushed tones then Faris himself exited the fort through the West Gate.

CHAPTER XXVII

Metallus arrived back at the smithy and was greeted by the children. Ruus was anxious as it was rare that his father left the workshop unattended. Ruus, Saima and Charlie were eager to hear Metallus explain the events of his day. How the key had brought an unexpected amount of money and how Faris had requested his help with the cart. It was at this last part where Ruus interrupted.

"Faris? Is that his name, the leatherworker from lower down the town?"

"Yes," exclaimed Metallus, "I told you."

"But you don't understand," Ruus replied tensely, "he's a murderer."

"What? Don't be ridiculous!"

Saima explained what Ruus meant.

"Ruus saw him shoot a soldier dead, but it seems they played some sort of clever trick because a while later he saw them together in a forest clearing. The soldier pretended to be dead then got up and ran away to their meeting place."

Ruus butted in, "He's up to something, I know he is. Now he's come to see you. I've no idea what he's doing but I bet it's not official."

"I only helped him with my cart, calm down everyone. I'm sure you're mistaken. Anyway, I've got the money to pay the fine so that means you're safe at least."

They nodded as they could see no problem with just helping someone but deep down it didn't quite feel right for any of them.

After supper, Metallus went to the tavern, the children sat around the cooking fire. There was a lot to think about. Charlie broke the silence.

"At least we know where the effigy is."

Saima wasn't so positive. "All very well, but how are we going to get it? It's all locked up in that gloomy room."

"Not exactly, it's locked up in the temple, but the room itself hasn't got a lock."

"Oh, that's brilliant then," answered Saima. "Only the temple's locked, not the room. That makes a lot of difference."

"What's biting you, midges from the marsh?" Charlie's voice rose to Saima's cutting remarks.

"I can't see the difference between one lock on the outside or any other on the inside. You're all, 'This is what I think, this is what I know.' Well, let me tell you what I think. You're a know-all and a liar. You've always got to have an answer. Just button up for once."

Saima had hit out hard. She felt so stressed and didn't want to be away from home any longer. She'd had enough, and Charlie was the only one who knew the reality. It wasn't his fault, of course, but the words had been said and couldn't be taken back; that made her feel even worse. She'd never done that before. No, that was a lie. She had done the same thing when Miss Dean had told her about her dad, the museum and the library. That thought was the killer and the one that drew shame and tears and hating herself. She couldn't stay in this company any longer. She ran outside just to give herself some time on her own, time to get away from it all.

After a bit, Ruus stood up and looked at Charlie. He could see that he was upset too, but he couldn't let Saima be outside alone; that might be dangerous. He went out onto the street and looked it up and down, but there was no sign of her. It was dark but the light of fires and oil lamps spilled out from the buildings. Flickering flames cast their orangey-yellow glow only so far before menacing shadows overtook them. A dog barked way down the street but could not be seen. Ruus carefully picked his way, searching the gaps between the dwellings for any sign of her. He reached the bottom of the *vicus*. It was lighter here. Stars shone, the constellations of the great Greek Gods winked in their heaven. There was Hercules, and to the north *Ursa Major*, The Great Bear that prowled the sky. Under him the river bridge was illuminated, and there a slight figure leant against its wooden rail. He approached quietly but without stealth. He stood at the northern end. Saima turned and saw him; she immediately knew who it was. She spun away as he approached. He stood beside her and stared out. Saima crossed her arms and wrapped them around her body.

Ruus kept his distance and spoke gently, "We were worried about you."

Her tears had dried, and she had got over her outburst but felt she couldn't face going back. She nodded and Ruus continued, "He doesn't mean it, you know? I reckon he's just scared like you but can't show it."

"Yes, I know, but I'm afraid we'll never go home."
She paused. "He seems so sure. He never seems to be
short of ideas. He's really a terrible liar. Everyone knows
what he's like. I just find it hard to listen to him over
and over again. Tonight, he had yet another answer.
It was too much. I'm never angry like that, but he can be
so annoying and I couldn't stop myself. Now, I'm
ashamed but I shouldn't be. It's not my fault. Oh,
I don't know where or what I stand for anymore."

"You must be true to yourself. That's what you were
when you shouted. It will have hurt you both, but it's
better out in the open. Perhaps now things will change."

She turned towards him. "You see things so
clearly," she said with her gentle smile and took a step
towards him.

"Somehow, I'll make sure you get home, both of
you."

"This is no time and place for young 'uns to be out,"
called a voice from the end of the bridge.

Immediately Saima and Ruus put a gap between
them, swivelled and like startled rabbits stood stock still
side by side. It was Metallus.

"Charlie told me you were upset and had gone out.
Thought I'd see if you were all right; seems you're fine."

He paused as they walked towards him, then grinned.
"Come on, you two, it's cold out here. Mind you, I'm
not sure that you would notice."

They walked back up the hill on each side of him,
feeling lighter and happier, telling him all about their
excursion to the temple. When they arrived at the door,
Charlie was standing waiting.

"Sorry, it's just the way I am, I suppose," he spouted
without waiting.

Saima didn't say a word. She looked at Ruus, winked, and then taking a decisive step, planted a hard slap on Charlie's shoulder, giggled and skipped inside. Ruus smiled and, putting an arm around Charlie's shoulder, led him inside too. They were friends once more.

"It's a big day tomorrow – *Calends* – the beginning of the month and the end of the last. Everyone will be at the temple. The statue of Janus will be brought out from the inner sanctum of the *cella* and placed on a plinth next to the altar outside. We will all watch the priest sacrifice to the oldest of Gods and say prayers in dedication," said Metallus as he sat with them by the fire.

Saima wasn't at all keen on the sacrifice bit but felt that this might provide a chance to get Janus back.

"Yes, *our* God of Truth and Lies, Beginnings and Endings, Doorways and Entrances. We must be there."

"And so we shall," replied Metallus, "After the ceremony, I shall be called upon to give my tribute."

Charlie was confused, "What's tribute?"

Metallus couldn't believe his ears; surely these children would know that. He looked astonished and seemed to be unsure whether these children were pulling his leg. Saima was again on hand to get Charlie out of a hole.

"You know, Caius, 'tribute'. It's when you say nice things about people. Metallus will have to say nice things about the Janus effigy. I expect he'll make a speech or something."

"No, not quite," interrupted Ruus. "My father will have to pay the money that Orcus demanded. You remember, he wanted twenty *denarii* for you two."

"Oh yes, of course, I forgot with all that's happened today. I'm so sorry, Metallus."

Ruus was a little disappointed neither had remembered the trouble his father had got into in order to save them.

Metallus shrugged. "I expect we're all a little overtaken by the day's events. At least I have the money safe and ready to pay. How lucky I've been that it's all worked out."

CHAPTER XXVIII

Vitus roused himself from his slumber in the darkest corner of the workshop. He was alert and keen to get started. It was well after midnight. Orion the Hunter had swung to the south-eastern sky and was pursuing the Great Bear. He drew back the leather hides under which he had slept and knelt, watching for any movement or signs of life. There were none. Using the charcoal under his belt, he smeared it over his arms, hands and face to camouflage himself among the shadows. Barefooted, he moved across to the workshop side wall. His eyes had grown accustomed to the dark, and he easily found the coil of strong rope and the plank with slats. He tied several knots in the rope and hung it over his right shoulder. He picked up the half dozen small sacks piled by the plank and arranged them around his body, tucking them into his belt to hold them in place. Finally, he picked up the saw and balanced the plank under his right arm.

Rain fell and puddles had begun to form in the alley between the workshop and the *praetorium*. The alley was unpaved and the surface of its hard-packed earth had become damp and slippery. Vitus nosed out carrying his tools. The damp earth started to ooze and cling to his feet. Turning to his immediate right, he hoisted the plank to an angle up against the wall of the workshop.

The plank with its horizontal slats could now act as a ladder. He placed the outside of his foot on the first rung. It was solid and held his weight with ease, so he climbed to the topmost rung where his waist was level with the terracotta *tegulae* of the roof. Uncoiling his rope, he passed the end of it behind the top of the plank and tied it securely in front, then he threw the coil up onto the roof. It unravelled as it went. Placing his hands shoulder-width apart on the *tegulae*, Vitus pushed and straightened his arms. He allowed the weight of his upper body to tip forward till his whole chest lay on the roof, now he was able to draw his legs up under him, and there he perched in a crouching stance.

The ladder was to act as a gangplank above the alley to cross onto the roof of the *praetorium*. The workshop roof, like most others in the fort, was constructed with *tegulae*, rectangular tiles. Vitus needed to find a beam supporting them. He ignored the first row as they were nailed on and removed some from the second and third rows. Soon he'd created a space large enough to slide the plank into. He lay flat on his belly, facing the edge of the roof, ready to haul up the plank with the rope he had tied round it earlier. Just as he started, the saw slid from the roof and fell with a dull thud at the bottom of the ladder.

"Can't wait for tomorrow. Five hours of freedom."

"Hail Janus."

The two soldiers laughed and slapped each other on the back as they passed the end of the workshop.

"Wait there a moment, I'm busting," said the first.

He moved round the corner and stood by the workshop wall next to the plank. Vitus had no cover. He could only flatten himself to the roof, but what about the ladder and the saw. He was sure the soldier would wonder why they were there and look up. The soldier stood by the wall for about half a minute.

"Come on," called his mate, "I'm getting wetter than that wall you're up against."

"Some things can't be hurried," said the first, pulling up his breeches. "Hold on, what's this?"

The second soldier came over as the first bent over and picked up the saw lying next to the plank.

"Here, some *stultus* has left this outside getting wet."

"Listen, mate, hurry it up. Chuck it inside if you must but let's get out of this weather."

He leant against the plank to pick up the saw, and the plank slid towards the wall causing the top to come away and threaten to fall. Vitus saw the rope slip and, in a split second, slapped his hand on top of it. The plank jerked and fell back upright against the wall. They looked up, but the darkness caused by the buildings being so close created deep shadow and obscured the top and the tied rope. It was fortunate Vitus had used the charcoal or he would have stood out like a beacon.

"That's dangerous leaving that there like that."

"It's only dangerous if some *stultus* leans on it," snorted the other. "Throw that saw inside unless you're gonna swap it for your *gladius*."

He guffawed again and pulled his friend by the shoulder back out of the alley. The saw was hurled back into the workshop.

Vitus waited until he was sure they had gone and then slid his legs over the edge of the tiles. With his feet swinging, he sought the ladder. His right foot caught on a sharp, rough edge of a slat. He pulled it away and stifled a cry. He had felt it slit the ball of his foot, but he hadn't time to worry about it; though painful and bleeding, he needed to get on if he was to complete his task before sunrise. He gingerly descended the ladder and inspected his foot. The cut was a couple of centimetres long but he had no way of covering it. He cursed the fact he had no longer got his sandals; if he'd had those this wouldn't have happened. He hoped the rest of the night would go better than it had started. Ignoring the wound, he went into the workshop and searched for the saw. He found it and once more climbed the ladder using his toes on the slats rather than the balls of his feet.

As before, he lay on the roof and hauled up the plank, untied the rope and coiled it, then placed it back over his head and shoulder. Vitus inched the plank out until it sat on the *praetorium* roof, hooking it over one beam and under another. He was ready to cross the makeshift bridge. He crept low and slow on his knees. He was a cat burglar slinking in the dead of night. Across he went. On the *praetorium* roof, he stacked the tiles so they wouldn't slip and give him away. He tied the rope to the end of the plank and let the knots lower down to reach the floor. There was room for a slim rope but nowhere near enough for him to get in. Using the saw, he cut out a piece of a beam and created a slot through which he could squeeze. Hand over hand, he descended the rope, the knots stopping him from slipping. At last, he was standing on the cold, flagstone floor of the strongroom, the *quaestorium*. He found that the coolness soothed his cut; perhaps that and the mud on his feet would help to seal the gash.

CHAPTER XXIX

The room was not in total darkness. On a shelf just inside the door was an oil lamp. At this time in the night, it was guttering. Its flame small and yellow as the wick had nearly finished sucking the small oil reservoir dry. He approached it, ensuring he trod quietly. He could hear sounds of chattering and laughing coming from rooms not so far away. That at least was good news; the noise would cover any small one he might make. He picked up the lamp and tilted it gently so that what little oil was left would trickle down inside the lamp and allow the flame to draw it upwards. Soon he had a much brighter light and was able to clearly see the room and, more importantly, the boxes. His eyes searched for the tell-tale straws he had been promised would show which ones to open.

"There you are. Come to Uncle Vitus, my lovelies," he whispered. "Soon have you tucked up in a new bed."

He picked up the lamp and, shielding the flame with his left hand, he brought it above an opened box. The yellow light caught the faces that stared back from a host of circular, silver *denarii*. For a moment, he feasted his eyes and then, placing the lamp on the floor, plunged his hand in and under the rippling, silvery sea. The coins tumbled like water through his greedy fingers. He set to work and filled the first three sacks, then lowered the lid. He could still hear voices and merrymaking, and satisfied with his work so far, he set about the second box and its contents.

He had nearly completed the same routine and filled two more sacks when the flame guttered, and the dim lamplight dwindled and withdrew its help. Vitus was sure that the early dawn light would soon be visible in the east. He needed to work fast. He scooped half a dozen handfuls of coins into the last bag, but in his haste, some fell onto the flagstone floor. His fingers scrabbled, trying to find the last few coins around his knees. Feeling no more around him, he closed the *arca's* lid. Six sacks in all to be raised to the roof. He climbed up, pulling two bags up after him. Then he made two more journeys grasping the rope with his hands closing just above each knot. Instinctively, he pulled his legs up under him and then thoughtlessly pressed the ball of his foot onto the rope with the top of the other foot beneath. He recoiled as the cut opened further and the ball of his foot started to bleed heavily.

Back on the roof, he untied the rope from the plank and scanned the ground, nobody to be seen. The sky to the east was indeed lighter. He replaced the tiles the best he could, although one or two were only just held in place by their neighbours where the beam had been cut. The sacks were pushed ahead of him back to the workshop roof. He repaired that too, then dropped them one at a time to the ground. He took a glance to ensure his way was clear to the cart and shoved the bags on, took the plank ladder back to the workshop and hoisted some hides on his shoulders. A glance out and he saw two *miles* who had finished their shift on guard duty and were returning to their barracks.

He ducked back inside. They paid the cart no attention and carried on past. Vitus moved out, threw the rope into the cart then clambered on board and arranged the hides randomly to cover both himself and his hoard. The sun breached the horizon. It would be a fine day for the dedication.

CHAPTER XXX

Metallus had slept well. He had his tax money to give as tribute, and soon enough life would return to normal, albeit with two extra children in tow. Even in such a short time, he had grown used to them and Ruus had never seemed happier than when he was in their company. The girl had certainly charmed him, and Ruus had definitely appeared more responsible since her arrival. She could stay as long as she wanted if that was to be the case.

There was a sharp rap on the post outside and a voice calling, "Metallus, are you awake? Metallus?"

The voice was urgent. Metallus, just wearing his leggings, shouted, "I'm coming…"

He made his way out to the front where he was met by Faris.

"Hail, my friend, how do I find you this glorious day?"

Metallus was not in the mood for small talk at this time in the morning, especially as he'd only just woken up. He could not, however, be impolite, seeing as Faris had provided him with work that would help pay his fine.

"Hail, Faris, you're an early bird. *Aurora* has barely dressed the day."

"Ah, yes, you're quite right, a beautiful dawn she sends us, but I am in need of a very small favour."

"Go on." Metallus was sure there was be bound to be something. After all, Faris wasn't going to give up ten *denarii* lightly.

His face must have shown disappointment, for Faris immediately smiled and said, "I'm a man of my word, Metallus. Our arrangement stands, and I ask no more than before."

"Why then do you hurry to my door?"

"Put simply, I have neglected a most important client and must attend to that business before all else this morning. It may take more time than I bargained for, and I can't afford to miss the dedication at the temple."

"So?"

"I merely ask that you might collect the cart without me and take it to my workshop. You know where that is. I'll unload things later."

"It will be too heavy for me to move on my own. I suppose the two boys could help me, though."

"Good, then that's settled. I'm much obliged to you. I'll get the cart back to you some time tomorrow morning then."

Without a gesture, he spun on his heel and was gone in a flash. Metallus watched him fairly fly down the road.

"His client must be very important to have to move that fast," he muttered, watching Faris disappear.

As he was out the front, he went to the water barrel and splashed his face with cool water. He returned inside to find Saima and Ruus down by the embers of the fire blowing gently, trying to reignite them. Saima had sprinkled kindling on top, and already flames wrapped their tiny fingers around the small pieces of wood. Charlie appeared, rubbing his eyes and pronouncing that he was hungry enough to eat a horse.

Metallus juddered. "Eat a horse? Where were you brought up, boy? He says he wants to eat a horse! Do you know how valuable a horse is? Have you any idea…?"

Saima came to his aid. "He doesn't mean he really wants to eat a horse, Metallus. It's just his way of saying he's hungry."

"Well, why didn't he say that then? It's unforgivable to say you want to eat a horse. I've never heard the like of it before."

Charlie thought he better say his bit, but as usual the lies dripped off his tongue like a drooling dog, "We always say that in our village. It's a well-known saying like 'beating a dead donkey' or 'biting the bullet'."

Saima shot Charlie a look that could have frozen the Sahara Desert. He'd already upset Metallus going on about eating horses, and now he was talking about beating a dead donkey. If that wasn't bad enough, he'd said 'bullet'. It was indeed fortunate that he was speaking Latin, for the word for bullet hadn't been invented yet. What came out was bull-ette.

"You have strange words in your village. We call that a calf. Ah, now that's much more like it. Yes, a young bull. That's much more acceptable and a lot more tasty, I say."

Ruus broke in and enquired, "What did Faris want?"

"He has other work to do and wants me to collect the cart from the fort. It seems reasonable enough, but I'll need your help."

Saima was very excited. A trip to a real, live Roman fort. How good would that be?

"Oh yes," she said enthusiastically. "When are we going?"

"We're going as soon as we're dressed. You're not. The job is not one for a girl. The boys will help. You can stay here and perhaps bake us some flatbreads on the fire for when we return."

Saima couldn't believe her ears. She was being left out just because she was a girl. Girls were as good as boys. Well, if they thought she was just going to hang around playing housemaid, they had another think coming. She was going out to explore, and no one would tell her any different.

CHAPTER XXXI

Metallus, Ruus and Charlie stood in front of the main gates.

A helmeted head called down from the tower, "State your business, Briton."

"We're collecting our work cart, sir," Metallus replied.

"Proceed then."

The three of them entered through the gates, and Metallus led the boys to the place where the cart had been parked the afternoon before. He instructed Ruus and Charlie to grab one of the arms while he took the other. They lifted the cart arms to the horizontal and turned it around, ready to exit from where they had entered. They pulled it with quite some effort towards the gates. Its wheels made a heavy rumbling sound as they rolled over the cobbles and slabs that made up the *Via Principalis*. Metallus was surprised at the weight and effort it took to move it. He didn't complain as he imagined it must be because the boys were helping him, and they would have a lot less strength than Faris.

"You're back quickly," called the guard.

"Yes, sir, we'll be out of your way as fast as we can."

Once more, the gates opened, and the cart was hauled through and went more easily now it was on its way downhill to the *vicus*. On they went past Metallus's forge and down to the bottom where, turning left, they came upon Faris's workshop. They tugged it round to the back where it had been left the day before. Pushing the arms down gently, they allowed the cart to tip and settle so they rested on the ground. Satisfied that the task had been completed, they set off back up the hill towards home.

Saima had watched them go out from the entrance of the workshop. Her arms folded across her chest and her shoulder leaning against a post; her expression was that of a Year 1 girl sent to the 'naughty chair'. She had never felt so humiliated or judged so worthless. The boys had reached the gates before she had made up her mind to go and watch the preparations for the celebration of *Calends* at the temple. She tramped with her arms still folded and chin tucked down towards her chest along the main street, then as the three children had done in the past, she cut down the alley past the field with the ox and out onto the hill overlooking the temple. Several people were around its precincts setting up lanterns and placing torches in the sconces for Janus, the bringer of light to the darkness, the changer of years, the first and the last. Heavy swags of greenery were being strung from the walls and strips of coloured cloth hung from them like bunting. Saima's mood changed, and she began to enjoy the spectacle. This was amazing to watch. How magical it would be when the afternoon became sunset and the torches and lanterns were lit. She imagined their flickering flames and the shadows that they might cast playing and jousting with each other in a light breeze. It must have been for a whole hour or more she watched under the warming sun, but then she was distracted.

Beneath her and to the east of the temple was the stream, the oath pool, and a little further the bridge that carried the road on which they had first come into the *vicus*. There, she noticed two men. They were pulling a cart, a cart with just two wheels that looked exactly like the one Metallus owned. It was this that piqued her interest and made her decide. She had to know who was pulling it and where they were pulling it to. She would surely be seen if she went directly down the hill, so she ran back through the alley out onto the main street next to the cloth merchant's shop. Picking up her skirts, she raced down the street until she emerged at the bottom of the *vicus*. The cart had gone. No wait; there it was, still moving away on the far side of the bridge. The road on the other side dipped a little before rising up once again towards the forest and the bend. She hung back and waited till they had climbed the rise and then they sank beyond the road's horizon. She would be a half-mile behind but where could they go? There was only one road. She watched them disappear and then started a purposeful walk in the same direction. As she crossed the bridge, she saw a woman place dishes in the oath pool. They were filled with common field-flower heads of whites and yellows. Perhaps they were daisies and buttercups. She wondered if Ruus might pick some for her later today. Her daydream caused her to trip, her toe stubbing on a raised plank.

"Concentrate," she told herself but grinned at the very reason for her lack of it. Her mind had wandered and she must keep on task. Reaching the far side of the bridge, she adjusted her thoughts and got back into gear. In a short time, she too was over the rise and approaching the forest and the bend in the road. Here, the road was less well made, and she could clearly see the shallow ruts formed by carts' wheels. She needed to go carefully now. There was no telling where the men may be. Saima was no fool and knew she needed to have some cover if she was to continue tracking. The ditches to the left and right of the road were deep but not so wide. She chose a suitable place and jumped across the ditch to her left, and then pushing past some gorse, she was among the straight silver birch, beech and oak trees of the forest edge.

Afforded this cover, she bent at the waist and jogged, keeping as low as possible. The forest on this side was becoming more dense, and she was forced to slow as she reached the end of the outside curve of the bend. She stopped for breath and leant her hand against a gnarled tree that had some low branches at shoulder height and others spaced equally as they rose, seeking the light. Saima raised her head to look up. It was certainly tall. As her eyes moved down to her hand once more, she was surprised to notice what appeared to be dried mud in the grooves of the tree's bark. She had no time to ponder and set off once more after the men. Just a minute later, she saw them. Well, not them but the cart at least, standing by itself on the road beside the far ditch. She waited for any sign of the men but there was none. Escaping the clutches of the low branches and their twiggy fingers, she vaulted the ditch and approached the cart. It was empty but it certainly was Metallus's. She would recognise that anywhere. But where were the men who were pulling it? Not on her side of the road, that's for sure. She looked down into the ditch.

"Aaghh!" she screamed and fell to her knees.

There in the grass, staring with glazed eye and its innards pulled from its body lay a dead crow. It was not a pleasant sight even though there was little blood. The purple stomach, ligaments and lungs had been nibbled, pecked, pulled and stretched out in a tangled mass that made her gag. Putting her hands to her mouth, she spun away and retched. The contents of her stomach were no less revolting than the mangled crow corpse. She was disgusted with herself. Her eyes watered from the efforts of her heaving stomach. She crouched and spat the few remains left in her mouth and pulled her sleeve across her lips. She could taste her sour breath on her tongue, and that revolted her even more.

"What might you be doing here?" said some sandals next to her on the roadway.

Sandals don't speak. She drew her face up, and to her side stood a soldier. He looked both tall and important. He was helmeted, and that had a crest across its crown, revealing he was no ordinary soldier; he was a *centurion*. His group of forty men, half a Roman century, were finishing their patrol and returning to the fort. Saima stood.

"Wait a moment, I don't know who you are but I recognise this cart. That was the one that came to the fort late yesterday afternoon. I'm sure of it. Who are you?"

Saima was awe-struck and stammered, "I'm Sabia."

The name tripped off her tongue without a moment's hesitation.

"Well, Sabia, this cart is blocking an Imperial highway. It must be moved. Who does it belong to and where is he?"

This was a perfectly reasonable question, but Saima found it hard because the two things didn't match up.

It was Metallus's cart but Metallus was nowhere near here. Her hesitation annoyed the *centurion*.

"Answer me, girl," he said in a more menacing tone.

Saima had little choice. She had no time for thought. All she could do was lie a little. It wasn't a big lie, just a small one that might be acceptable.

"It belongs to Metallus, sir; he's gone into the woods."

There was a laugh from the ranks of soldiers for some joker had called to his mates, "He'll be back in a minute, love, he's only gone for a—"

The *centurion* turned smartly and glowered in the direction of the voice. The *centurion*'s gaze took in his troop, and they stood stock still without a murmur.

"Well, wherever he is, the cart cannot stay here. If I push it in the ditch, no doubt at the next rains the road will flood because of it."

He turned once more, and selecting the most likely candidates who might have made the joke, he ordered them to place their equipment in the cart and pull it back to the *vicus*. This would be a great idea, thought Saima, but really she wanted to know who it was that had been pulling the cart in the first place and why they had suddenly disappeared. Still, there was no help for it, and as the troop marched off, she sat on the back of the cart examining the symbols drawn on the soldiers' shields. Not such a bad way to travel, and at least she didn't have to walk. A bit like going to town on the bus, except she didn't need her bus pass. She grinned at the thought and sang a little song that sprang to mind – 'The Wheels on the Bus'. It seemed appropriate as, after all, bus was just the short version of a Latin word, *omnibus*, meaning by, with or for everyone. After a couple of verses, the soldiers pulling the cart had learned the tune and were humming along. Soon the whole group were singing, whistling and humming as the cart was trundled over the bridge and up into town. They were delighted that the *centurion* was turning a blind eye to it all. This *Calends* was going to be special indeed.

CHAPTER XXXII

Charlie, Ruus and Metallus had returned home. Saima wasn't there. Strange. Why would she not be? They searched out the back and around the sides of the workshop but there wasn't any sign of her. Ruus was particularly concerned. Metallus, as practical as ever, decided she couldn't be far away and formed a plan.

"Ruus and I will make a search. Caius, you stay here in case she returns before we do."

Charlie agreed to wait, so off the two Britons went, searching around the backs of houses, down alleyways and in shop doorways but still no sign. Finally, they arrived at Faris's place. It was all shut up and no one was around. Going to the back, they saw that the cart they had left there earlier was also missing.

"I thought he said he was going to unload it and bring it back later. He made no mention of using it again."

Ruus was also intrigued. "That's a heavy cart for just one man to pull any distance; he must have had some help."

Strains of singing were coming from the road, and as they had no answers nor had they found Saima, they themselves set upon a path home. A hundred metres in front of them, the singing continued, and they could make out the rear of a column of soldiers. At the back, two were hunched over and were labouring to a task on their journey. Finally, these two soldiers stretched their backs and moved off at pace to catch up with the column who were already entering the fort. There, in plain sight, was the cart, and so was Saima who slid to her feet as the cart tipped backwards on its axle. Ruus couldn't contain himself and ran up the hill.

"Where have you been? Why were you on the cart? We've been frantic worrying about you. We even went out to find you; now we find you swanning your way home towed by some Romans. Didn't we say stay at home? I don't believe you even know the dangers you could have faced. I mean not that I suppose you'd be in any danger with your new Roman mates."

Saima listened to Ruus's rant and couldn't stop herself from fighting back. "You just expected me to stay at home, eh? Not worth much else. Keep the fire going. Make some flatbreads. Yes sir, no sir, three bags full, sir. I'm not your slave. I'm me, I'm free and I have free will. I'll do what I want, when I want, and don't you ever forget it!"

The shouting had started to draw a small crowd of neighbours who gawped at the two youngsters and were quite enjoying the slanging match. After all, it broke up their day a bit and gave them an excuse to stop their work, even if just for a short while. Metallus was not so keen to have a mob outside his front door, so, putting his hands on both their shoulders, he urged them inside away from prying ears and eyes.

The glares continued even if the yelling stopped, and it wasn't until Charlie came in from the back that their faces had returned to something closer to their natural colour.

Charlie hadn't really understood why Ruus and Saima were so mad at each other. He was pretty sure she'd have been okay and so she was. No big deal. He hadn't read the tell-tale signs that had spilled into a huge ball of worry for Ruus and indignant anger for Saima. There was a good deal of caring between them, and that had passed Charlie by. His first thought was what everyone in the room wanted to know but hadn't yet asked.

"So how come you were on the cart then?"

Saima hesitated, then seeing that they were ready to listen, sat and related her tale of her spying and how it had ended.

"What I don't understand is where they went or why," she said.

Ruus looked down into his lap, not yet ready to look Saima in the eye.

"I think that following them was extremely dangerous," he said, "but I'm sure I know where. The question is still why."

"What's your theory then?" Saima was still a bit aloof and it showed in her voice.

Ruus went back over the story of how the soldier had been shot and how he had followed him into a clearing a distance from the road. Then how he had hidden and escaped by the skin of his teeth.

"I'd have cuffed you soundly if I'd known all that. Still, what's past is past, you'd better finish."

Ruus continued, "When Saima mentioned the crow, that did it. I knew it must be the same place where the 'dead' soldier got up and went down the path to that clearing. I bet that's where they were today."

"So, the soldier was in the clearing, but who was with him?"

"Oh Caius, don't be so dense," Saima cut in. "The other one must have been Faris, the one who borrowed Metallus's cart."

"Of course, that's it," said Metallus. "They must have put something in the cart and taken it up the road then went off to the clearing, leaving my cart stranded by the ditch. Charming."

"Yes, so that's why he wanted to give the cart back later. I wonder what will happen when he finds it has gone? Especially when he finds out we've got it back already."

This was getting deeper by the second.

"I have just had a terrible thought." Saima frowned. "What if he thinks we know what he's up to and thinks we followed him?"

"Well, he wouldn't be wrong with most of that, would he?" said Ruus.

Saima smiled. Her mood had melted a little, but then she issued a note of caution, "If he's up to no good, and he suspects we know, then isn't it likely we'll be in danger?"

Saima's logic had once again cut through. She was right, and they should indeed be worried.

CHAPTER XXXIII

Faris and Vitus had carried three sacks of *denarii* each up the path towards the clearing.

"We must dig a pit to put the sacks in," Faris said, giving the impression that this was all decided by their masters, Drusus and Orcus.

"That's what I expected. I don't think I need to be told that."

"Look, I haven't a clue why, but that isn't the only part of the instructions."

"What else then?"

"They say it must be deep and wide."

"That's ridiculous. Why?"

"I don't know, and I don't care; that's not the point I'm trying to make. I've been told we dig, and it must be wide and deep."

"For six sacks of silver?"

"Do you want to get paid or not?" said Faris losing his patience. "As far as I'm concerned, if they want wide and deep, that's what they'll get. You start and I'll gather leaves, brushwood and brambles to hide our work."

Faris went to the forest edge to begin his collecting, but as soon as he was out of sight, he sat down with his back to a tree and waited.

"Oh, that's great, I get all the hard graft and he goes off collecting," Vitus snarled under his breath, but he reckoned the quicker he started the sooner he'd be paid off, so he began to dig. The earth beneath his feet was soft and he made rapid progress.

He was already nearly a metre down and a metre wide by the time Faris decided to return, dragging a mass of foliage in his wake.

"This enough?"

"No, not yet. It needs to be just a bit deeper yet."

"Are you sure?"

Faris gave him a glare that stopped the question in its tracks.

"Right, okay, I get it, but it's your turn now anyway. Take my arm and give me a hand out."

"You've nearly finished, my friend. No point in both of us getting filthy, and you've done a great job there. I'd never have managed that as well as you. Let's just say a bit deeper. I'll go and get the rest of the covering while you finish up."

There was little point in Vitus arguing. He was almost done and he was quite proud of his efforts. Soon be finished now. Faris left him to his work and went to the opposite end of the clearing from the path on which they'd entered. From behind the trunk of an ancient oak, he retrieved what he'd hidden before. Holding the two objects behind his back, he returned to the edge of the hole.

Vitus turned and asked the question, "Will this do now?"

Faris took a pace back but bent over to peer in. "Perfect," replied Faris.

"Good, then give me your arm and pull me out of here."

Vitus reached down to retrieve his spade and offered his right arm upwards. Faris stood stock still. In his very capable hands, he held a bow and an arrow that was already nocked on its string.

Vitus laughed, "Oh yes, very funny, Faris. Now quit messing about and get me out of here."

"You've worked brilliantly and if I might say so, you will be a perfect fit."

"Wha—"

The word never finished for the string had been drawn and released in the twinkling of an eye. The arrow struck Vitus's neck precisely and, from such short range, killed him instantly. The body slumped to its knees as Faris had calculated it would and with its head lolling, bent forward at the waist and bumped against the side wall. Faris dropped his bow and got to his knees. He fished the spade from the pit and began to refill the hole with the stacked earth. There certainly seemed to be a fair bit left when all was done, so he spread it around as best he could. The scrub he had gathered was strewn over it to give it a more natural look. Next he moved to the back of the glade and dug a much smaller pit into which he placed the sacks of coins, again refilling and tramping to ensure that as much of the soil as possible was filled in, then he arranged branches and twigs to cover it.

The cart was gone! How was that even possible? Faris had returned to the road and was startled that Metallus's cart had mysteriously vanished. He searched up and down but there was no sign. He had no idea how that could be, and equally he had no idea how he would explain its loss to Metallus. He knew, however, he must not loiter here. His sandals, hands and clothing were still streaked with mud even though he'd done his best to clean himself with damp grass. At a trot, he loped back to the *vicus*, pondering all the time on the story he should tell Metallus about his cart. Perhaps he could say he'd taken and left it at his important client's house. That would at least give him some more time to investigate. Of course, the trap would be set even more firmly now and no suspicion could possibly fall his way. He would go to the fort first thing in the morning.

CHAPTER XXXIV

The afternoon was drawing to a close, and the preparations at the temple had been made. Torches were ready to be lit and the walls had been decorated. Inside the *temenos,* people were scurrying back and forth with bowls of fruit and bread, and large *amphorae* holding wine and oil were standing like sentries. A pen for animals had been constructed and its makeshift gate stood open in readiness. There were some benefits to having Roman Gods and their feast days. Out from their houses, workshops, and the smallest of hovels came the residents of the *vicus.* They had dressed for the occasion and wore clean tunics and best dresses fastened at the shoulder by metal pins or ornate brooches fashioned with intricate workings. It was party time, and who wouldn't dress up for that. The only fly in the ointment was the donation of taxes, but once that was out of the way, the celebrations could begin. The main street was lined two or three deep in places to watch the passing parade.

Inside the fort the *Via Principalis* thronged with *miles, optios* and their *centurions* all in fine array with burnished armour and plumes of horsehair on their crested helmets dyed in reds and yellows. The *miles* had polished their helms and they reflected the setting sun. An order rang out and the great gates were pulled to stand fully open. The column turned a sharp right angle outside the *praetorium*, and more soldiers were drawn up in three columns stretching away down the *Via Praetoria*. On the *praetorium* steps was a six-man guard of honour, three on each side in front of its door. At the base of the steps was a chair with a canopy over the top and a wooden base on which the chair sat. The whole construction had four short, sturdy legs, and by each longer side were metal loops through which poles had been inserted. These projected both backwards and forwards, and beside these were stationed four men dressed in ghostly white togas. These were the slaves who had been selected to carry the ceremonial chair on which *Publicanus* Lucius would sit and who would be carried to watch the events unfold at the temple as befitted his status. Waiting behind the chair was Orcus and near him was Drusus and the rest of his *contubernium*. They would flank the chair four on each side; the Guard of Honour formed a rank of three in front and then a rank of three behind Orcus and the chair. They carried two empty strongboxes for the tribute. Another order rang out, and like a great human armadillo in shining armour plate, the column began to move. The crowds on either side of the roadway nudged each other as they told their neighbour of its approach. The cheers rang out and also a few jeers, although it was not a day for protest.

As the column moved through the town, the crowd filled in behind and followed their route. Down they went; the ribbon of bright metals and red tunics followed closely by its tail of citizens, some in their wools and yet others in tartan breeches, all converging on the eastern gate of the Temple of Janus. Like a film being played backwards, it seemed as though they were liquid streaming back into a bottle as they filed through the gap in the wall and spread out to get the best vantage point to watch the proceedings. Some like Metallus had barely got through the gap, and still others strained to look in from outside or even stayed high above in the meadow and gained a view of it all looking down from a distance.

The priest had set himself on the steps of the *cella*. He also wore a toga but of ivory white, and one of its many folds had been drawn over his head in a cowl down to his forehead. He already held the statue of Janus. The crowd hushed and soldiers formed a line from the base of the steps to the plinth beside the altar. Stepping with sombre care, he descended and crossed the short distance to stand in front of the crowd behind the plinth. The *Publicanus* rose from his chair and took up position on the left, and Orcus moved to the right with the priest between them. Then with great ceremony and with such slowness it appeared his arms must surely drop from the sheer effort, he lifted Janus above his head and spoke.

"*Ave, Ave, Ave!* Oh Greatest God of All, we call upon you and worship you."

The crowd roared as one in reply, "*Ave, Ianus Maximus!*"

Without pause, the priest continued, "We beg and urge you to favour us and cause the might and power of Rome to prosper that we all may live in your glory, *Ave Ianus Maximus.*"

The crowd raised their arms in the air and repeated his final three words in unison.

Charlie was fascinated but couldn't understand why those in the *vicus* seemed so fond of worshipping a Roman God. Ruus tried to explain,

"Look, Caius," he said, "it's like this. Firstly, most people here don't want any trouble, so they go along with whatever the Romans want. Secondly, it's a holiday. Look at all these people, some of them are slaves, and they get the day off. It's about the only day they have to themselves where they can relax. Thirdly," he turned the volume down to a whisper, "don't you believe for one moment that old Janus there is anything special. We've got our own Gods, you know. It's just that when he says Janus, we all say Janus, but we think in our heads of *Lugh* the sun God or *Taranis* the God of sky and thunder, or we even pray to the mysterious Green Man of the forest who saved me the other day when I had to hide. Lastly, when was the last time you got to eat ox?"

Charlie thought then said, "Don't think I've ever eaten ox."

"Well, there you are then, that's the whole point. We get to eat great food and we don't have to pay for it. We just have to pretend that we're praying to their daft statue and the meal's all ours."

While Ruus had been talking, Saima had been listening intently and understood a little more how things worked. All the time the priest had been declaring this and proclaiming that from where he stood. The crowd in front of them was quite dense, and they could barely see a thing. Suddenly there was a bellow that cut short, and the crowd let out a great, 'Aaaaahhhh,' as though the whole place had blown out its breath all at once.

"What's going on?" asked Saima, straining to see through the crowd of bodies but without managing to.

"That's the ox," said Ruus.

"What do you mean that's the ox? I heard a great sigh from all around us."

"Well, I didn't exactly mean *that* was the ox. What I meant was, that was the people watching the ox."

"What ox? What was it doing?" asked Charlie. "High jump?"

"No, it was being sacrificed."

"Sacrificed!" yelled Saima, horrified.

"Well, yes, of course. You must have sacrifices all the time like we do, don't you."

Charlie cut in, seeing this was another one of those things that they had heard about in the classroom, but the reality of it hadn't entered their heads till now.

"Yes of course we have sacrifices, don't we, Sabia?"

He was nodding frantically in her direction, trying to get her to agree.

"Er... yes, sorry, but I'm a bit squeamish, and actually we don't have big animals like you have here."

"Yeah, usually it's a mouse or a guinea pig or something," helped Charlie.

Saima raised her eyes to heaven. What on earth would come out of his mouth next? That boy could lie for England, she thought.

"You certainly have strange ways, where you come from. I've never even heard of a guinea pig."

"Oh, it's just Caius's way of saying a piglet. You know a small animal, like he said."

Now she'd caught herself at it too, lying. Lying because he'd lied. Lies upon lies to cover lies. Oh, what was to become of her? Fortunately, Metallus interrupted their conversation.

"This is it. The time for the tributes to be paid."

Some of the crowd moved back as they would not be involved, and a gap appeared through which Saima could see a trail of blood leading from the hard flagstones in front of the altar. Both *Publicanus* Lucius and his clerk, Orcus, had blood all over their togas. Saima, although disgusted, could not look away and asked, "Did they do the killing, the sacrifice, I mean?"

"No, that was done by the priest," said Metallus opening his *bursa* of coins ready to count into the strongbox.

"Why are the others all covered in blood then?" she asked.

"Oh, they'll have wanted to get as much blood on them as possible. It is the Romans' belief that sacrificial blood will give them long life perhaps never to die at all."

Saima had no answer to that other than to just place her hand on Ruus's arm and watch what was unfolding. Ruus smiled and put his hand on hers.

It was time for Orcus to take centre stage. Lucius retired to his chair, and while the statue stared down from its plinth, Orcus called on Drusus and another guard to bring a strongbox to the front beside him. A table was brought forward, and a list was presented to Orcus with the details of names, amounts and types of tribute to be collected. He settled his bulk on a stool that had been placed behind the table. The legs creaked and threatened to break out from underneath him. The two soldiers passed quick, knowing glances but were pulled back to their work when Orcus mouthed a name. It was a guard beside Drusus who was to call it out, and both Orcus and Drusus were to check the amount was paid as expected.

"Pallius! Pallius the weaver, to give tribute of three tunics for the Imperial army of Rome."

Pallius had urged his way from the second row and halted at the table. Across his arm were three red tunics as requested. He laid them on the table in front of Orcus.

"Pass them to the guard, man. Think what you're doing; you'll ruin my accounts."

Orcus had barely started his collection and already he was into push and shout mode. Charlie reckoned he'd hate to be last if this was how it was going to be. It could only get worse.

"Hodic!" shouted the guard, "Hodic the goatherd, two goats as tribute to the glory of Rome."

Hodic brought them forward but seeing the problem Pallius had he stayed well back from the table. Orcus made some marks and indicated he was satisfied. Hodic was directed to leave his goats in the pen that had been constructed and had earlier housed the poor ox.

And so the names continued to be called and the tribute paid until, "Metallus, Metallus the metalworker; twenty *denarii* as tribute to the glory of Rome."

There was a sharp intake of breath from all assembled. The air tingled. Now there would be trouble. There was no chance that Metallus could possibly have raised those funds in such a short time.

"Metallus! I call on Metallus."

The voice lifted over and among the crowd.

"Here he is!" shouted one.

"Go on then," roared another, giving him a push from behind.

This was going to be a spectacle, and just like at a road traffic accident when it seems everyone wants to slow down and have a good look even though it's thoughtless and unkind, so it was here. It wasn't going to be them in trouble but someone was, and they wanted to see it in all its gruesome detail. Metallus spilled out from the throng, the children following him through the gap to the front, waiting to see what befell.

"Ah, Metallus, I remember our little natter. How are you?" enquired Orcus.

His voice was full of icy nastiness, and he scanned the crowd, loving the audience and the mood. Then his eyes fell upon the children. He turned to Drusus, who wheeled away out of sight.

"Now," beamed Orcus, "Imperial Rome needs her full dues. As you can't pay, I'll take what I'm owed."

At that, three soldiers roughly parted the crowd and fell upon Charlie, Ruus and Saima, grabbing their arms and pulling them behind their backs. Drusus and his two fellow soldiers had crept behind them while Orcus was speaking. They pushed the children forward beside Metallus.

"Leave us alone," shouted Charlie.

All that got him was a hard cuff around the ear. He started to cry.

"Oh, that's big of you," spat Ruus. "You're really strong beating up a little kid, aren't you?"

That was enough to send the crowd into uproar, laughing and pretending to thump each other. Then one shouted out, "Go on, soldier, hit the girl. I hear she bites!"

The crowd started barking and yapping this time. This was becoming a joke, and it couldn't continue. *Publicanus* Lucius got up and moved to Orcus.

"Get this rabble under control or I'll have you whipped in front of them."

Orcus issued an order, and a detachment of soldiers left the main column and stood with shields and spears at the ready in front of the crowd. That calmed them and Orcus continued.

"As you are unable to pay, I take these as payment."

The children were grabbed once more and were shoved towards the animal pen.

"Wait!" Metallus called out, and the soldiers forgetting their orders did just that.

"I *can* pay."

Once more the crowd gasped as Metallus eased the coins from his *bursa* and into his large, gnarled hands.

"What trickery is this? Where could you have possibly got so much money so quickly?"

Orcus was shocked. On the table in front of him, Metallus counted out twenty silver *denarii* and placed them in a line so all could see. Orcus slammed his palms onto the table and it buckled, spilling the coins in all directions. A soldier at his side just managed to save the strongbox from tipping to the ground. Orcus had been outwitted and it was obvious it hurt, but everyone had seen Metallus pay and more to the point so had Lucius. There was no help for it, Orcus would have to let him and the children go. He stood and the stool breathed a sigh of relief and gathered its legs back in.

"This will not be the last you hear from me," he hissed, "I have your measure and you will not escape my clutches, and that may be sooner than you think."

All Metallus did was turn the corners of his mouth into a wry smile and walk back with his children into the crowd. The crowd loved that bit of theatre, and now everyone was clapping him on the back instead of baying for his blood. Orcus resumed his place.

CHAPTER XXXV

With the formalities over, *Publicanus* Lucius made a boring speech about the way Rome looked after its citizens all over the Empire, and the priest made final offerings of wine and food at the feet of the effigy on the plinth before some closing words. He then invited the people to enjoy the bounty spread before them. The ox was already being roasted over a large fire to the side of the *cella*. Huge joints of meat turned on iron spits, held aloft by sturdy triangular obelisks. The soldiers filed back to the fort in similar order to that in which they had left. The festivities were to begin, and apart from a skeleton guard placed at the entrances and on the watchtowers, the rest were dismissed. Soon they streamed back down into the *vicus* to eat, drink and make merry in their few hours of freedom.

Orcus had been invited to dine with the *Publicanus* as had the priest and several of the higher dignitaries who farmed the larger, outlying estates. They entered his private quarters where he had several rooms, one of which had a table laden with choice meats, fruit, olives and wine. Around the table were long couches, *triclinia,* on which Lucius and his guests leaned and were served by the few slaves who hadn't been fortunate to be given free time; they talked into the night.

"What was that business with the metalworker all about?" asked Lucius.

"My Lord, I was set upon by his slaves in the street only a few days ago. I was lucky to get away with my life to be honest. It was fortunate I had a bodyguard or who knows what might have become of me."

Lucius raised his eyebrows; he couldn't imagine anyone setting upon the massive figure of Orcus and especially with a unit of soldiers to guard him. He continued to question him.

"I thought you told me he was going to make you a new strongbox key. I see you still wear your old one. You took some money to pay for it, I believe."

"Yes, sir, that is completely correct. My old key was given to the smith who returned it, as you have pointed out."

"You haven't had it from your finger at all since then; you guard it well. However, that still doesn't answer my question about the incident at the temple."

The other guests had stopped their small talk and had turned their ears to this bit of intrigue and gossip. They had all seen his furious response, and they wanted to know why he had flown off the handle. Orcus gave the impression he was most troubled to have behaved in this rather outrageous way.

He said in a positive, clear tone that all could hear, nodding to each as he spoke, "My lord, gentlemen, friends; that man could not possibly have raised such an amount of silver in two days. I am positive he has obtained it by some sly, underhand dealings. I intend, sirs, to find out how."

"But you yourself gave him half of it," said Lucius. "You asked me to give you ten *denarii* for the key to be made. It's a lot, I know, but he could have made up the extra somehow."

"Ah, you are very astute, sir, and you are right he may have been able to gather a few extra coins to make it up after my payment."

"Well, there you are then. I really am disappointed in you, Orcus, causing such a scene in front of the lowly *populus* and *plebs* of the *vicus*."

The others, lying on their couches, made noises of agreement and looked with some disgust in Orcus's direction. However, Orcus hadn't quite finished, and he'd judged this a perfect time to release his bombshell.

"You would all be within your rights to find me guilty of a gross error but for two small items of information I haven't yet mentioned. Firstly, I have not received the new key. *I* have not been to fetch it."

This first part was certainly true, although he failed to mention that he knew that Drusus had picked it up. This first statement was enough to arouse more interest.

"I still think you are overreacting. What's your second point?"

He pulled a *bursa* from his belt and spilled ten *denarii* into an empty bowl beside him.

"I haven't paid him yet."

He allowed his words to sink in. The *Publicanus* swung his legs so he was in a sitting position. He fingered the coins and looked at the purse in Orcus's hand.

"So let me get this straight, you only have your old key and the impression for the new one has been taken, but you have not received that key or had a chance to pay for it."

"Exactly, sir."

"Ah, now I understand your issue, and I realise why you are so concerned. Such a sum is not gained quickly or easily. That makes me suspicious, too, Orcus. I apologise and commend your reasoning. I want you to investigate this more thoroughly tomorrow. There should be a logical reason, and perhaps a simple answer will be found but..."

The *Publicanus* paused and some alarm revealed itself in the lines that deepened into creases at the corners of his mouth and on his forehead, "...there's no smoke without fire."

The conversation in the dining room now started to buzz as theories both wild and more down-to-earth were voiced and discussed at length. Money always talked, or in this case was talked about till the early hours.

CHAPTER XXXVI

Faris approached the gates and announced himself and his business. New guards were on the gate, and although he was a frequent visitor, they either hadn't remembered him or not seen him before. As usual, he was checked for weapons, but as he was on his own and had already stated he'd come for a cart their search and questioning was short. He walked the same route inside as he had done previously. He went straight to the place where the cart had been parked near the workshop. It was just before mid-morning and he had calculated that several artisans would be busy at work by this time. He stood in full view of them and made a play of moving up and down searching. Then he just stood scratching his head and turning on the spot, looking perplexed. He called inside to anyone in general who might hear him,

"Hey, anybody seen a cart? I had a cart here and now it's nowhere to be seen."

The noise from the workshop drowned him out, and almost all of those inside had their heads bowed to their work and paid him no attention. He moved inside up to a bench on which spear shafts were being prepared.

"Hey!" he called loudly.

"What's up? No need to shout."

Faris raised his eyes to the heavens and repeated, "I had a cart. Have you seen it?"

The worker looked bemused, then shouted above the noise of others, "No, thank the Gods. Probably the beer last night, eh? Not seen it or smelt it; thanks for the warning, though."

He laughed and, shaking his head, settled back down to his work.

How difficult was this going to get? thought Faris. He shouted even louder above the din.

"No, not fart! Cart, cart! You deaf old…"

Across in front of the workshop, at the same time as Faris was yelling, a small unit of soldiers headed by a *centurion* appeared and behind them Orcus.

"What is all that noise about?" enquired Orcus.

The *centurion* peered inside and at once recognised Faris. It was he who had been on the gate when the cart had been brought in.

"What's all the fuss, Faris? You're disturbing the peace and for that matter some important work."

"Sorry, sir, I was just asking about my cart. I left it here the other day and I have returned to collect it, and some nasty piece of work has moved it or worse stolen it. Either way, I'm trying to establish just where it might have gone."

"A cart, you say. I found a cart beside the road yesterday. So it was yours then?"

"No, not exactly; it belongs to Metallus. If you remember, he helped me bring it in."

"Now you mention it, I do remember."

"Metallus, the metalworker?" Orcus had intervened. "Where did you leave the cart?"

"Yes, my lord, that's him. I left it outside the workshop just over there."

"*Centurion*, send a man to the gates. I need to know if and when the cart has gone from the fort and if it did leave who took it."

Then turning back to Faris, "Show me where you left it."

Faris led the men just a few metres away around the side of the workshop. Orcus noted the wheel marks where the cart had been stationed; however, it was the *centurion* who looked more closely.

"Excuse me, sir, but I am intrigued by this."

Orcus stared at the ground beside the crouching soldier whose finger was pointing to a muddy footprint. It took but a few seconds before another had been found and following that a further two. In front of these was a thin rectangle impressed into the earth about thirty centimetres or so from the wall.

"Why would anyone be barefooted in the rain?"

The soldier sent on the fact-finding mission returned. He'd hurried back at a trot from the main gates. He slapped a fist across his chest and stood to attention in front of Orcus and the *centurion*.

"Well?" said Orcus impatiently.

"A cart was seen leaving yesterday morning, sir. The guard reported that it was pulled by a man and two boys."

"Metallus," spouted Orcus, "I guessed it was him, but what would he want with a cart of Faris's leather?"

"Two boys?" quizzed the *centurion*, then he explained that when he had found the cart the previous day, there was just a girl beside it.

"The guard said that the cart seemed heavier to move than it should be but thought nothing of it as it was children who were helping."

"Heavier than it should be. Of course, that's the reason for it then."

"Will you be letting us in on your analysis or must we guess, *Centurion*?" Orcus was becoming impatient. He needn't have worried. The *centurion* was enjoying his detective work and was happy to share his thoughts.

"What if the cart was heavy because the girl was hidden under the leather hides. The question then becomes why would she need to be covered over and why was she left here that night?"

His face creased. Answers were not forthcoming. Orcus had had enough waiting around. "Split up your men and make a thorough search around the immediate area. Leave no stone unturned. There will be an answer, and I want it found, *festinate*!"

The *centurion* divided his unit into groups to search near the granaries behind the workshop, another around the nearest walls and a group to scour inside the workshop itself. The craftsmen inside were ordered to line themselves up in the road near the stables that lay close by. Five *miles* systematically pulled the workshop apart. They cleared the tops and under-shelving of the workbenches, pulled tools from hooks on walls and flung them into the narrow alley. A few minutes later, a keen-eyed soldier noticed that the floor was damp inside near the end wall. There was no bench or liquids anywhere near that could possibly have caused it. Looking up, he could see no gaps or light coming through between the tiles. He called the *centurion* in to look.

"How can a roof leak with no holes or gaps? That's impossible."

"But it's plainly happened, sir, so it must be possible."

"Yes, soldier. So the only way that can have happened is if…?"

"The tiles were moved and then replaced, sir," said the exultant soldier.

"How right you are. We must investigate the roof then."

Almost immediately after, a soldier called out from over by the wall, "Found out how they got up there, sir."

The makeshift ladder was lifted outside, and immediately it was obvious how the rectangular mark in the muddy earth had been made. It was leant up against the wall, and one of the guards climbed to the top and looked out across the roof. Then he scanned the roof of the *praetorium* opposite and called down.

"It looks as though there's been some disturbance on the *praetorium* roof, sir. Some tiles appear scraped of moss and askew."

"The girl climbs the ladder and gets onto the roof. She somehow gets across to the *praetorium* roof and removes tiles there because…" Orcus couldn't finish his sentence because the *centurion* jumped in,

"Because below her is the strongroom."

Bingo! Orcus had allowed the soldier to solve the crime for him, and now he must quickly engage the *Publicanus* in the search there. Soon Metallus and his children would be firm candidates for execution. Drusus's plan was masterful. Orcus could see how he could have been such an asset if only he hadn't blackmailed him to start with. What a team they could have made. With rapid waddle, Orcus and the *centurion* presented themselves at the door to Lucius's office. They were admitted and stood before his desk. Faris was obliged to wait outside.

"Excuse me, my lord, but we believe that there may have been a serious crime committed. It is possible someone has gained entry to the strongroom through the roof."

Lucius was a decisive man and spent no time pushing back his chair and ushering them out of his room and down the dimly lit corridor to the rear of the *praetorium*. The *quaestorium* door had a lock on its outside. A slotted key on a chain around Lucius's waist was produced, which passed through the wards inside the lock and when turned shot the bolt of the door back. The heavy wooden door was opened. Torches on the inside near wall were set ablaze and the room was illuminated. At first glance, nothing seemed out of place. The *centurion* removed a torch and moved towards the strongboxes. He raised it and looked up, remembering that it appeared the tiles had been disturbed.

"My Lord, look, the beam has been cut away."

The two officers barely examined the gap. There was a more pressing matter.

"Never mind that," Lucius said sharply. His eyes had fallen on some coins in-between two of the boxes that had caught the light.

"Orcus, that box there. See if it's open."

Orcus dropped to his knees in front of the box. The *centurion* and Lucius cringed as his bare knees hit the flagged floor.

"It's unlocked, my lord."

"Well, those coins didn't jump out by themselves unless you've been careless. Open it."

"I can see this job must be painful for you," said Lucius watching Orcus get up with difficulty. He gave the *centurion* a knowing glance.

"Why do you say that, sir?"

"Your knees, I had no idea that this job would cause you to spill as much blood as my soldiers on the battlefield."

"I haven't spilled any blood, sir."

"Well, I think those dark-red stains around the boxes give a lie to that statement. You show commendable fortitude, Orcus."

"Please, sir, I don't mean to contradict you but…"

Orcus turned to face the *Publicanus* and lifted his tunic above his knees.

"Orcus, what are you doing? Please, that's enough."

The *Publicanus* was horrified. The folds of his tunic were gripped in two tight fists as Orcus rested them on his thighs.

"Look, sir, my knees are red but the skin is unbroken. It wasn't me who bled here."

"Well, somebody certainly has, and if not you then who? Anyway, we are getting side-tracked; let me see in the box."

The *Publicanus* moved forward as the *centurion* brought the torch closer to give more light. He ordered the *centurion* to lift the box out so that it could be examined. The *centurion* was certain this was going to be quite a task to lift. To his astonishment, the box had hardly any weight and he had no difficulty in lifting it at all. This was equally apparent to those watching. "Open it," ordered Lucius.

The lid was lifted, and the *centurion* flipped the box upside down. The lid hung and swung like the mouth on a ventriloquist's dummy. Lucius's jaw was almost on the floor, too, and his gaping mouth was catching flies. The box had been emptied and apart from a meagre few coins scattered around, it was clear a major theft had taken place. The other boxes were opened, and it was discovered that only silver *denarii* had been taken from two of them.

"Why *denarii*?" questioned Lucius. "Why, when there is all that gold and jewellery here are those boxes untouched?"

Orcus gave a space of time. He had sown the seed earlier, and now he wanted strong roots to ensure his story conveyed real weight and justification. A few seconds more he waited, then...

"My Lord, I believe I have an answer to your question. It is only a theory but I am sure if you think about it, this can be the only possible solution. I believe the thief needed *denarii*. Gold *aurei* hold too much value and are too eye-catching. Our thief enters through the roof, probably by a rope. He or *she* has a key and opens the boxes, discovers the ones holding *denarii* and steals them away like thieving *Mercurius*."

"No, Orcus, that can't be. How in Jupiter's name would he get them out of the fort?"

"The cart, that's how they did it, with a cart," again the *centurion* had his answer.

Orcus had sown the seed, created those strong roots and as if by the power of *Solus* himself, the fruits of his sowing were being picked and eaten by the tonne.

"The girl was beside the cart," continued the *centurion*. "She must have been hiding in the cart with the silver covered by the hides. The man and the boys pulled the cart out of the fort under our very noses."

"What man?" The *Publicanus* had followed the story but not who had carried out the raid.

"Metallus, sir. He had a cart; he left it here overnight. He has two boys and a girl, and the most telling evidence of all is that he paid his tribute, which he couldn't possibly have raised in so short a time, in silver *denarii.*"

"It's a convincing tale, Orcus. All the elements seem to fit. We must arrest this man and get some evidence, some indisputable proof."

The *centurion* decided this was his area of expertise,

"You just need a confession, sir. If you arrest just the man, he may not crack. Arrest the girl as well, and there's your leverage. I don't know any man who would see a child suffer for his own wrongdoings. Start to persuade her, if you get my meaning, while he watches on, and you'll soon have all the evidence you need."

"I'm not a squeamish man, *Centurion,* and even for me, your method is extreme. However, in this case, I believe you may well be right."

CHAPTER XXXVII

Charlie, Saima and Ruus had left the *temenos* late in the evening on *Calends*. They had feasted and danced and watched men arm-wrestle for large wagers that had each man's backers cheering wildly as each strained to force the other's knuckles to the table. They'd watched a play in which the actors had worn 'happy' or 'sad' masks with huge rectangular mouths that told how the character being played was feeling. There were no speeches, it was in mime, yet the play was easy to understand as the players used great big gestures. They were full of the day's events and kept laughing as they remembered Orcus's face when Metallus produced the tribute. They thought of different ways to describe his flushed features.

Ruus offered, "Redder than a *centurion*'s crest."

"Redder than a soldier's tunic," said Saima.

"Redder than a Ferrari," chimed Charlie, pleased with his addition.

"Redder than a what?" asked Ruus.

Saima sighed; she was fed up helping Charlie out of holes.

"He's just making up words 'cos he can't think of anything to say," she sighed. "You know what he's like by now."

"Well, he seemed pretty sure of what he was saying, but I've never heard such words before. I think you lot are holding back on me somehow."

Saima had to change the mood and swing the conversation.

"Look, I haven't a clue what he meant either, but we should really be deciding what to do about where I found the cart today."

That got them all back to working out what would be best to do next. Eventually, they all agreed on their plan for the following morning.

CHAPTER XXXVIII

Saima was to see what was happening in and around Faris's workshop. This wasn't because she was a girl and it was easy, far from it; this was equally as dangerous as the boys' task they'd all decided upon. It was because a girl would go unnoticed wandering around shopping areas and workshops for fine goods; boys would be seen wanting to steal or create havoc. Ruus was going to lead Charlie to the spot where Saima had found the abandoned cart. They would find the path over the roadside ditch and go to the clearing. Once there, they could investigate together and see what they could find. So, leaving each other outside the workshop, they split off to do their separate tasks.

Ruus led Charlie onto the hill and down past the temple. He had no desire to meet up with Faris even by chance. He worried that Saima was taking on her dangerous duty alone, and that was into the very place he and Charlie were avoiding. He reasoned, however, that their choices were for the best and Saima herself had seemed keen to carry out that particular part of the investigation. So he forged on, Charlie in tow, over the bridge and across the ditch into the scrub and trees just as Saima had done the day before.

It wasn't long before they both stopped by the oak with low branches that Saima had found. Ruus asked

Charlie to keep watch and whistle like a bird if he saw anyone. Charlie had never whistled like a bird in his life and hadn't a clue how he would even begin, so he decided he would pick a blade of grass and place it between his thumbs. If anyone came, he'd blow that instead. Ruus meanwhile climbed the tree and scanned the road. He could make out both ditches and had a brilliant view around the bend. Charlie had rather switched off and was leaning braced against the bark of the trunk. Idly he began to blow between his thumbs for want of anything better to do. Forgetting himself entirely, he let out a blast of air from between his lips and the grass reed bellowed its raucous trumpet. Ruus nearly fell from his perch and scrambled down quicker than a squirrel that'd eaten a bowl of chillies. He almost trod on Charlie's shoulders and had to jump the last metre and a half to the ground.

"Where are they?" he asked, crouching low.

"Oh, sorry, that was just me practising."

"You *stultus*! You gave me the fright of my life. I reckon Sabia was right about you."

"Why, what did she say?" Charlie shuffled a few steps away from the tree. Charlie's body language became very defensive and he clutched his chest with both arms. Almost always his behaviour was an act. He'd always cover up somehow; make out he was in the right or knew the answers, yet in reality was insecure. He felt everyone else was more intelligent or more worldly-wise than he was. That's what he believed, and so he lied or shouted or made great gestures. Small vessels making the greatest sound held true for Charlie. That was him, all bluster. Right now, he hadn't a leg to stand on. He'd been in the wrong and he knew it, and worse, he didn't have a way out, an excuse. He was just plain wrong and it hurt. What hurt even more was Saima had spoken about him with Ruus. He thought they'd grown to be friends. Friends and allies through adversity but no, Saima had confided her private thoughts about him with Ruus and he was out in the cold. His chin went down, not able to face the truth.

Meanwhile, Ruus ignored Charlie's outburst. His mood had changed at the flick of a switch and here he was examining tree bark.

"Caius, look."

Charlie didn't move. Confidence and feelings in tatters, he preferred to bundle himself up in his own self-pity and use that as his security blanket.

"Come on, snap out of it; this is important," Ruus spoke encouragingly and Charlie looked up.

"Look, halfway up this part of the tree, see?"

Charlie dropped his arms to his side and wandered over. He tried to make a joke, "Oh yes, it's as clear as mud," he quipped.

Ruus shook his head and explained, "I climbed up, okay. I sat on a branch, and I had a clear view of the road."

"So?"

"How does mud get halfway up a tree? Answer: It doesn't unless someone's climbed it and mud from their sandal has squeezed it there."

"Still don't get you."

"This has to be the tree that the murderer used to shoot from. Faris must have climbed this tree to have a clear view of the road and his target. The fox path I told you about will be on the other side just a few metres along the road across the ditch."

All animosity shelved, the boys emerged from the bracken and gorse, crossed the ditch and walked slowly up the other side looking for the path. Just as Saima before them, they came upon the decaying crow. Charlie put two fingers in his mouth and pulled down his lower jaw and tongue while making a throaty, vomity noise.

"Gross or what?" he exclaimed.

They jumped over and Ruus led the way down the path towards the clearing. This time, as they approached, Ruus put his finger to his lips and signed for Charlie to lie flat and move using his elbows and knees. They skirted the space and came upon Ruus's previous hidey-hole. Laying low and elbowing their way up the bank, their eyes scanned left and right. Ruus cupped his ear and mimed that they should stay still and just listen. The forest was silent, no birdsong, no rustling of a thrush turning leaves for tasty slugs or spiders. Not even a breath of wind wafted the thinnest of branches. All was clear to explore.

They rose and scampered down the short slope onto the grass. They saw the marks where the branches that covered both pits had been dragged, and it was pretty obvious where the earth had been disturbed. Charlie rushed across to the biggest patch and began to pull the covering away, revealing a mounded patch of earth.

"X marks the spot," he said eagerly over his shoulder and started to scrabble away with both hands, scooping double handfuls of soil back between his knees.

"We need to be careful, Caius. There's no telling when someone might turn up."

"So the quicker we get to it the better," was Charlie's immediate response.

Ruus had no option. This time he had to go with the flow, and anyway he was as curious about the dig as Charlie; so he set to work from the opposite side of the hole. Ruus was sweating and sat back on his heels wiping his brow, while Charlie scrabbled deeper.

"AAAAGGGGHHHH!!!"

Charlie had scrabbled, and in his hands along with a soft cake of mud, he'd come across something a bit tougher that his fingers ran through. Wondering what it might be, he had tugged and pulled until with a jerk it came free. In his filthy hands, he was staring at a hank of hair. His shock had paralysed his limbs and he screamed over and over. His breathing was shallow and rapid, then all went blank as he fainted and tumbled over the hole, his face pressed against the top of Vitus's partly bald head.

Ruus, with his strong arms, hoisted him back up. Charlie had regained consciousness but still clung on to a chunk of Vitus's hair. In a panic, he flung his palms at each other and brushed them furiously together. The mud and the hair clung on tight. Every sweep of one hand seemed to transfer it to the other. He started to do a wild dance flicking his hands, then he rushed to the trees surrounding the clearing and smeared the whole hairy mess across the bark of a gleaming, white, silver birch.

Ruus caught up and put his hands on both of Charlie's shoulders to steady him and help him regain some calm.

"It's okay, Caius. I'm here."

Charlie was shaking, but his breathing slowed and he sunk to his knees.

"I didn't sign up for this," he coughed and caught his breath. "Who is that?"

"I don't know but I do know we can't afford to stop now. We'll never get another chance. Caius, we've got to be brave. We need to dig the other patch too. Perhaps that will make things clearer. I know you've had an awful fright but we can do this, together; you and me, a team. Yes?"

Charlie looked up at him. Ruus cared; he could see it in his eyes. He cared that Charlie was okay. He needed someone strong and was willing to trust him with all his faults. Charlie also knew that this was a chance to shake off his shell, to do something heroic, bold and fearless, the like of which he'd never done before; a new Charlie.

"Yes," he said after a short pause, and a grim determination showed in his clenched jaw and tight lips.

The second pit was easier and shallower to dig. This time it was Ruus who uncovered leather. Like a fussy archaeologist, he picked the earth from around it with care. He had no desire to end up with another head in his hands. Charlie eased soil away from the other side, and soon he too had revealed the top of yet another sack which overlaid part of the first. Together the boys forgot their prodding and poking and giving each other a wink of agreement, they tugged the topmost sack out from the hole. It was heavy and bulbous, but as they lowered it onto the grass its shape flattened out.

"Well, that's not a body part," said Ruus winking, and he grabbed the corners at the bottom of the sack and tipped it. Coins slipped from the neck of the sack and formed a silver puddle in-between them.

"OMG," whispered Charlie.

"What did you say?"

"Um... I said, OMG. Orion's Mighty *Gladius*, yeah?" Charlie had made up an explanation on the spur of the moment and hoped it sounded ancient enough to convince Ruus.

"You have the weirdest sayings," Ruus said, shaking his head. "Let's see what else we can uncover."

Soon six sacks, all containing the stolen silver *denarii*, were in a tight hexagon on the grass beside them. The coins from the first sack had been replaced inside it. All that remained was to decide how to proceed. Charlie had a germ of an idea in his head, and being devious he was quite used to thinking up ways in and around things on the spur of the moment. As more sacks had appeared, his plan became firmer in his mind and he hoped Ruus would agree.

"Before we go any further, I want to put an idea to you. At first, it may seem a bit of a long shot and not a little dangerous, but I reckon if we play it right, we can get our just reward."

Charlie explained what they should do, and Ruus saw the sense of it and without hesitation agreed. He was beginning to believe Sabia may not be wholly correct in her estimation of Caius and his ways.

CHAPTER XXXIX

Saima had taken the scenic route. She had visited the stalls on either side of the main street and kept an eye out for Faris as she did so. She decided that if she saw him, she'd just nip inside the shop that she was at and let him go past. She wound her way down the street, fingering fabrics or cooing over jewellery and trinkets the like of which she had never seen before. A brooch of a horse grabbed her attention. It was inlaid with bright blue stones. She asked what they were and was told they were *lapis lazuli* mined in the Orient in far-away Bactria. The stones had come many miles across land and water. She pulled herself away, only wishing she had the money to buy it. At last, she rounded the corner and slipped down the side street that gave onto the rear of Faris's home.

Drawing herself stealthily along the back wall, she listened by the back door flap. The only sound was a faint drip of water coming from a small leak in a water butt on the opposite side of a simple sheet of leather that formed the door. Saima pushed it aside and crept inside. This was Faris's living quarters with a bed to one side and a rough table in the centre. She took little notice of these and started to search. Her task was made easier by light from the open front of the workshop spilling through to the back and illuminating the space.

As she examined the room, she noted a coil of rope beneath the bed against the wall. She crouched down and pulled the rope out. A coil of rope under a bed in a living space? Why would that be? Shouldn't that be in the workshop? Why is it knotted? She shook her head.

"For goodness sake," she spoke aloud, "stop thinking everything is a mystery. Perhaps it's just a convenient place to put it. C'mon, Saima, get your head together."

She pushed it back into place, and despite searching everywhere she could see nothing out of the ordinary. She'd even been into the front workshop and kept a low profile while searching there. Nothing. Back she came into the living room and edged her way past the table. With little else to see or find, she made her way to the door flap, then she stopped and spun on her heel. The table, something had drawn her back to the table. What was it? It was staring her in the face. Why hadn't she thought about it straight away the moment she came in? Faris lived by himself, yet here on the table were two bowls still with the remnants of dried food stuck on the sides and two drinking cups. This hadn't been breakfast, and from the look of it they'd been there a while. Each bowl and cup was on an opposite side of the table as though two people had shared a meal together. She moved to the seat nearest her and moved a plain stool to get a closer look. She inspected the bowl, cup and table and then from out of the blue...

Slam!

A hand clamped over her mouth, and an arm around her throat squeezed her breath from entering her lungs. She had no time to struggle let alone bite or kick. Her eyelids felt heavy and she rapidly became dizzy, and without further warning she collapsed in her captor's arms. He pulled the rope out from under the bed and winding it tightly, secured her arms behind her back and pushed her legs into a kneeling position. Then he finished by tying her ankles up to the rope, securing her hands behind her so that her legs were bent right back at the knee. She was rolled onto her side and lay there trussed like a chicken beside the table.

"Thought I hadn't seen you, eh? How wrong could you be? What're you doing here then, a sneak thief perhaps?"

Saima coughed and her eyes fluttered open. Faris had no cause to be anxious about what she might have found because, after all, there was nothing to see, but she was here and there had to be a reason. That reason alone could be his undoing, a serious cause for concern. He must find out what she knew.

Saima pulled at her hands. They were tied fast, and when she pulled, the rope bit into her ankles and made her shout out in pain. Faris was in no mood to mess around being gentle. He pulled an evil looking blade from a shelf and gently knelt down beside her placing its slick, keen edge to her slender neck. Her struggles stopped as she felt its faintest touch on her skin. She held herself rigid, scared that the slightest movement would cause it to slice her open.

"Well?"

"I can't speak with that thing at my throat," she hissed. It was amazing how defiant she felt even at the very gates of death.

"That's a shame," he sighed and grasped a hank of her hair, then with a flick of his wrist cut it off as easily as a hot knife through butter. He returned the blade to just below her ear and bent in close, holding the hair in front of her eyes. Saima's eyes brimmed with tears of fear and loathing. How would she ever get out of this alive? She had to think quickly and clearly, yet her mind was hardly in a functioning state.

"Now, let's try again, shall we? What are you doing in my home skulking around?"

He pulled her hair once more so that her face was directly in front of his, a mere thumb's length apart.

"Tell me!" he shouted, getting more aggressive and less patient by the second.

"Ana abnat 'akhik," she cried, making tears stream down her face, which wasn't hard considering the circumstances and what she was suffering.

"I'm a slave. Can't you see that I'm a slave? Bought and sold and made to go wherever my masters took me until I escaped and found myself with a family once more. Not my family, not *our* family but a family that cared and looked after me. When I saw you the other day with that cart, I knew it was you but I had to be sure. You look just like my father, your brother. I am your niece!"

Faris sat back and pulled the knife away.

"My niece? My brother's child? Where is he? What of our family?"

Saima's masterstroke had delivered. She had tried a few words of Arabic that she had learnt when she was growing up. Simple words like I, am, daughter, mother, father, brother and sister were among those she remembered. She hoped something yelled out loud would either bring someone to investigate the screaming or perhaps, if she was lucky, he might recognise some of her words. All her real family apart from herself had quite a few brothers and sisters, so she made a guess that Faris might too. Luck had played its part. The lie had worked.

"Ana aibnat 'akhik, I am your brother's daughter," she repeated. "When I was taken as a slave, the traders separated us all from our families. I have no idea where they are, but I have now found you."

Faris's shock at the revelation turned to wonder. "It's a miracle," he gushed. "What can I say? What should I do?"

"Well, you could start by untying me," Saima offered.

"Gods forgive me, yes of course."

He clenched the knife and leant towards Saima who let out a shriek, but he deftly sliced the knot then allowed her space to sit up and rub the reddest, rawest places where the rope had chafed.

"Thank you." Then thinking she must get away from him as quickly as possible said, "I can't stay you know, Metallus will wonder where I am."

"Oh no, I can't let you go."

"Why not?"

"You are in the gravest danger; the soldiers are coming to arrest you and Metallus. He has stolen silver from the fort and you are also a suspect."

"Me?"

"Yes, you must hide here, and I will try and find a way for you, for us to get away together. Whatever you've done, I don't care. We shall be family again."

Saima had lied and it had saved her life, but now she was trapped and could see no way out this time. She asked for some water and sat at the table, trying without success to find another story, another lie. Faris, of course, knew full well that Saima wasn't involved in the theft from the fort, but he couldn't have her giving her version of events as that would incriminate him. He couldn't be sure either if the family story Saima had told him was true. It sounded reasonable but it somehow seemed too convenient. Until he could question her more thoroughly, he'd keep her here under watch. He guessed she wouldn't leave if she thought she'd be arrested as soon as she stepped outside. Similarly, he was sure there would be no reason to search his house, so for now all was safe.

CHAPTER XL

Earlier at the fort, the *Publicanus* had thanked Faris for his input and sent him on his way. The *centurion* was instructed to arrange for the arrest of Metallus and Saima as quickly as possible, then turning to Orcus, he ordered him to create an account of how much was missing and present that to him promptly so that he would have the full facts of the theft before him.

Orcus went straight to his small office and pored over his accounts. Lucius could be very demanding, and his calculations needed to be careful. At the same time as Orcus was about his counting, the *centurion* started to gather together a small unit to arrest Metallus. He moved to the barracks and, selecting a few off-duty soldiers, informed them he wanted them armed and on parade at the gates in five minutes. The selected band dressed and presented themselves in good order at the gates. Drusus had been watching the activity from his guard duty on a gate tower. He had seen the conversations in front of the *praetorium* and watched Faris leave. The *centurion* called for his unit to form up.

"*Procedite; Gradum Servate.*"

Before they had gone a Roman pace of two steps, there was a call from above the gate.

"Excuse me, sir."

"*Consiste!*"

The unit halted and waited as Drusus descended.

"These men are in my *contubernium*, sir. I wonder if I could know where they're going?"

"This is most irregular, soldier. You are delaying me. They are going to arrest the smith, Metallus."

"Sir, I was with Clerk Orcus when Metallus attacked him. He is devious, sir."

"I am arresting him for theft, not trickery."

"But I have been to his workshop, sir. I know its layout; after all, it was I who gave him Clerk Orcus's key to copy. He may well try and escape through the back, so I would split my force to cover that, sir."

"Oh, would you? Are you telling me, your superior officer, that I wouldn't have thought of that? You are on dangerous ground, soldier. Stop wasting my time."

The *centurion* was about to set off once more when again he was interrupted,

"Evidence, sir. As much as Metallus might confess, it will be no good unless the *Publicanus* has his evidence. He's a stickler for the rule of law, sir. I think I know just where such evidence may be hidden."

"Enough, you have wasted enough of my time already. He and the girl could be halfway to *Eboracum* by now. Join your unit then, if you must, but let's get on with it."

The detachment moved out of the fort and split into equal groups, one tracking right behind the smith's workshop and living quarters. The rest, including the *centurion*, marched down the road, ready for a frontal assault. Without waiting, they barged in under the small, sloping roof and spread equally spaced from wall to wall. Metallus was caught totally unawares. He was heating a rod of iron in the forge's furnace and now stood holding it out in a gloved hand; in the other fist was a heavy hammer.

"Drop those now!" bellowed the *centurion* looking Metallus straight in the eye. The four soldiers at his front lowered their *pila* towards his face and chest. Those who had been sent round the back appeared with *gladii* drawn and ready to strike if and when ordered.

"Where's the girl?"

A soldier in the line behind Metallus replied that there had been no sign of her, nor had they seen her escape.

"She can't be far. We'll find her quickly enough. Search the place. You're looking for anything that may give me evidence of a theft – coins, a strongbox, anything."

Three soldiers stood at Metallus's sides and back while all apart from the *centurion* pulled the place apart piece by piece. Jars, bowls, cups, shelves, mattresses and tools were strewn about, leaving the whole place a wreck. Outside, they turned the cart upside down and just for pleasure it seemed used hot coals transported from the furnace to set it ablaze. Not a jot of evidence was found.

"You, soldier, what's your name?"

"Drusus, sir."

"Drusus. Well, Drusus, your little scheme of finding evidence is a failure. I'll get my evidence back at the fort, and I will have you cleaning latrines for the next month, so help me…"

"We have one place we haven't searched, sir. I think there is nowhere you are more likely to find what you need."

Drusus led them all out to the front.

"There is nothing here, Drusus." The *centurion* looked puzzled.

"Stand back, sir. I would hate you to get wet."

Drusus moved a metre or two towards the outside front wall and, with a heave, pulled the brimming water butt onto its edge and then with force threw it to the ground. Litres of water gushed into and down the street, its flow carving a rill as it went, and as the torrent subsided, there staring up was the bright, new, strongbox ring key.

"Evidence, sir."

CHAPTER XLI

Charlie and Ruus had made a large detour after their exertions in the clearing. They crossed back over the road and, keeping the river to their left, headed north. The going was easy, and although they had to make the odd stop to rest their arms, they arrived at a small copse of trees around half a kilometre from the temple. This place was ideal. No one strayed this far from the road. From here, they could see the eastern side of the *vicus* and the river at the bottom of the hill. Directly away across the stream bridge was the temple entrance. The two boys dropped to their knees behind the trees. The two sacks of coins that they had carried sat squat on last autumn's decaying leaf-litter.

Ruus spoke softly, "We'll never manage to break the ground here with our hands; we're going to need a spade. For now, let's just scrape leaves over them and get back here as quickly as we can to bury them."

"Great idea." Charlie smiled. "We'll have our conversation on the way."

"If we cut back to the road and walk up to town, there'll be a chance to talk then."

"Okay, let's get home and pick up what we need."

They cut straight back to the road by the small bridge and started their walk into town. As they moved towards the top, a group of townsfolk were drawn up on the far side of the street. It was obvious that something serious had happened, and seeing the overturned barrel with its broken staves dressing the street, they ran full tilt till they stood outside and stared into the wrecked interior. There was no sign of Metallus. Ruus swung round and glared at the gathering glued to the spot opposite.

"What's going on?" he yelled in a blind rage. "Where's my father?"

The reply from the closest man was short and not the most helpful, "Taken."

"Taken? How? Who? Why?" howled Ruus, "Didn't one of you lousy neighbours support him? Didn't anyone try to help?"

"He's a thief," said a thin woman at the back. There was a murmur of agreement from them all.

The first man spoke again, "We saw the key he'd made lying right there on the road. Straight out of the barrel it came. We saw him pay his tribute at the Festival of Janus. How could he manage that, eh? Your father is a liar; a dirty, low-life, sneak thief, and he deserves all he gets!"

Again, there were nods and agreements. Ruus flew from where he stood and head-butted the man in the stomach who fell winded to the ground. Ruus jumped on top of him and started to pummel him with his fingers curled into wicked fists. It took three others to haul him off, and they threw him onto his back in the middle of the street.

"You're obviously no better," one shouted.

"Gutter boy," sneered another.

Ruus made to get up and start his assault again, his rage fed by the hateful words, but Charlie grasped his shoulders and, with all his strength, held him tight.

"Listen to me," he whispered with his mouth almost clamped to Ruus's ear, "they're not worth it. We know the truth, and we'll make the truth play out. Don't lose it now; there are bigger fish to fry than these *stulti*. We'll show them who has lied and who tells the truth."

Ruus's rage subsided, and as they sat in the middle of the road, the smaller boy with all his faults held his friend tight. Of all people to show their true emotion, Charlie believed Ruus to be the most unlikely. Yet Ruus's chest heaved and, with his head back, howled his tears of frustration and pain to the heedless sky. Charlie was aware that this spectacle was not to the neighbours' taste and they started to drift away, tutting about how they had suspected Metallus all along and speculating what would become of him now.

Ruus recovered a little and clambered to his feet. He looked about him and, running to the far side of the street, caught a man by the arm.

"Sabia," he said, "the girl, where is she? Was she taken to the fort too?"

The man shrugged away his hand and grudgingly said over his shoulder, "Girl? There was no girl here."

He continued to amble away, shaking his head.

"Did you hear that? Sabia wasn't here. Where is she? What's happened to her? She should have been back by now." Ruus became agitated again. This was turning into a nightmare. His dad arrested and Sabia missing. Charlie had much to ponder as well. Not only was Saima missing and Metallus arrested, but they hadn't even had a chance to think about getting the statue and finding their way home. Too many things were just piling up and blocking any sort of attempt to find a plan for that.

"Look," said Charlie as they started to clear up the mess that the soldiers had created, "Sabia was going to scout out Faris's place. We know what he was up to, and we have the evidence. Now would be the perfect time to sow the seeds of our plan."

Twenty minutes later they arrived at Faris's workshop. He was out front, sharpening a wheeled leather-cutter on a stone. Its scrape set Charlie's teeth on edge.

"*Salve,* Faris, I hope we find you well."

Ruus was hoping his polite and easy approach would be recognised as a pleasant and friendly greeting. He continued in the same vein,

"We were wondering if you had seen *Sabia.* She said she thought she'd head down this way this morning."

Faris appeared calm and was about to deny any sign of her when from the back Saima, having heard friendly voices, came rushing out. She had never been so delighted to see her friends, but she had to make sure they understood the situation.

"Ruus, Caius!" she exclaimed. "You needn't have worried, I'm in safe hands. You'll never guess; Faris is my long-lost uncle. I know, amazing, right, but it's true."

She started to give an explanation of the events that had led to her discovery. The boys gaped but understood they had to play along with it. As always, Charlie had a few words to chip in.

"Oh yes, you said, it was cobblers, didn't you, and this is the cobbler?" Charlie smiled in Faris's direction.

Saima didn't understand for a moment. What on earth was he talking about? Then the penny dropped; he'd let her know in his colourful language that her story about the leatherworker and shoemaker had been made up.

"Yes," she said, "that's it. Faris has two faces just like Janus, a cobbler and my uncle."

Now Charlie knew that she'd made up a lie, saying one thing and meaning another.

Ruus had no idea what this chit-chat was all about but decided he needed to up the stakes and set their plan in motion.

"Sabia, my father has been arrested. We need to go somewhere safe together before we're taken too."

Faris cut in, "She's safe with me; they won't look here."

"We have to be together, away from town; even here is too dangerous. Someone is bound to look for her and us sooner or later. Anyway, we've found a place. It's perfect. No one will think to look there. It's in a clearing a short distance from the road up in the woods, but we need to move quickly before the search widens."

Charlie added his little gem, "Yes, it's a great hiding place. It's weird there, though, loose earth has been scattered around, and tracks of brushwood dragged about. Could be badgers, I suppose. Anyway, we can investigate that when we get back there while we wait till the heat dies down a bit."

Faris was now less concerned about the welfare of Sabia and more concerned that his hoard of silver or Vitus's body would be discovered.

"There are patrols along that road all day. You could be seen. Look, this is the best place. I'm happy for you to stay safe together here, all of you, at least until say midnight. That would give you a chance." He made a good case, but for their plan to have any chance,

Saima needed to get away. Somehow, they'd have to work her escape.

"Okay, that seems a good idea. Thanks." Charlie couldn't think of how to turn him down.

Faris breathed a sigh of relief. That fact was not missed by the boys, and they nodded to each other. Saima, however, was very confused. Now they were all trapped. What were the boys up to?

Faris went back to his work but seemed agitated and had hardly settled to it properly when once again he appeared in the back and spoke to the children,

"I need to get on with my work. Make sure you stay here in the back and keep out of sight."

CHAPTER XLII

"What are you doing?" Saima whispered when the scraping of the sharpening stone started up once more. "And what's all this about Metallus being arrested?"

Ruus spoke, "They have accused him of stealing and say they found the new key he made in our water barrel."

"But that's impossible; he gave the key to that soldier and was paid for it."

"I know, but that's what's happened and what they'll do to him doesn't bear thinking about."

Charlie interjected, "Look, Sabia, we've got a plan. You are the only one who can make this come right."

"Why me? What on earth can I do?"

"You've got to be arrested! The soldiers know you were with the cart when they found it. They've put two and two together and think you're another one they want."

Charlie then explained what the plan was.

"What if they don't believe me? What if you're wrong about Faris?"

Charlie tried to reassure her, "We can't be wrong about Faris. What with him and the cart and the money we found. It all adds up. You always tell the truth. You always tell it with such conviction. No one would believe me. I'm hopeless at the truth. They will believe you, I know they will, but you must only tell *Publicanus* Lucius."

"Why him?"

"Look, we're not exactly flavour of the month with the fat man Orcus or his henchman Drusus. The *centurion* found you by the cart, so even he's not going to believe you. No, you've got to hope that Lucius will listen and see what you're saying is the only possible alternative truth."

"Charlie is so sure, but I'm not. I'm not sure we can ask it of you. You will be putting yourself in great danger," Ruus added.

"If it has come to this, then I have to trust you both and hope your plan will work. Have you got a Plan B?"

The two boys looked at each other, then back at her and shook their heads.

"Thought so. Well then, I'll have to do it and suffer the consequences if it all goes wrong. What else is there? *We* have to let the truth be told and hope it's enough."

Not long after, Faris prepared some food. The children were ravenous and tucked in. Faris watched a while then returned to his work. He had no desire to join the children, so stayed out front keeping an eye open for a sight of soldiers searching.

As it grew dark, Charlie moved forward into the workshop. It was nearly time. Faris spun at the sound of his coming; his face showed a hint of anger at Charlie's approach. Charlie could see he was on edge, truly tense. Faris had to be distracted, so Charlie sat close by and spoke quietly, "We... er... wanted to thank you for your help. I mean, not everyone would be as kind as you, especially in the circumstances."

Faris waved a hand as if to say don't concern yourself.

Charlie continued, "So Sabia's your niece then? It's great she found you after so long. What about your brother? Did he work leather like you? Did your dad teach you both?"

Faris lifted his face and searched Charlie's eyes. A child's question. What possible interest could this boy have in his family? He resumed his hunched position and continued to sharpen his tools.

"I would have loved to have helped my dad and learn his skills, but things didn't turn out that way," Charlie added.

He wanted to try and keep this conversation going, so he was making it up as he went along hoping that Faris would buy into it. Faris seemed to be in a state of limbo, listening but immersed in his own private thoughts. So it was a surprise when he said, "My brother was a coward."

Charlie was shocked at his outburst, but he had him hooked and questioned him further, "Why do you say that?"

"When the Romans came to our town, they burnt our houses and enslaved some of the women and children and killed many old menfolk. My father was murdered in his own house. My brother was older than me. He lived away from the town, herding his goats and living a simple life with his wife. Even before the attack, he never once came back to see us or help us, and now I have his offspring in my house, calling me her long-lost uncle."

During this time, Ruus had quietly pulled back the flap, and Saima had slipped out and away. Ruus had heard the conversation, and after letting Saima out, he waited a few seconds for her to get away then threw a stool to the ground. Charlie and Faris jumped up at the sound and ran into the back.

"What's going on?"

Ruus answered, "Sabia, she's gone. She heard what you were saying about her father and her family and couldn't stand to hear it anymore. She said that she was a burden to you and that could never be permitted. She decided it was for the best if she just went away and never troubled you again."

Faris's shoulders slumped. He couldn't believe his words had carried and created such distress and offence. Of course, it was too late now to turn back the clock. She'd gone. Charlie turned the stool upright again so that Faris could sit. They almost felt sorry for him. He was a husk of a man without a family or a country. A nomad, yet bound to serve those he hated most and tied to the Romans by his trade.

Charlie had to speak and needed to prevent Faris himself from disappearing too soon.

"We have all suffered under the yoke of these invaders, yet we must stay strong. Besides, we may find her. Who knows? However, it is getting dark, and we would have little chance of finding her at night. Perhaps she'll find the clearing, and we can explain your words were all a terrible misunderstanding and you meant her no harm, but we need to wait a little while longer yet."

This was accepted. Faris realised the sense of it. He sincerely hoped she wouldn't be at the clearing later or her fate would be the same as the boys.

CHAPTER XLIII

Saima passed through the town going over her part, what she must say and do. For that's how it seemed to her. It was all an act. How could any of this be real? Yet here she was; flesh and blood. She even pinched herself to test she was living this nightmare. She emerged from the top of the *vicus* and was within a hundred metres of the gate. She could see the armed guards, two on each tower. One pair were in some kind of conversation with each other, but the ones to her left had already spotted her. Light spilled onto the roadway from torches placed at either side. Every precaution, it seemed, had been taken against a frenzied attack by a ten-year-old girl. She couldn't back out now and continued her journey up towards the fort. Fifty metres away she halted and stood stock still staring towards them. The guards to the right had forgotten their conversation, and one had immediately disappeared from view.

Inside the fort, there were several urgent commands, and as quickly as the guard had disappeared, both gates were swung back. Facing Saima was a century of eighty men in full battle dress. At their head was the *centurion* with his horsehair, crested helmet. He bellowed an order and at double time they ran at her, a rattling and clanking dragon of death. Its fire the *pila* and *gladii* held behind their rectangular *scuta*. On it came raging and pouring from the gates of Roman hell, the metres between consumed by burnished scale and stride as the reflection from their *lorica segmentata* flashed in the torch light. She put her hands to her eyes yet couldn't turn away. Almost upon her now, she could hear the pounding, rhythmic tread that would crush her into the paving and her blood would spill and flow to fill the gaps between; so many soldiers with their spears and swords for just one small girl. A command snapped out. This was it. She awaited the fatal blow. Another command, she felt the breath hot on her cheeks and deafening orders beside her ears. A stamp in unison was followed by a single thud that blunted the air around her.

She opened her fingers and peeped through. In front of her stood a tall, impressive man and on his head the transverse, crested helmet of a *centurion* while behind him the empty road that led to the gates were still standing wide open. On each side of her at the edge of the road were soldiers standing with their shields held firmly against the road's surface. Each was spaced so that, should she have dared, she could never have breached the wall they created. Behind her, blocking her retreat, soldiers were similarly placed.

The *centurion* spoke, his tone matter of fact, there would be no argument, "You are under arrest. You will accompany me, and you will be held until his Lordship, the *Publicanus*, deems it fit to pronounce his judgement upon you. Move."

The *centurion* rounded her, and the soldiers flanking the road stiffened their grips on their shields and withdrew their *gladii,* creating a wall that was even stronger and more impenetrable than before.

Saima realised that this was the time to summon up her courage. She would show some Boudicca spirit. She remained rooted to the spot. The *centurion* was in no mood for games. He pushed her hard and roughly in the back. Saima stumbled two steps forward and pitched onto her knees. She looked neither right nor left nor at the man behind her. She just got to her feet and planted them once more.

"Don't try my patience, child."

A rougher, harder shove brought her sprawling once again. Her knees grazed and bleeding now, but as before she got up and just held herself still. The *centurion* was becoming extremely angry; he was being bettered by a child; worse still, his whole century was watching the scenario play out. The authority none of them dared challenge was being threatened and beaten by a little girl. He moved to her side and spoke directly into her right ear.

"If you don't move in the next three seconds, I'll skewer you where you stand and leave you for the crows."

Saima didn't budge but summoned up her largest voice so that the whole century could hear, "You didn't capture me. I came to you. Don't you find it strange that a person you're searching for has come to you willingly? Think. When was the last time an enemy or a fugitive came and gave themselves up. I bet that has never happened, has it?"

Saima looked at the soldiers nearest to her, and she could see that her words had hit home. It was true. No one gave themselves up, ever.

She continued, "I am no fool. I know what you think I did. I know what you think Metallus did, but you have no idea what the truth is. Only I know. Only I can unravel the mystery of the missing silver. Kill me if you must, *Centurion*, but beware the anger of the *Publicanus* when he knows that you have murdered the only person who can help you find the silver and help you know the real truth."

She paused for breath, then turned one hundred and eighty degrees and stared at the tall Roman without a single blink of her eye and beckoned for him to listen to her whisper.

"I must speak to the *Publicanus* without delay. Take me there now. It is a matter of life and death to delay further."

Having spoken, Saima didn't hesitate but turned and walked briskly up to the fort and inside its gates. The *centurion* had no time to argue or even reply, but with a swift wave of his hand, the ranks formed behind him and returned to the fort. The gates were closed and bolted.

CHAPTER XLIV

It was time for Charlie and Ruus to leave. There was no clasping of hands or fond farewells.

"Thanks, maybe see you around," was all Charlie said to Faris.

The light was extinguished and they stole into the night, out through the back door. A cloudy sky and moonless night gave them excellent cover, but Ruus was determined to keep away from the road and make their way across country.

"You sure this is right?"

Ruus ignored the comment and ploughed on. He had an impeccable sense of direction and knew the terrain. They arrived back at the copse but didn't linger to search for their leaf-smothered bounty. Ruus led them on, following the road but at a safe distance from it. He held up his hand and halted their progress, listening. All was still, so he cut closer to the bordering trees picking up the trail they had used earlier. Charlie was quite breathless. His stooping run constricting his chest and lungs. He wasn't as stealthy as Ruus, who several times had to turn and put his finger to his lips. At last they reached the tree Ruus had sought.

"The Killing Tree," he mouthed.

Charlie understood. Not far now. They'd have to chance their luck on the road for several metres to find the path. Hovering in the ditch, they scanned for movement. There was none so they were up, out and running along the road without anyone in sight.

"Here. It's here."

Ruus jumped first, landing softly on the far side of the western ditch. Charlie was not so successful. He got seven-eighths of the way across before toppling forward on the sharp incline and sliding into the water covering the bottom.

Ruus leaned down and grinned. "*Stultus.*"

Then without another word, he ran down the fox path. Charlie followed though he thought the squelch of his sandaled feet would be enough to wake the dead. The trees began to close on them; leaf, twig and branch ushering them ever inwards. The clearing when it came offered no relief, a stifling, troubled, airless space. An arena of souls seemed to fill it.

"Bloody creepy," said Charlie. "Feels like all my free will has been sucked out of me."

"The God of the Forest will protect you."

"Didn't protect that poor dead bloke whose hair I wrenched off, did it?"

Ruus had more courage and entered the glade. Charlie followed warily, looking about him for ghouls, sprites and witches on broomsticks.

"We've got to take off that brushwood first."

Ruus began the work. The sticks and leaves that covered the smaller pit were piled at the end of the clearing but left in full view.

"Let's scrape the earth away; we've got to make this look genuine."

The boys made a mound of scraped soil beside themselves as they knelt and bent over the pit. The chill of the night was creeping into Charlie's bones and he shivered. It took quite a while, but when they had finished, the digging had kept him warm and occupied. Now they waited. How long had they been hunched like this? An hour, two? Occasionally, one got up and walked about just to get the blood circulating and get rid of the pins and needles that seemed to return almost as soon as they got back in place. It was Charlie that broke first, of course.

"It's hopeless, I'm sorry." Charlie looked across the short space at Ruus. "This was stupid. Why did I even think this plan might work?"

"Dawn is still some time away. We can't give up yet."

"No, I've messed up again and we're wasting our time."

Self-pity had raised its head and Charlie couldn't take being wrong yet again.

"It always was a long shot. I'm sorry but I'm not hanging about. It was worth a try but it had only a slim chance, and now I'm more worried about what will happen to Sabia?"

"Caius, stay here; have faith. It's really not too late yet."

But Charlie was adamant. He stood and mooched away back towards the path across the clearing. Ruus watched as a dejected Charlie dragged his soggy feet away through the grass. When he reached the far side, he turned and shrugged.

"Sorry, mate, got to... Urf!!!"

A hand clamped around Charlie's nose and mouth, an arm across his chest. He was lifted powerfully off his feet and brought back into the clearing, wriggling like a hooked eel.

"Faris, what are you doing here? Gods alive, put Caius down," Ruus pleaded.

He moved towards him then stopped sharp. In the hand of the arm across Charlie's chest was a sickle-like blade, a small but deadly *jambiya* with its point against Charlie's heart. One twist was all it needed.

"Stand still," Faris menaced. "You've already interfered too much. I see you've started to dig. Don't let me stop you."

"We've finished," said Ruus, holding up one of the sacks of excavated coins.

Faris marched Charlie across the clearing towards the hole then stopped a couple of metres back, peering in.

"Not nearly deep enough. Get started."

Faris made the blade flick against Charlie's tunic, and a small slit appeared as well as a drop or two of blood.

"You surely don't want me to go further."

The hand holding the *jambiya* slid up and closer to Charlie's cheek but the other covering his mouth prevented him from turning away from it. Faris placed its point against his skin. Ruus needed no further encouragement and scraped the damp earth with both hands.

"I think it needs to be wider. Here, use this." He pressed Charlie to the ground and, placing a heavy foot on his neck, unstrapped a small spade that had been at his back. He tossed it across the short space.

"Remember, one false move from you and your friend here dies."

The work making the hole wider was harder than Ruus expected. There were roots getting in the way of his digging as he was getting closer to the tree line. Faris didn't seem to be in any hurry; he settled cross-legged on the ground with the blade upon Charlie's throat. He was pleased he'd got them both but still needed to catch Sabia. He relaxed a little and spoke, "I believe you all lied to me, even that girl. There is only one truth that matters; I hate Romans and their ways almost as much as children."

"Yeah, but not enough to stop working for them. You stole those *denarii*; you and that poor bloke buried over there." Charlie found it hard to stay quiet most of the time, and this was another occasion he couldn't stop himself.

Faris glared down at the boy beneath his blade.

He grabbed the rough, frayed wool of his tunic and pulled him up to within a hand of his face.

"Listen, boy, I've worked for that scum for years, but only so I could get to know their customs and become friendly with one or two. I chose carefully, and when I'd found a soldier who wanted the same things as me, I decided to join forces with him."

"What could a soldier want that you could possibly want too?"

Ruus had stopped digging and joined in, having listened to the conversation. Faris deftly drew a line a cross Charlie's cheek with the *jambiya*, a small scratch but one that caught Charlie and Ruus unawares. Charlie screeched and felt the wetness on his face that could only be blood.

"Dig!"

Ruus didn't hesitate and was back to work. His intervention had nearly killed Charlie. He wouldn't make that mistake again.

"What did we want? Freedom. Freedom to live our own lives, and what buys freedom? Money. What could be sweeter for us both than stealing from the very hand that oppresses us? So, we had a plan and it worked. That is until you stuck your noses in. Well, you won't be sticking your noses in much longer."

Indicating for Charlie to stand, he thrust him towards Ruus. Faris looked at the newly dug hole.

"Not particularly deep but sufficient, I suppose. Get in."

Ruus stepped in. Faris moved round the hole with his back to the tree line. He took Charlie with him and pushed him forwards so that he too fell into the hole beside Ruus. Charlie stood back up, his waist level with the top of the hole.

"Good. Any last words?"

Faris grabbed Ruus by the hair and pulled his head back to expose his throat. The *jambiya* was switched to his right hand and he held it high. Tears now streamed down the faces of both boys as they realised that their fate was to die here and be buried.

"No? Excellent, I hate speeches."

He brought his hand and the edge of the blade close to Ruus's throat.

"No stop, wait, Uncle, please!"

Across the clearing stood Saima.

"Ah, the third one. I'm glad you've turned up. It'll save me a search."

He beckoned her forward towards him. Tears coursed down her face too.

Then another deeper voice called out, "We have heard your words but would hear more. Leave the children be and let us come to an arrangement."

The clouds had shifted, and shafts of moonlight broke into the glade picking out the shining breastplate of the *Publicanus* Lucius in cold spotlight.

"What possible arrangement could you have for me? Crucifixion?"

"No, not at all, just let the children go. Tell me the name of your accomplice. The name of that soldier, and we'll settle things."

Behind Lucius, a group of six soldiers entered the clearing and fanned out on either side of him. He clicked his fingers and one broke away back into the trees.

"It wasn't just one. How little you know. What guarantee have I got?"

"I can't give you one other than you won't be harmed by me. Let the children go. We can talk money if that's what you want. I need the truth. I need to know their names."

Faris lowered his dagger and began to speak.

"Do I have your word?"

"I guarantee I won't touch you."

He thought about his chances and, having weighed them and finding nothing to lose, said, "Very well. There was Vitus, of course, but the other man you seek is D—"

The sentence was never finished, for a gladius rammed straight through Faris's back and its double-edged blade sliced out through his chest. Drusus had crept up behind him through the trees and delivered the blow. Faris stared at the dripping point, not believing his life was done. In a few final gasped breaths, he burbled, "You said you wouldn't harm me."

And as his eyes closed, Lucius said, "I told the truth, *I* didn't," then directed his words to Drusus, "Soldier, I will see you in my quarters."

"Yes, *Publicanus*, my lord."

Drusus withdrew his sword, then bent down and, using Faris's tunic, wiped it clean, a trace of a wry grin flashed upon his face.

Saima ran full pelt across to the boys, and without waiting for them to step out of the hole, she embraced them both and the three friends hugged.

Lucius ordered the soldiers to retrieve the four sacks of silver beside the hole. He looked pleased at first, then a perplexed expression came over him. He ordered the other pit to be exhumed and soon the body of Vitus was laid on the grass. It was fitting that the hole from which he was removed became the burial pit for Faris. Dawn was beginning to break and birdsong filled the trees. The gloomy atmosphere had lifted. The children, Lucius and the troop of soldiers left the clearing the way they had come, four carrying Vitus's body on a shield and the other two *miles* that included Drusus took the four bags of silver.

CHAPTER XLV

The *Publicanus's* office door was closed. Drusus and the three children were aligned in front of the desk. Lucius was seated, and he pushed two scrolls aside, clearing a space in front of him. He leaned forward.

"There are several things I need to clear up," Lucius began. "Let me say first of all, I am grateful to the young lady in front of me. I am indebted to her for her truthfulness and honesty."

The boys wondered just how honest she'd been. Had she told the *Publicanus* about the missing sacks?

He continued, "It is obvious to me now that she had nothing to do with the theft from the strong room. She tells me it was your plan, Caius, to try and lure Faris to the clearing. I would not normally have believed a child, but Drusus was sure she was correct. I need to let you in on a secret of my own. Can you be trusted to keep it?"

They nodded.

"It is essential that you keep this between yourselves. Firstly, the case is not closed. I'll explain in a moment; I think we may need your help just once more. I know that it appears as though you or Metallus had stolen the new key because, of course, the *centurion* found it."

"But we didn't steal it and neither did my father." Ruus was flushed with anger. He knew the key must have been planted, and there was only one person who could possibly be responsible, Drusus.

Ruus couldn't contain it any longer. He stepped out of the line, and with arm outstretched and with his index finger aimed straight at Drusus, he said, "It was him! He asked for it to be made. He bought and even paid for it, and he must have been the one that planted it after my dad gave it to him, and he was the one that found it, not the *centurion*."

He now directed his tirade directly at Drusus, "It was you. Go on; admit it, you and you alone!"

Exhausted from his declaration, Ruus's boiling rage subsided.

"Will you tell him or shall I?"

Lucius leaned back in his chair, allowing Drusus the chance to speak, but Drusus said nothing and held his place.

"Very well then, Drusus here is not what he seems. He was summoned to serve me by the governor of this province under direct orders from Rome. He is helping me investigate the constant dribble of funds that disappear from our treasury. Drusus was a member of the *praetorian guard*, the most elite force that guards the emperor. He is a very skilled agent, who was sent here a while ago to help investigate crimes against the state, and as you can see, he has even fooled you. I ordered him to kill Faris in the clearing, as I couldn't have his identity revealed yet. The information I am sharing with you is not to leave this room. We believe that Orcus has blackmailed and worked with others to help him steal thousands. Drusus has managed to retrieve a *defixio* that states he wants me dead. Certainly that is enough to condemn him, but it does not get us close to the missing money and treasure. I must find it or the governor will hold me responsible."

Drusus took up the tale, "I was sure that Orcus must have a way of getting the silver out of the fort. It had to be someone who came to the fort regularly and left again without suspicion."

"Faris," the three children chorused together.

"Yes, but where did he put the money after it was outside these walls? I checked his workshop; no sign there."

"So you set Faris up," said Saima.

"I told him we could be rich, and we needn't think about including Orcus. He jumped at the chance, and he made a leather—"

"A leather 'lifesaver', of course, so the soldier didn't die, and I saw him follow Faris after you left with that patrol."

"Did you?" Drusus was a little taken aback but continued, "That was Vitus. He volunteered. I knew he had several large gambling debts, so he was an obvious choice. However, I didn't expect Faris to kill him later."

"I guess you hoped that all the treasure stolen would be buried in that clearing then," Saima added.

Lucius decided to finish the discussion. He needed to get on and he didn't want any more delay. "Yes, once you had told us about what you yourselves had set up, we thought we'd catch them and retrieve all the missing *denarii* as well as the rest he had stolen."

The *Publicanus* continued, "We now believe that Orcus and the priest, who has to be involved, are storing that in the *cella* of the temple."

Charlie spoke up for all of them as he could see that, like him, he had no idea where this was leading,

"OK, that kind of makes sense, but I want to know what's happened to Metallus. He's done nothing wrong other than be pulled into the scandal without knowing it."

Saima and Ruus were surprised that Charlie should have thought of Metallus before anything else. A pride arose in Saima, an acknowledgement that Charlie may have changed his ways. The selfishness had gone, at least for now.

Drusus spoke at a nod from Lucius, "Metallus is well and unharmed; in fact he is at this moment eating his fill. We cannot, however, let anyone see him other than those we trust to keep quiet. If we let him free or allowed others to know, then it would be obvious we no longer held the major suspect in the case. This would alert Orcus and the priest, and they may well shift the treasure before we could retrieve it. It is enough for you to know that as soon as this is over he will be released."

Charlie continued, "So, what about the treasure and the priest? I don't see what we can do to help with that. Why don't you just batter the door of the *cella* down and look for yourselves?"

"Ah, that's not possible," Lucius explained. "What if the money is hidden elsewhere? We would have made a grave mistake. They would then be alerted and we'd never have a chance to recover it. You are the ideal people to help us. We are soldiers, and it would be a terrible crime to enter the most sacred part of the temple in such a way. Janus is the oldest and most revered God. We would never be forgiven if we barged into his house, let alone battered the doors down. No, we need you, innocent children to find a way of getting inside. Perhaps persuade the priest to let you help him.

Children can do no wrong and are not usually subject to the rules that apply to adults."

"Blimey, I wish you'd tell that to my parents and teachers," said Charlie.

"What did he say?" asked Drusus.

"Take no notice of him; he always says weird things," said Ruus.

"In fact," said Saima, giving Charlie a sidelong glance, "we think he may be a bit simple, you know not the sharpest gladius if you get my meaning."

Then Saima faced Charlie, licked her index finger and drew a number one in the air.

"Enough of this childish prattle." Lucius was losing his patience. "Will you help or must I put *you* in chains till all this is resolved? If you find what I believe is in there, then we can arrest the priest and Orcus in the full knowledge of their criminal acts and enter the *cella* peaceably and in reverent fashion."

"When you put it like that, I don't see we really have a choice. We might as well follow this through to the end if we can."

Then with a sly aside to Saima, Charlie whispered, "It'll give us a chance to get close to the statue."

"Good, then it's up to you. It needs to be accomplished quickly. Drusus will escort you to the gates. If you find he's being a bit rough, just remember he's got to make it look right; it's only for show."

"Oh well, that'll be alright then," said Charlie, raising his stripy eyebrows.

CHAPTER XLVI

Despite a few more bruises on their arms and shoulders thanks to the doubtful but effective acting skills displayed by Drusus on his way to the gates, the children made it safely out and beyond. They eventually collapsed on a bench in the forge's back room.

"Any ideas?" Charlie asked, yawning, as he found three unbroken cups and filled them with some sour ale from a small barrel.

They were shattered. A night with no sleep and then the revelations in the fort had dulled their senses and inspiration. They sat as if a spell had been cast upon them, and each nodded off, collapsing against the wall at their backs and their companions' shoulders at their sides.

A while later, Ruus awoke with a start. It was early afternoon and the sun warmed the rear wall. His cup was empty and had spilled to the floor, leaving a dark stain. Those belonging to Charlie and Saima clung to the cliffs of their knees held by curled fingers, quite improbably still full. He rubbed an eye which watered and noticed with the other that the furnace had died to a feeble glow among a grey, cool ash. He must revive it or it would take an age to rekindle. He blew gently, coaxing the coals to reignite and as he blew, the glow increased and when he stopped, eager flame emerged. As the coals flared, Ruus emptied still more cold nuggets of blackness upon them from a hide bucket. They crackled and spat and caught at their edges till their hearts glowed too. Their blues, purples, oranges and yellows swirled. At last he stood back and felt their warmth. Saima and Charlie became aware of those small changes too and roused from their slumbers. Charlie stretched and put his cup on a bench. The tarry smell of the coals couldn't entirely remove the acidic aroma of the ale. Ruus looked up and smiled. Charlie crouched.

"We're so close," he said. "So near and yet so far."

"We'll come through, all of us together." Ruus had found some true friends. His words touched Charlie's thoughts and rebounded.

"Ruus; I, that is we, Sabia and me, we can't stay. When this is over, we have to go back."

"I know but you can visit me, can't you?"

"No. As much as we would want to, that would be impossible."

"How far away is your village then, surely not that far?"

"Our village?" Charlie hesitated. "No, I suppose it's not far really."

Saima listened as the two boys spoke. Their backs turned away from where she sat.

"Tell him." Saima's voice cut through between them, and they turned their heads to face her.

"Tell him the truth, Caius. Just for once, tell the truth."

Ruus turned back and looked towards Charlie. What possible truth could he reveal? Charlie looked into Ruus's grey-blue eyes and stuttered, "She's not my sister; we're just friends... innit."

The words that came from Charlie's lips were a truth, but not the one Saima needed him or expected him to say. He'd ducked his responsibility. He hadn't changed at all. His whole body must be wrapped in cling-film with truth held tight inside. It could see the outside but would never escape. His own world was wrapped tight around him, so tight no one could break in or eke the truth out.

"Oh, Caius, must it always be me?" Saima took a long slow breath, then hesitating no longer declared, "What Caius has failed to tell you is... *this is our village*. Right here. Well, not exactly here, more just over a bit on the far side of the river. Beyond the temple is our school, and beyond that our houses. Among our houses, there is one single shop, my shop, my mum and dad's shop."

Ruus laughed out loud.

"Come on, enough games. What are you talking about? There are no houses or shops out there, just grass and woods."

"I'll tell you truth, and you have to believe me because that's all I can do," Saima's voice wobbled, "We don't belong here. Our time is yet to come."

"Oh, who can't say it now then?" said Charlie. "Give it him straight, you said. Okay, here it is, Ruus." He paused so that each word would bear no trace of doubt. "We're from the future."

Ruus wasn't so sure about these friends any more. Leaving the top arm of the bellows to sag its breath into the fire, he paled and shrunk back as far as he could from both of them.

"You're beginning to frighten me. Can you stop now? It was funny to start with but now it's just scary."

"Ruus, we can't keep the secret any longer. Not even we understand how we came to be here. But that's how it is, truly. We believe that the Janus effigy transported us back in time. Perhaps to solve this crime with you, who knows? But there are three things that have to happen. First, we must get inside that *cella*. Second, for us to return home to our time, we must have Janus, and third, we have to ensure that your father Metallus is freed. So we must find that lost money. We have become friends, we are true to each other, and you are right we'll come through this together, but we must then part. Who's to say we won't come back some day, but for now we must concentrate on those three things alone."

Charlie had never put a bigger speech together in his life. He bent at the waist and put his hands on his knees, still looking at Ruus who had pressed himself to the far wall.

"Help us get home. Help us help your dad. Please." Saima saw the first ray of understanding cross Ruus's face.

He peeled from the safety of the wall.

"If any God has power, the most likely to have it is Janus. Your ways have been strange in part, that is true, but you have never done me harm and always been my friends, so it would be odd to think you would harm me now. I think I trust you, for that seems to be right. Let it be us one more time… together."

They moved to the centre of the room and, in a tight huddle, hugged each other.

"Together," they said.

CHAPTER XLVII

The three sat staring into the fire. They had a new energy born of their sleep and started discussing how they might get into the *cella* unnoticed and then out again unharmed.

"We could try the same idea we used before," said Saima.

"Do you think he'd fall for that a second time? I'm not sure he would," replied Ruus.

The conversation between them ticked and tocked backwards and forwards with ideas and how they might or might not work. It wasn't just the getting into the *temenos* unnoticed; they would have to get past a door to the *cella,* with a large lock clamping it shut. Charlie hadn't spoken at all. His practical mind had been thinking through the puzzle, and he was ready to try it on his companions.

"If someone keeps you talking, you don't generally look away from them. Just as an example, Lucius spoke to Faris in the clearing, and he had no idea that Drusus was behind him."

"Ugh, that's a lovely memory, thanks, Caius."

Saima pulled a face of disgust.

"I'm just saying, distraction is a great way to fool people. We need to distract the priest to give us time to get into the *cella* unseen. We also need to come at the job from two opposite angles, so someone comes in at the front and distracts; the other approaches from behind."

"That all sounds good, but you've forgotten the lock on the front door. How are we going to get past that?" Ruus had just put a great big spanner in the works, and Saima nodded.

"Unless we can get past that, we might as well give up."

"We could steal the key," Ruus was warming to his idea, "I could sneak into the priest's house then search it out and run across to the temple …"

"No chance," Charlie scotched his plan. "First, you've got to find the key. Do you know where he keeps it? And what if he's locked his own front door? You'll need to have a key for that too. I know you're quick and can be pretty stealthy, but there's no way you can get from the house to the temple and up those steps without being noticed."

"OK, it was only a thought," Ruus was crestfallen.

"I know, and in other circumstances it might have worked, but this has got to be as neat a plan as we can make."

"So we're back to square one then," said Saima dejectedly.

"Not quite." He smiled and looked at Saima. "Do you remember the day I made rather a mess of a library book and Miss Dean told me to take it away? Well, I did, and I still haven't returned it."

"Why doesn't that surprise me?" she said. "Anyway, what's a chocolatey book got to do with anything?"

"Its title was *The Roman Era in Britain*. It was dull and boring. I only picked it up because it was in the wrong place, but some of the pictures and diagrams were OK. One chapter near the end was all about locks. Call it a coincidence, but the lock on the *cella* door is just like one in that book."

"Great, so you have a book with a picture of the *cella* lock."

"And," said Charlie pausing for effect, "it just so happens there was also a picture of its key right beside it. If I can draw it and if Ruus or you can help me with remembering the size of the lock, we could be in business."

"How will a drawing of a key help open a metal lock?"

Ruus had grasped Charlie's idea. "That's brilliant!" he exclaimed.

"Will you boys let me in on your little appreciation society?"

"Sabia, Caius will draw the key as best he can from our memory of the lock size. I will try and make the key in the forge from that drawing. What is it you two say, simples?"

They all laughed, and Charlie set about asking Saima and Ruus questions. He drew three pictures of the key on the hard floor with a sharp, charred stick, one from the end, one from above and the final one from the side. Ruus could match up his metalwork to these and get it exact.

"Look," he said when he'd finished drawing. "All the key has to do is push two bits of metal shaped like an arrow back in towards its shaft. The key is just a flat bit of metal with a bend at the end that's got a suitable square hole in it."

"It's not hard to make at least," confirmed Ruus. "I've helped my dad shape metal loads of times."

"How will you make the hole?" asked Saima.

"I'll use one of these, a punch."

He grasped a tool shaped a bit like a pencil but fatter, and before it tapered to a point it was cut off sharp and flat.

"When the metal becomes white-hot, I'll need to use a hammer. It'll take a few heatings to make it properly. I just hope we've drawn the size right."

"I reckon you can make the key as thin as you like, then we'll be sure it'll fit in the key slot. The important part is the square hole."

Ruus began heating a piece of scrap metal bar he found in the workshop store. He hammered the punch onto the white-hot surface. It made an indentation about a quarter of the way into the surface. But quickly the metal cooled and had to be reheated. This time the punch drove down, but Ruus stopped before going right through.

Charlie was curious. "Why did you stop?"

"I want to have a clean cut."

Ruus turned the bar over so Saima and Charlie could see. The back of the bar had a little bump the same shape as the punch hole on the other side.

"Can you see the bulge on this side? If I heat the bar again and punch from this side exactly on top of that, we'll have a clean-cut, square hole with no ragged edges."

He turned back and put the bar in the coals to heat. After a minute or so, he took it out and hammered one more time then offered it up to the drawings on the floor to check for size. It fitted perfectly, the neatest hole they could have ever imagined. Saima burst into spontaneous applause.

Charlie just murmured, "Wicked."

Fortunately, Ruus didn't hear, or there would have had to have been another whole heap of explanations and little lies. There was a further bout of hammering that brought the hole round at a right angle to its thin, flat bar, and so it was finished. The key was plunged into the bucket of water to be quenched, and a rapid, boiling sizzle of steam filled the air.

"Right," said Ruus, emerging like a genie, "what next?"

"We have to make sure that the priest doesn't find us by chance. That means we need someone to engage him in conversation while someone else breaks in with the key."

"We'll need to go round the back of the *cella* and climb over the wall; that way we'll be out of sight," said Saima.

"OK. So, Ruus, you are the wall climber and you will use your key to get in. Saima and I will come in through the main entrance in the east wall."

"I'll need a rope."

"No problem," said Saima, remembering the one that she'd been tied up with in Faris's back room.

"How will I know that you're talking to the priest and can come round to unlock the door? I won't be able to see you."

Ruus had made a good point, and at once their plan was looking shaky. There was no way they could shout out, wave their arms or even pull the same trick as last time when Charlie threw himself to the floor. Their joy at having a plan and a key evaporated as quickly as that cloud of steam. Saima broke the silence.

"I'm going outside for a walk and some fresh air. I need to think."

The boys watched her go, realising that she probably needed the space anyway. Saima gave the street a good look up and down and drew in a long, slow breath. This was all getting a bit much. She wanted to be home, safe and secure. She looked to her left and saw the imposing fort, the soldiers standing guard on the wall walkways. She'd seen enough of that to last her a lifetime. There wasn't any chance of her deciding to walk in that direction, so turning right she set off down the street between the awnings, workshops, houses and shops that lined the route. Nothing drew her attention, nothing sparked her imagination, but at least the sun was shining and the air was warm. After a while, she found herself outside the shop where the trinkets and jewellery were being sold. This was one place she didn't mind stopping, and the array of necklaces, brooches and rings drew her towards them like a magnet.

The lady who spoke to her before smiled. "You come back for that brooch then? You'll need a few *denarii* to buy that, you know."

Saima smiled back. She had no *denarii* and was unlikely to have any. The woman could see she wanted to see it, hold it even. She also had a good feeling about the girl. Trustworthy.

"Come round here, dear," said the woman.

Saima did as she was told. There was something rather familiar about her. Saima supposed it was just that she'd met her a short while before. Picking up the horse brooch with its deep blue inlay, she pulled Saima towards her by her tunic.

"I know you can't afford it, love, but that don't mean you can't try it on."

In a moment, the woman had Saima's robe in a gentle grip at the shoulder and pushed the two small rings through the coarse fabric, then she carefully threaded a blunt needle through the rings so that the brooch was held fast.

Saima's jaw dropped open, and she gushed, "Oh, it's beautiful, thank you."

"Here," said the woman collecting a finely polished metal mirror from the table. "You can see it better with this."

She handed Saima the mirror. Saima held it up close to the brooch near her shoulder. It was indeed wonderful.

"Now give me the mirror; you can't see yourself properly with it close up like that."

Saima handed her the mirror, and the woman moved around the table to the outside of the shop. Then, telling Saima to face her, she held the mirror so that she could get a larger view of herself, the robe and the brooch. The woman held the mirror steady for a few seconds and then moved around the table back towards Saima. It was as she did so that Saima let out a gasp.

"Are you alright, dear?" asked the woman who'd put the mirror down and moved her hands softly onto Saima's shoulder to remove the brooch.

"Oh yes, thank you. I'm fine. I just felt like a queen wearing that," she lied easily.

"Well," said the woman, having removed the brooch and holding it in her hand, "I'm not surprised. It's very special, isn't it?"

Her green eyes sparkled.

Saima nodded and skipped around the table back to the street. She waved and then ran, with a broad grin on her face, back to Metallus's workshop. She knew how she was going to put the plan back on track.

When she arrived back, the boys had hardly moved from the positions in which she had left them. They noticed that her mood seemed lighter than when she went out.

"You feeling better?" asked Charlie.

"Yes, actually," she said brightly. "I wanted air, space and inspiration."

"And?" Ruus was keen to find out what had made her so happy.

"I want to take you and show you, but we'll need some money."

"We've got plenty of that," said Charlie.

Ruus hushed him. He was still worried about anyone hearing anything about their windfall.

The companions under Ruus's direction headed across the hill and crossed the spring stream where it was narrow, near the top of the ridge, then cut down further still. Charlie understood; he could see that Ruus didn't want to give any clue to anyone who might be watching from town. The hill on this side masked them from view. The copse came into view, and they skirted its edge until they came upon the stacked leaves covering the two sacks of coins.

"So, how much do you need?" Ruus asked Saima, allowing a handful of coins to trickle through his fingers and back into their sack.

"I suppose I shouldn't need more than five at the most."

"Is that all?" Charlie was quite put out. "I thought you'd say at least a hundred."

"We just need to go and see a nice lady and make a small purchase."

Ruus gave Saima the five coins. She held them tight in her fist as the boys scraped soil over the sacks and spread the leaves once more.

"Don't you two come anywhere near me. Your hands are covered in mud, although I'm not sure it's only mud judging by the smell."

They made their way back to where the road crossed the river by the bridge. The boys scrambled down the shallow bank and washed their hands, then came back up and stood in front of Saima for inspection.

"Perfect," she said and then, "Follow me, we're going shopping."

CHAPTER XLVIII

The lady at the stall greeted Saima like a long-lost daughter, "Hello, my dear, brought your friends to see your brooch, have you?"

Her emerald eye winked. She picked up the *lapis lazuli* horse brooch from its bed of soft cloth at the back and raised it to show them.

"Here it is," she said. "You boys going to buy it for her?"

"Is that what you want to buy?" asked Charlie, wondering how on earth she could possibly use it to get Ruus's attention behind the temple."

"No, of course not, though it is lovely; anyway it's far too expensive for us," she said, explaining as much to the woman as to the boys.

"Excuse me, miss," said Saima, ever polite in her ways. "How much is the mirror you used to show me the brooch?"

"That's made of silver, dearie; it's fifteen *denarii,* I'm afraid."

"Oh."

Saima was crestfallen. She hadn't expected that. The woman could see her disappointment.

"How much you got, love?"

"Only five *denarii,* not nearly enough."

"As it's you, I've got a smaller one here, but it's not so pretty."

"How much is that?" asked Ruus.

"Well, it should be eight *denarii,* but as your friend is so polite, I'll let her have it for five. How's that?"

"Sick!" exclaimed Charlie.

The woman looked confused and thought that he meant even that was too much. She shrugged and started to put it back on her table.

Saima chirped up immediately, "Oh no, don't put it back. It's lovely. Just what I want." Then glaring daggers at Charlie, she said, "Please ignore him. He really isn't all that bright; you know, the temple steps don't quite reach the *cella* door."

The woman grinned and handed the small mirror over to her in exchange for Saima's fistful of coins. They thanked her once more and said their farewells. Once they arrived back at Metallus's workshop, the boys waited to hear Saima's explanation for her purchase. She took them through the shop and out to the back so that they could look down the hill towards the temple.

She asked them to sit, and so she began, "You can see the whole of the temple from here. The East Entrance, the altar, the *cella* and the walls of the *temenos.*" She spoke as if she was explaining a military assault. "Ruus will come over the back wall of the *temenos.* He'll need a signal to know when the priest is talking to us. This afternoon the sun is, of course, in the western sky, so if I am in the east, facing the sun, I can reflect it using the mirror. Ruus will be able to see the reflection on the shadowy north wall. That will be his signal to go."

The boys were impressed.

"How clever is that? Blimey, Sabia, anybody'd think you'd been at Sandhurst not Wicton Primary."

Ruus had a confused look, and Saima explained that Charlie was just spouting his usual rubbish and that he was to take no notice. She did, however, feel a kind of smugness and knew she had gone up in their estimation of her abilities.

"So, we need a sunny afternoon, which means that there is no time that looks better than the present," said Ruus.

"Hold on." Charlie was unclear about the last part of the plan that had not even been discussed. "How will we know if the loot is in there? You'll be inside, and we could be anywhere that the priest decides to take us."

"Look, once I've seen what's in there or not, I won't hang about. I'll make a dash for it up to the fort if necessary. He won't be quick enough to catch me even if he does see me coming out. All right?"

The other two weren't quite so confident, but in the absence of an alternative they guessed that this was really their best and only choice. First, they went to Faris's back door and Saima coiled up the rope. As she handed it to Ruus, she gave a short exclamation.

"What's wrong?"

"Nothing much. What do you remember about Vitus's body?"

Charlie was straight in, "What, do you mean apart from the missing hair?"

He thought this was hilarious. Both Saima and Ruus just stood and stared at him, waiting for him to calm down.

"Finished?" she said. "Good. No, I mean, did you see his feet?"

They shook their heads.

"He had a gash on the ball of one foot. This must be the rope he used to get in from the roof," she said as she pointed at the dried blood stains.

"She's not only a general, she's Sabia Holmes as well," quipped Charlie.

This time he was totally ignored. Saima and Ruus were already outside and waiting.

"Off you go then," said Saima taking charge of the situation.

Ruus set off with the rope slung over his shoulder and carrying a short bar of metal in his left hand. He went back onto the main street and jogged down the alley beside the paddock in which the ox had been. He came out onto the hill to drop down to the north-west corner of the *temenos* wall. Once there, he crouched and waited for the other two to appear on the road. He watched them descend as far as the small bridge over the stream before they were lost to view when they turned towards the temple. Now he had to carry out his first job, scaling the west wall. He moved along it, keeping his eyes peeled for any small gap or nick between the bricks at the top. In most places, they were perfectly joined. He retraced his steps and was pleased to find one that he had missed and was suitable just around halfway.

He made a noose at the end of the rope and then cinched it tight around the metal bar. Coiling the rope, he swung the bar in a circle then released it, and up it flew towards the wall, but his throw was short and the bar clattered into the bricks before it had cleared the top. The noise of the bar clashing against the wall was enough to wake the dead. He hunched down, waiting to hear footsteps running from any and every direction. None came, not even a shout. His luck had held. He readied the rope to try again. This time he released it well and the bar soared over the wall. He dragged it back towards him, but he missed the notch between the bricks and the bar and the rope fell in an untidy heap at his feet. This was not as easy as he thought it would be.

Saima and Charlie had crossed the grass and made their way around the votive pool. They reached the eastern entrance and stationed themselves several steps from the altar. They had no idea when or if the priest was even about, but the plan relied on them being his sole focus, so they held their positions and waited.

Ruus had gathered his rope and flung it up for the third time. Success. He pulled it back, edging it towards the notch. The rope fell in and the bar caught. Ruus tugged it so that it held tight behind the bricks. Using the knots, he hauled himself up almost horizontally and with a final pull, he flung an arm over the top and scrabbled his legs up beside him. There he sat, breathing hard, astride the top of the wall as if riding a horse. He switched his rope to the inside of the wall and made sure the bar was swapped to the outside. The descent was much easier and quicker than the climb up, and he crept near to the northern end of the wall to await Saima's mirror signal.

CHAPTER XLIX

If Charlie had been a rabbit, his whiskers would have been twitching twenty to the dozen. Saima was no calmer. She fiddled with her sleeves and shivered despite the warm western sun. They were out in the open and felt vulnerable. So it was little wonder that as the door to the temple opened, a disastrous chain of events unfolded. Charlie, shocked and tongue-tied, goggled at the door. He nudged Saima. She had her feet stuck to the ground and her bottom lip bitten down hard. The only parts of her that could and did move were her buttery fingers. The mirror, seeking its freedom, slipped from her grasp and fell towards the ground, but as it did so it caught the strong afternoon sunlight and splashed a signal across onto the north wall. Ruus thinking this was his moment, lowered his body and ran full pelt along the columned *ambulatory*. Without a second thought or even a snatched glance, he turned the corner towards the drooling jaws of the great east door and collided with the priest who had just emerged. He fell prone on the floor.

The priest stamped his foot down onto Ruus's arm and held him to the ground.

"Run!" Ruus shouted. "Run for your lives."

Charlie and Saima needed no other bidding and spun on their heels to make a dash for it.

Bang! Two large, train-buffered hands hit them square on their faces, which lifted them clean off their feet. As they fell onto their backs, they looked up into spiteful eyes that speared them with menace and foreboding: Orcus.

"A scheming trio of snakes, we've caught. Now what could they possibly want?"

"We…" Charlie spoke, but his words were cut short by a stamp on his stomach. The air was driven from Charlie's body and he groaned in agony. Winded, his knees doubled up towards his chest.

"Why are you here, boy?"

Charlie was in too much pain to speak. Orcus raised his foot to stamp again.

"We came to ask if we could help," said Saima bravely.

"Oh yes, of course you did."

Orcus bent his considerable bulk and snatched her up, holding her off the ground with his face pressed against hers, his foul, fish-sauce breath making her wince.

"I saw you… all three. You're a little liar, and I don't think liars deserve to live."

Without warning, he released her, and she dropped like a stone to the ground and creased in two. The priest wasn't so keen on violence and didn't exactly favour Orcus's methods.

"This is too public. Let's at least get out of sight before we decide what to do with them."

Orcus's evil hands grabbed Charlie and Saima by an ankle and dragged them towards the *cella*. There was no fight or resistance. All that had been well and truly knocked out of them. Not stopping to consider their wellbeing, Orcus continued to drag them up the stone steps. As their shoulders scraped off each tread, their heads fell back and cracked against them. On reaching the top, Orcus made no ceremony but dragged them inside, followed by the priest who had gripped Ruus's collar and twisted an arm behind his back. All three were thrown with great force against the plinth upon which Janus was perched.

Janus wobbled. Janus staggered. Janus rocked and reeled and swayed and hovered and then crashed full length on the unyielding flagstones of the floor. It bounced, first head, then feet and over again. A chink, a ding, and it came to rest, head and body separated along its cast neckline.

"Look what you've done," cried the priest.

"Look what *I've* done. You're as much to blame. Calm down or I'll break your neck too."

The priest's mouth closed as tight as a drum and he eyed the big man uneasily.

"I need time to think. Lock these three in here; they can't escape. We need to do some serious talking."

The outer door slammed, and the friends heard the heavy bolt of the large padlock click into its keep. Slithers of light from under the door and around the jamb played on Charlie's face. Silent tears washed his cheeks as he clutched his aching stomach with one hand and his head with another.

Their eyes gradually became adjusted to the gloom. Ruus, who had been the least assaulted, was able to stand and made his way to the door. He placed an ear against the heavy wood and listened. Not a sound. He braced himself then rammed his shoulder against the door. Instead of the door giving way, it was his left shoulder that took the brunt of the charge. He lurched back, stooping and clutching it with his right hand.

"I shouldn't have done that," he managed to say before sitting down once more with his back to the plinth. "That door is as solid as a rock. There's no chance of getting out. We're stuck, and I'm sure those two won't be long in thinking of a way to deal with us."

"Well, I'm not just going to let them kill me," sobbed Saima.

"It'll be okay, Sabia." Ruus tried to put on a brave face and change the mood. "We need some weapons so when they do come, we'll be ready for them. That plinth doesn't look too strong. We could dismantle it and use that. We've got to try something."

Charlie and Saima saw Ruus's logic but were not at all convinced.

"I'll push it towards you, and you two pull it."

He edged around the plinth, still feeling particularly sore until, "Wow! Oh wow!"

The other two ran to see what the matter was, and they too stopped dead in their tracks.

There were four large chests settled before them near the back wall, the gloom not nearly enough to hide them.

"Let's see if they're locked," said Ruus going down onto his knees and trying the lid of the one closest. It lifted open with ease as did the rest. He went from one to the next, and all four chests lay open in front of them full of coin, jewellery, gold and silver.

"So, the *Publicanus* wasn't wrong, was he? Look at that lot," said Saima.

"Not that it's much use to us at the moment, unless I swing this at them."

Charlie picked up a silver necklace and whirled it. He wished he hadn't as he crumpled with pain from his earlier encounter with a hefty foot. He crawled away, trying to ease it by shallow breathing. The discomfort in his stomach subsided, but then he cried out in pain as he stabbed his hand on something sharp.

"Janus has got some explaining to do," Charlie seethed as he picked up the headless body of the effigy, avoiding the sharp break at the neck where his hand had so unfortunately been placed only moments before. Then his voice died, and he was totally silent, quieter than he had ever managed in his whole life.

He sat holding the body for a few seconds more, then said, "I've got a plan."

"Without seeming ungrateful," called Ruus, moving to sit beside him, "our plans aren't that successful, are they?"

"It's not my fault the priest was in the wrong place and Orcus saw us," said Saima, feeling somewhat offended. "Anyway, we all agreed on different parts of it, not just me."

Charlie pulled the pair up short and said, "This is no time to get angry with each other. Let me tell you what I'm thinking, then we can decide."

He put the body down and retrieved the severed head.

"Guess what I'm thinking, Sabia."

Charlie leaned over and pushed Janus's head into her hands. Saima took just an instant to realise what Charlie meant.

"We can't." Her disgust was clear. She stared hard at him, her eyes narrowing at his suggestion.

"Why not? As I see it, it's our only chance. There's no other way out."

"I can't believe that after all we've been through *together,* you are suggesting we leave Ruus to face those monsters on his own. I'm ashamed of you."

Her face was now a picture of astonishment and horror rolled into one.

"No, you don't understand. If we can get outside, then we can unlock the door and set Ruus free."

"You can't take the key with you. It'll disappear just like our clothes did when we arrived."

"Okay. Well, he can squeeze it out to us through a gap when we come back."

"That's a better idea."

"Give me any alternative."

Charlie waited. Saima couldn't think of anything, and time was surely running out. If they were going to do something, it had to be now before the men came back. Ruus had listened to this conversation and was utterly mystified as to what they were talking about.

"What are you two going on at? We're locked in a building with high walls, no windows and a heavy door, and you are talking about using a key from the outside."

"Sabia and I have already told you that we are from the future. This head," said Charlie pointing it out, "has a power. It transported us here through time. It can transport us back. In our time, the temple is a ruin. We can go forward in time and escape, then return to help you."

"Sabia," said Ruus, "tell me this boy is lying again; tell me what you're really going to do."

"Ruus," said Saima, "for once, Caius is telling the truth. It is how we came here, and it is our only chance of saving you and ourselves."

Without further ado, Saima sidled over to Charlie. She wanted to believe that this was going to work but was so frightened that the head would prove a false hope. Charlie's hands enclosed Saima's; the head held between them.

"I'm amazed. You're mad. I was almost taken in by you for a while there."

Ruus couldn't believe the rubbish he had just heard, and his eyes didn't lie. Two fools clutching the head of a statue and saying they were going back to the future to save him. He could stand no more of this nonsense and wanted to distance himself from it. He wanted to get away from these two as far as possible and get his life back to normal. Perhaps he was in some living nightmare. No matter, he knew what he would do, and that was to ignore these idiots completely. He rounded the plinth and sat with his back to it and the childish game they were playing. Saima saw him go, saw his face as he got up, saw his rejection, saw that her hopes were dashed when nothing happened and that Charlie's big ideas had failed again. Tears welled in her eyes and fell between her fingers, down onto Charlie's, onto *Janus's* head and into his eyes.

There was no flash, no rushing lights, no roaring sounds that pounded their ears. Everything just dissolved once again, a kind of melting away. Saima could feel the head vaporise under her fingers. Charlie could feel Saima's hands liquidise. Saima saw Charlie's hands do the same. Then they disappeared. The process continued up their arms across their bodies until there were just their necks and heads suspended in the *cella*. Now, it was their necks and on up past their chins and mouths. Strangely, the tops of their heads were fading downwards until all that was left of the two children were pairs of eyes opposite each other, surrounded by a sombre, ochre glow. The eyes gawped, just white spheres with discs of blue in one set and brown in the other. They were gone.

CHAPTER L

As before, the first to appear was the last to have gone; eyes of brown and blue materialised then foreheads, hair, noses, mouths, chins, feet, legs, bodies, arms and finally hands still clasped together holding... nothing. For a split second, they seemed to be in a hovering position, and then there they were in the middle of the ruined temple, sat on the grass and staring at each other.

"Charlie, it worked. It was my tears that must have done it. I was crying the first time, remember?"

Of course he did. He'd sort of insulted her and her dad without thinking.

"OK, let's move; I reckon the door was there," she pointed, "So if we go a bit further, we'll be on the outside."

She got up and ran to her chosen spot. Charlie also got up but didn't move.

"We can't go back."

"Why not? You said we could. I don't see why you don't want to save Ruus."

"I do, I really do, but..."

"But what?"

"*Janus's* head... the head's gone!"

Saima looked. Moments before, their hands had clasped together around *Janus's* head, now their hands were totally empty.

"Search the grass; it must be here."

Charlie was already frantically searching, brushing his hands this way and that in an effort to seek out the missing head.

"Stop!" Saima had a sudden brainwave. "Where was the last time we had the head?"

"Here, in the temple."

"No, not in Roman times, in our time; you know, present day."

"Oh no, are you thinking what I'm thinking?"

Saima hadn't waited to give her answer; she was running for the gate that gave out onto the road. Charlie caught her up as she pushed through it.

"We'll have been missed, run!"

They crossed the bridge and ran as fast as they could along Temple Street. They passed Hornbeam Lane on the other side of the road and sprinted to the crossing opposite the library. No cars in sight, they dashed across and reached the outer library doors.

"Your face is all red, Charlie."

"I'm not surprised, yours too. You're panting like a steam train. We can't go in like this."

"We have to; we've got no choice. We must get back before they notice we're gone."

"We've been gone a bloomin' week," wheezed Charlie, catching his breath too. "Heaven knows what they think has happened to us. This is not going to be easy to explain."

The two children, recovering some of their composure, pushed the doors open and slid inside. They crept quietly past the desk where Miss Dean stamped the books and were just entering the library itself when from up the corridor came Miss Vearn.

"Just where have you two been? I've looked high and low for you. Saima, I'm shocked at you. I might have expected some antics from Charlie, but I thought you were the sensible one." She didn't stop there; on she went, "Five minutes, five minutes I've been searching for you. Do you hear me? I've been frantic with worry. Frantic. Just a metal head staring at me from the middle of the desk."

A wry look passed between Saima and Charlie.

"Five minutes, Miss? I didn't realise we'd been gone that long. I mean, I only took Saima outside because she was feeling faint and thought she could do with some air. Look, you can see she's a bit short of breath. Has the library been painted or something? Perhaps it's the fumes that affected her."

"Painting, fumes what utter nonsense. If you're having me on, Charlie Hipkiss, you'll be for the high jump, I'm warning you."

Saima spoke, "It's true, Miss. Charlie said I shouldn't go outside alone so he went with me."

"Well then, I'm relieved, Saima. It seems you've done a good deed, Charlie. But nonetheless it is most irregular, and I think it best you return with me to the museum."

"But, Miss, we haven't drawn the head yet. Please just give us a few more minutes to have a go."

"Very well, but only five more minutes."

"I love history, Miss."

"Another of your lies. You'll drive me to distraction, Charlie Hipkiss."

CHAPTER LI

Mrs Vearn walked them back to their table and went off to tell Miss Parton that the two had been found. No sooner had she rounded the corner than Charlie and Saima resumed their places.

"Five minutes, that's all the time we were away, just five minutes."

"Yes, and I bet that five minutes was the time it took us to get from the temple back to the library, which means that if we can mark the spot where we appear in Roman times; we should be able to end up back in the library with no lost time at all."

"The bottom of that soggy ditch you mean, ugh."

At that moment, Miss Dean appeared. "It's an interesting piece, don't you think? So, how should I put it? Moving."

Then she whisked herself away without another word.

"What on earth was she talking about?"

"Don't be a *stultus,* Charlie."

"OMG. She knows. She knows what the *Janus* head can do."

"Come on, we're wasting time."

They placed their hands on the head and upon each other's as they had done before. Elbows leant on the table, and their eyes met. Truth and lies mingled. Saima thought of home, her father and mother while Charlie was drawn to thinking of football and Alfie and the way he treated him. There seemed little reason why they thought of these things at this time, but the tears the thoughts provoked were true and slipped between each other's fingers into *Janus's* eyes.

CHAPTER LII

The ditch was drier than it had been when they arrived for the first time. They had no need to wonder about how they got here or where they were. They did, however, make sure that there was no one on the road above them then climbed the bank. Saima piled some stones to mark the spot.

"No time to waste," said Charlie, setting off in the direction of the bridge over the river.

Saima jogged behind him and caught him up quickly; to tell the truth, she was faster than Charlie and had been the quickest girl in her year since the infants. She was actually quicker than most of the boys, too, and would undoubtedly win on sports' day in Year 5 this summer. They crossed the bridge and continued until they got to the stream, then stopped and caught their breath. It was Saima who decided their next move.

"Listen, you know how that lock works, and I'm quicker than you, so it makes sense if I go up to the fort and tell them what we've found and you get Ruus free. That way we cover all bases; Metallus being released, Ruus free, Orcus and the priest arrested, the money recovered, and not to forget, getting back hold of Janus's head."

Before Charlie could even agree, Saima was already heading up into the *vicus*. He turned his attention to the temple. He edged past the *votive* pool and flattened himself against the temple's eastern wall. Crouching low, he nosed around the corner of the entrance and checked left and right. Then just for good measure, he looked behind him, not wishing to be caught out a second time. He was in luck, no one in sight.

"If I'm going to do this, I suppose it better be now," he whispered to himself and summoning up as much courage as he could, he dashed straight across to the front of the *cella* and up the steps. He sprawled on the cold, stone slabs and spoke to the gap under the door.

"Ruus, Ruus, give me the key."

The voice that came from inside was not complimentary.

"Leave me alone; you two are as bad as one another. I'm fed up with your stupid lies. You don't need a key. You need an axe to get out of here, so just leave me alone, unless you just so happen to have found one of those lying about in here too."

"Hurry up, give me the key. They'll be back soon, then we'll all be done for."

"Oh, in Jupiter's name, shut up! Here, have the blasted key."

From where Ruus sat, he threw the key back over his head and the plinth behind him, aiming casually at where Charlie and Saima had been sitting minutes before. The key clattered to the ground, clinking and skidding away.

"What was that? What are you doing?" Charlie was becoming agitated.

Ruus was at the end of his tether. He'd had enough of money, of Romans and of being a detective. He'd particularly had enough of Charlie and stood up ready to tell him what he really thought face to face.

"Will you just be quiet and leave me be. I'm sick and tired of hearing your voice giving out your stupid instructions. Be quiet or I'm going to... eh?"

"Ruus, will you please bloody well hurry up!"

"Caius, Sabia, where are you?"

"I've already told you, I'm outside. I need the key, now."

"How?"

"Don't worry about how; just get the key passed under this door and I'll get you out too."

Ruus hesitated no longer. His only problem being that as he'd chucked the key, it wasn't so easy to find in the dimness of the room. He got down on all fours and swept his hands back and forth in front of him. He found it eventually where it had slithered up against the side wall. He picked it up and was across to the door in a flash. The longish handle slipped easily beneath the door, and Charlie lifted and wriggled it till the short, bent end with the square hole popped out.

"Wait there. I'll have it open as quickly as I can."

"I'm hardly going anywhere, am I?" said Ruus, barely holding his temper, then recovering some composure, he said begrudgingly, "Sorry."

Charlie pushed the short end into the padlock's slot, lifted the handle and tried to engage the hole in the key over the springs inside. It wasn't working. What was wrong? Charlie pulled the key out and examined it. Of course, the bend was too shallow; it needed to be at right angles. It must have bent out of shape while he was wriggling it under the door. He held the handle vertically and banged the short end on the step.

The noise was small but metallic, and it echoed off the walls surrounding the *cella*. As Charlie banged it for a fourth time, he managed to get it much squarer, and he went back to the lock, inserted the key and lifted the handle once more. He felt it slide over the springs and grate to a stop. Now all he needed to do was push hard, and the sprung, arrow-shaped bolt could be pulled out and the lock would be open.

"They're escaping!"

A shout from across the other side of the *temenos* bounced off the *cella* wall and rang in Charlie's ears. The priest was rushing towards him while, at a distance behind, Orcus the steamroller bowled in the temple's direction. Charlie pulled the bolt free; the other half of the lock fell to the ground. He pushed hard against the door and it started to swing inwards. The priest was nearly on him at the top of the steps. Charlie pushed himself in through the opening.

"Quick," yelled Charlie. "Close it; they're here."

As he shouted, an arm and shoulder pushed its way into the gap that still hadn't been closed. Orcus arrived and added his considerable weight, and the gap became wider. The priest's head was almost through now. It was only a matter of seconds before they would be at the men's mercy.

"Use the bolt," puffed Ruus, trying unsuccessfully to stop the gap widening.

Charlie understood without further prompting. He raised the sharp arrow-spring bolt and stabbed the priest as hard as he could on his shoulder. There was a shrieking scream, and the priest's head, shoulder and arm were gone. The two boys slammed their bodies against the back of the door and sat braced against the next attempt.

Outside, another shout rang out. Arrayed in and across the entrance and moving swiftly to cover the walls inside the *temenos* were eighty armoured *miles* of the third century. In front of them was their *centurion* with his crested helmet, and at the bottom of the steps stood *Publicanus* Lucius and beside him Drusus.

CHAPTER LIII

Orcus spoke, "Great timing, sir. We've trapped two filthy criminals inside."

He grabbed the priest and threw him down the steps.

"I've been watching this one a long time too, sir; that's where our money's gone."

Lucius beckoned to Drusus beside him, who withdrew a small piece of lead from a *bursa* and started to unfold it.

"That's not mine, sir. That's a fake."

"I wonder why on earth you would think it *was* yours or even recognise it unless *you* wrote it."

Drusus held out the *defixio*, its words clearly condemning Orcus.

"Drusus wrote it, sir; he was blackmailing me. He wanted me to give him money or he'd show it to you. He came to me with it, sir. He's a criminal, sir; a lousy, criminal thief."

"Now that's interesting because you see Drusus has been working for me. He is a trusted agent of the emperor himself. It was I who sent for him and asked him to watch you and all that you got up to. I needed evidence and I got it. I also found out about your 'friends', your partners in crime. The children helped me with that. You are the liar and thief. You are a loathsome creature, Orcus, and you will be flogged.

If you survive, which I doubt, you will be bound to slavery for the rest of your days as determined by Roman law."

Orcus slumped to his knees, but the priest had recovered sufficiently from his fall to be able to speak, "He wrote it, my lord. Orcus wrote it. Spare me. He made me help him. I had no choice."

The priest's voice shook as he realised that he would be on the receiving end of the same fate.

"Enough."

Lucius beckoned once more, and out from the back, Saima and Metallus were brought forward. Drusus marched up the steps flanked by soldiers who took Orcus and clamped his hands in iron manacles.

"Come out, you pair of *stulti*, you're safe now," he bellowed.

Two faces showed at the crack of the door, and as it widened, Ruus stepped out warily and then came Charlie holding Janus's head under his arm. Below them, they saw the soldiers and Lucius, but most of all they saw Saima and Metallus. They rushed down the steps, and the three children were enfolded in Metallus's arms. He hugged them tight. Lucius's face creased into a smile.

"Brave warriors all. We should be grateful to them for their service to the emperor and Rome."

The *centurion* raised his gladius, and the soldiers gave one huge resounding cheer.

"*Ave, Senatus, Populusque Romanus!*"

Lucius ushered the four to the side. "I am sure that the Senate and the People of Rome would wish to salute and thank you," then without pause, "*Centurion*, scour the temple and be sure not to mislay any of the contents."

There was a rapid command and bustle as the soldiers carried out their orders.

Lucius spoke one last time to the children and Metallus. He was brief and with true regard and pride in their work, he said, "Go home. Your work is well done."

Drusus came forward and clapped his hand onto Charlie's shoulder. "Got your souvenir, have you?"

Charlie stiffened. Here he was in trouble again. He took out the head from under his arm and offered it to Drusus.

"What do I want with that? You did a good job; keep it. Whoever made it obviously hadn't a clue about proper casting. Perhaps Metallus can make a decent new one for us."

He nodded in the smith's direction and then went off back to the fort, following Lucius and the remaining soldiers with the priest and Orcus in tow.

CHAPTER LIV

Metallus, Ruus, Saima and Charlie walked slowly together out of the *temenos*. They crossed the worn grass that led back to the bridge over the spring.

Saima pulled Charlie's tunic and said, "We can't go on. We have to go back, return home."

Charlie knew it and had to agree.

"I guess she's right," he said to both Metallus and Ruus. "There's never a right time to say goodbye, but I'm afraid that time has come."

"Can't you stay a little while; go tomorrow or perhaps in a couple of days," Ruus tried to persuade them.

"Your kindness will always stay with us. I think you'll always be in our thoughts."

Saima winked. "That's the most sense I've ever heard you utter, Caius."

"I'll never forget you either, but what about your share? You know the silver *denarii*."

"We can't take it. It's hard to explain, but there's an opening, a kind of door if you like that we found. Remember in the temple? You wondered how I got outside? Well, I had Janus's help, he helped me through the door, but he doesn't let everything pass through, just Sabia and me. Not keys, not money, just us two. Do you understand?"

"No, not really, but you saved our lives, and however you did it, we'll forever be in your debt. By the way, I picked this up; I suppose you can't take that either."

Ruus held out the mirror towards Saima and she sadly shook her head.

"Will you never come back?"

"We can't say never. Who knows? But we know this place, and perhaps one day we may do, in the future," said Saima with a little wink in Charlie's direction.

"Well in that case, I'll make sure you can find your share somehow should you ever decide to return."

He grasped Charlie's wrist in the now familiar handshake, then he kissed Saima lightly on the cheek and bowed his head to her as he stepped back. Metallus put a strong arm across Ruus's shoulders. Charlie and Saima watched them as they turned and walked up into the *vicus* for the last time.

The tears weren't hard to come by as they sat at the bottom of the ditch. Each had their own memories, and they were more than enough to trigger the response that trickled down through their fingers. Feet, legs, bodies, arms, necks, fingers and finally eyes stared at each other back in the library.

Mrs Vearn had just got to the museum door and called, "Just five minutes, you two, that's all, just five minutes."

No time had passed, and here they were with blank paper in front of them and pencil in hand. They didn't talk, just started to make their sketches; Saima, with her neat, careful strokes and Charlie drawing a cartoon head that bore little resemblance to the one between them on the table. It seems some things never changed. In all too short a time, Mrs Vearn appeared accompanied by Miss Dean, who leant over the desk, and with her gloved fingers, lifted Janus into her keeping.

"A fascinating object, don't you think?" she said to them. "I suspect that was quite an ordeal."

Mrs Vearn had to put in a word, "With respect, Miss Dean, I don't see that drawing a head can be much of an ordeal, but looking at Charlie's drawing, perhaps you're right."

Miss Dean held the children with her unblinking green eyes for a moment or two. A dark tunnel spun them round and down until she broke her gaze and they jerked, startled at the strange influence she had placed upon them.

"C'mon, you jumping pigeons, get into the museum. The class are going to thank Miss Dean for an exciting morning."

As the two children walked up the short corridor between the two rooms, Charlie hissed, "Blimey, exciting's not the word I'd have used."

CHAPTER LV

In the museum, the children sat on the hard parquet floor. Alfie was clutching his drawing of the bricks and tracing his finger around the wooden flooring blocks. His mind happily bound in the patterns he was creating. He started to use his fingernail, and soon little piles of dirt from between the blocks were piled up at their corners. He stopped suddenly when Miss Parton made her announcement.

"I'd just like to personally thank Miss Dean for this opportunity to see some of the museum's wonderful artefacts first hand and to be able to actually touch real history."

It was Saima sitting next to Charlie who did the whispering this time, "I've touched enough history to last me a lifetime."

"So," continued Miss Parton, "can you please all say a big thank you to Miss Dean for her kindness this morning?"

The whole class, acting as if they were back in Year 1 of the infants, bleated in unison, "Thank you, Miss Dean."

Alfie, however, had still been with his blocks and had only half heard and, as if by remote, called out, "Good morning, Miss Dean. Good morning, everyone," then smiled, pleased with himself. Most of the class burst out laughing.

"I think we'd best be off," said Miss Parton.

The class were chivvied into twos and, holding onto their drawings, clipboards and pencils, filed out of the building and made their short journey back to school in time for lunch.

Lunchtime play was usually the longest and therefore the best for having a match with a few others. Today, however, Charlie had no desire to play football or anything else for that matter. Mrs King, the midday assistant, noticed he was sitting by a sunny wall in the playground on his own.

"Hi, Charlie, no football for you today. You feeling okay?"

Charlie nodded, not really acknowledging her.

"Not like you to miss out on running around on the field. Alfie's out there, you know, wondering where you are."

He stared out across the field from where he sat and watched. There was the match, and nearby some children were doing handstands. Not far from them, some Year 3s were teaching each other dance moves and singing into pretend mics.

"Thanks, Miss, just don't feel like it today, that's all."

What he really wanted to do was try to understand what had been happening to him. He played scenes from the past few days over in his head. The worst of them always seemed to bubble back on top; Vitus's hair torn out with his own hand. The image wouldn't go away. He needed Saima, but she was doing monitor duty in the hall, helping clear the tables and scrape the plates into those disgusting plastic bins. What a privilege that was. Still, she was happy to do it, and unlike him, she was trusted.

He'd have been delighted to know that Saima wasn't exactly feeling top-notch either. She had scraped one plate and missed the bin completely. A midday assistant had to come and mop up the baked bean juice and mashed potato leftovers that dribbled down the side of the bin and had formed off-white islands in an orange sea on the floor. She was relieved of scraping duties and asked to collect up water cups instead. She finished that soon enough, then wandered to the end of the hall and pushed the double doors open. Alfie flew inside from the opposite direction and bumped into her. He'd grazed his knee and needed to go to the medical room.

"Watch out, you *stultus*!" she cried.

"Er... really sorry. I didn't mean it. I've got to get my knee fixed. What'd you call me?"

"Never mind," said Saima. "Go and get a plaster or something, just be more careful."

She waited a second or two longer, then her brush with Orcus kept replaying itself in her head. She left the building and, walking along a short tarmac path, turned left and faced the sun. It felt warm on her face. If only she could spend the afternoon soaking it up she might feel less weary. At the end of the building, she looked across the field, then glancing to her left saw Charlie propped against the wall. He looked as bad as she felt. She took herself over and plonked herself down beside him. He gave her a sidelong squint with a hand raised to shield his eyes, then turned back to look across the field as well.

The sun caught the river at the bottom of the slope; its ripples and runs shimmered. Further to the left, the temple ruins sat squat on their meadow and up the hill past that was the *vicus* and the forbidding fort – but nowadays nothing; hardly a sign. They had been told almost all of the stone had been robbed away and used in other buildings, perhaps even some of the older ones in the village itself.

"I'm lost."

Charlie said just two short words. Saima listened and nodded.

"Think I am too."

"Do you ever think we'll recover, you know, be ourselves again?"

"Not for a while, I suppose. Eventually we might make sense of it."

"Do you feel any pain? You know, where you were kicked."

"No, nothing. I noticed that had gone as soon as we got back. My hair's normal too. Remember where Faris hacked at it?"

"I just feel so empty, like my insides have been sucked out and I'm just a walking, talking shell, yet my memory of it all is so sharp."

A whistle blew a million miles away. Children filtered in, and they saw some kids arguing about a last-second goal that went in as the whistle blew. Alfie was collecting the ball which had hurtled past him. He was one of the last to come in, being hurried along by Mrs King.

"Come on, you two," she said, collecting Saima and Charlie into her little flock. "You're usually first in, Saima. What is up with you two today?"

Through the doors across the hall, now scattered with yellow plastic signs saying CAUTION: Slippery Surface, where the hall had been mopped, and the yoghurt ponds and baked bean boats had been wiped away. Another set of doors and a swift right turn brought them into their classroom. Miss Parton sat in her comfy chair in the window corner. The children sat at their desks of six. Register over and sent on its way to the office, Miss Parton explained that this afternoon she had drawn and photocopied a template of a Roman temple to colour, cut and stick as this would be part of their class's 'Our Village' display. The *cella* and its roof and the altar stone block were to be made from cardboard cuboid nets, and the roof was a folded rectangle, but that was it. These pieces were to be stuck onto a larger square of card. The class were relieved that the usual literacy and numeracy sessions had been cut from the timetable for today. The whole afternoon was to be spent with old friends; PVA glue, a pair of round-ended scissors and a plastic spatula. The class loved the latter because often the glue had dried hard on their one, and it was a kind of joy picking it off like an old scab.

All the class set to using the recently sharpened pencil crayons and chattering quietly, except that is for Charlie. The temple was wrong. Why couldn't they see that? Where were the steps, the columns, the *ambulatory*? So instead of colouring, Charlie started drawing on the part of the card that had been set aside for the base, twelve columns and the other parts that would make it right. Mrs Vearn sat and helped her usual group, and Miss Parton, as she always did, sat at another table and made one of her own so that the children could see her construct it, but really it was for a bit of her own light afternoon relief. The time dwindled on, sounds of infant play from the playground filtered through the open windows and inside requests for more glue had Mrs Vearn out of her seat pouring small amounts into green milk bottle lids that served as glue pots. Some of the colours being used on Mrs Vearn's table weren't exactly accurate, nor was the sticking, but by five past three everyone in the room seemed to have finished.

"Alright now, can you all put your spatulas and glue lids on the trays? Table monitors, please put them by the sink."

Miss Parton gave other instructions regarding collection of scissors and scrap card then said, "If you could leave your temples in front of you on the desk and stand up, we'll all go round to each table in turn to look at each other's work."

The chairs scraped as they were first pushed back and then shoved under. Each desk was instructed to move in rotation to look at the next. Off the children went and polite oohing and ahhing arose until suddenly, "Oh wow! A-ma-zing. That's cool!"

A press of pupils crammed together while others from tables further away grabbed chairs to stand on so that they could see what the fuss was about. Miss Parton was almost overwhelmed and needed Mrs Vearn's help to restore some order. The children parted before her and allowed her to come to the table. There, in front of Charlie's chair, sat his temple. It shone out against the others. Its card still in pristine condition, uncrayoned but beautifully constructed in the way that he had seen it in real life. Nina Parton could only stand and gaze agog at what lay before her.

"Whose is this?" she uttered, gathering herself back together.

"Mine, Miss," said Charlie, sheepishly raising his hand, standing at the far side of the desk.

"Well, Charlie, it is truly a work of art, a masterpiece. You'd better come and tell us all about it. Everyone, sit in your places and Charlie will bring his model to the front."

The class immediately did as they were told. Miss Parton stood beside Charlie, who was holding the temple in front of the class.

"It's a wonderful model, Charlie, but I'm not sure how or why you decided to change my design. Can you tell us about that?"

Charlie needed to think on his feet and could think of no answer. For once in his life, he was tongue-tied, but a knight in shining armour came to his rescue in the form of Saima.

"Please, Miss," she said, putting up her hand at the same time, "I think it's my fault."

This was unheard of; Saima being at fault for something was unknown.

"You see, Miss; when we were in the museum, drawing, I told Charlie all about my research into Roman life. I explained how I'd been researching on the internet last night, and I'd seen their temples and what they looked like. I didn't think he was listening, but he must have been. So I guess that's why he chose to make it as he did."

What a most wonderfully convincing lie. The most trusted pupil in the class giving an account of her extra homework and sharing it with someone who couldn't care less. Brilliant. Charlie could hardly believe his ears. Saima had lied for him, lied to save his skin. A little lie but such a big rescue.

"Well, all I can say is well done to both of you. I think your model will have pride of place in our exhibition, Charlie. Saima, perhaps you could write a little bit about the parts of the model for people to read."

The end of the day had arrived, and classes had been dismissed. Charlie began his walk home and was caught up by Alfie, and then surprisingly, Saima joined them.

Alfie was delighted, "You two are safe," he said as his stride bobbled between them.

"Thanks," they said together and smiled at each other, safe in more ways than Alfie could guess.

"See ya tomorrow," said Alfie. They split up and went their several ways home.

CHAPTER LVI

Although time had passed, Charlie and Saima's shared memories didn't fade. They talked about them less, but occasions arose when the two could be found just sat staring across at the 'mount' where the *vicus* and fort had once stood. It was nearing half-term, and on this last Friday playtime the sun was beating down. Charlie had been running up and down, chasing, tackling, shooting, defending and was quite exhausted even though there was ages to go. His first thought was of himself but then pondered if it was a kindness.

"Hey, Alfie," he gasped, gulping in bundles of warm air, "I'm knackered. I'll go in goal if you like; you come and play centre-forward."

Alfie couldn't believe his ears, "Really, you sure? Magic, thanks!"

It was like all his birthdays rolled into one. Charlie had never seen Alfie so excited. He was pretty sure he'd have loads of saves to make now Alfie was in the outfield. That would keep him in the game, and Alfie could enjoy his newly awarded freedom. It didn't work out that way, though. Alfie was like a boy possessed. He tackled hard and slipped into spaces for passes that he smashed through the opponent's goalposts. Charlie was gobsmacked. Who knew? Alfie was almost better than he was. He defended for all he was worth, too, and even with subtle skill diverted a defensive header into Charlie's arms.

"I'm going for a drink," he called and sped off across the grass towards the water fountain on the outside of the classroom wall. Charlie watched him go.

"We're going to have to find a new goalie. I reckon me and Alfie will tear any team apart," he bragged. "He'll be back in a mo', we'll have a rest, boys."

Alfie had reached the water fountain and there was a short queue. In front of him were two Year 6 boys. One pulled the handle down and placed his thumb over the spout so it squirted at his mate, who laughed and jumped sideways to avoid the spray. Unfortunately, the spray didn't miss Alfie; it splattered over his shirt and down his trousers.

"Ha! He's wet himself. You need to go to nursery and get some dry pants."

The boy at the fountain squirted at Alfie again.

"Here, drink this."

The two roared with laughter once more, that was until a football smashed the squirter flush on the side of the head and sent him crashing to the floor, clutching his red cheek and wailing loudly.

"Don't like it being done to you, do you? That'll teach you not to mess with my mate Alfie."

Alfie was stunned. Charlie had fired the football from barely ten yards away to defend him. Not only that, Charlie called him 'my mate'. First playing out of goal, and now he was apparently Charlie's mate. There was no doubt *he* liked Charlie, but up until now he didn't know what Charlie thought of him. He did now.

"Get inside, Charlie Hipkiss." Mrs Marsh was running across the playground, having been supervising some long rope skipping. "I saw you kick that ball. Get in and stand by the office. Your teacher will hear about this."

Charlie didn't even wait to explain. What was the point? Mrs Marsh wouldn't believe him anyway.

"Harry, take your friend to the medical room; he'll need a cold compress and a note to take home."

"Please, Miss…"

"Not now, Alfie. I've got enough on my hands dealing with a nasty injury."

She marched off in hot pursuit of the boy clutching his ever-reddening, tear-streaked cheek. The ball was returned to the game but Alfie had no wish to go back to it. It was Saima who found him roaming the edges of the playground on his own. It was his fallback. Before Charlie had asked him to be in goal for him a while ago, that's what he'd do most playtimes. Other kids would ignore him or give him a wide berth. He wasn't someone you went out of your way to play with, the offers never came. Saima joined him on his circuit.

"Not playing football?" she asked.

Alfie didn't lift his face. "Charlie's in trouble. I don't want to play anymore."

"What's he done?"

Alfie explained as best as he could. It was all a bit disjointed but Saima understood. The whistle went, and the children dripped through the doors back to their classrooms. Many were sweaty, and there was a huge queue at the fountain. Mrs Marsh, who had reappeared, was trying to prise them away with only a smidgeon of success. When Saima and Alfie arrived at the classroom, Miss Parton wasn't there. It was Mrs Vearn who had taken charge.

Saima had to make an excuse, "Excuse me, Mrs Vearn, I found a key on the playground. Can I quickly take it to the office?"

"I suppose so, but be quick, I need to start the lesson. Miss Parton has an incident to deal with."

Saima left the room and crossed the cool hall. She pressed a button beside the reception doors. She called it the 'airlock'. It was to stop visitors going through into the school without being invited or taken in. The door buzzed and she pushed it open. To her right was the reception desk and to her left some chairs upon which sat a boy clutching a damp, blue paper towel to his cheek. On another was Charlie with his teacher standing in front of him.

"Excuse me, Miss. I need to speak to you, please."

Miss Parton left the boys and went to her.

"Can we speak in private, Miss?"

"I'm just trying to find out what's gone on at playtime, Saima. Can't it wait?"

"Not really, Miss."

"Very well but quickly; you need to be back in class."

Saima explained how Charlie had been good to Alfie and that Alfie had been victimised by the two Year 6s. She explained that Charlie was too small to confront them and being Charlie had kicked the ball at them to help his friend.

"I see. That doesn't make what Charlie did right, but I can see he had a strong sense that these boys were bullying. That makes more sense now you've explained it. Charlie wouldn't say a word."

"I think sometimes when he tells the truth, some people don't believe him."

"If he didn't tell so many lies, perhaps we might. Thank you, Saima. Tell Mrs Vearn I'll be in class very soon."

A short while later, Charlie walked sullenly across the classroom followed by Miss Parton.

"I think we need to get started, don't we, Mrs Vearn?"

Mrs Vearn nodded and said, "Maths books are out, Miss Parton; dated and ready on a new clean page."

"Literacy and maths are the two subjects we must always try and fit in, what with SATs next year and end of year assessments," Nina Parton said to the class. "Let's see if we can attempt to learn a bit more about – symmetry. So, Mrs Vearn, if you could take your group and work on line symmetry? I'll work with the rest."

She handed Mrs Vearn some photocopies. Then using the smart screen started to explain 'order of rotational symmetry' to the others. She called several different children up and asked them to count how many times they could rotate a shape so that it fitted exactly on itself, and then she explained that the number of times is its 'order of symmetry'. She then gave out tracing paper and placed coordinates on the board.

"Use the coordinates to mark the corners of a shape. Join them up, then use your tracing paper to rotate the shape and find its 'order'."

Normal service had been resumed.

CHAPTER LVII

The lesson finished. Lunch was consumed. Lunchtime play came and went, and back they came to class. It was reading time, twenty minutes of heads down and look at a book. This wasn't as boring as it might have been. Nina Parton liked to introduce a bit of lightness so that reading was fun rather than a chore. Of course, there were those like Saima who would delve into her novel and thoroughly enjoy it, but that wasn't everyone's cup of tea. Miss Parton had introduced them to graphic novels, comics and football magazines, to name a few. These she hoped would promote enjoyment, and perhaps lead to a child picking up a chapter book and it seemed to work. Charlie wasn't a novel reader, but he liked anything mechanical, so she'd find him car magazines or instruction leaflets for garden or DIY tools. He loved them and would pour over them for the whole time. It was almost a shame when the sessions ended, and of course it allowed the class to cool and calm down before settling to afternoon lessons. This afternoon, however, Miss Parton asked them to tidy their trays for a fresh start after the half-term break. She'd had a system for this because every child ended up with the oddest assortment of things in their trays apart from their usual exercise books.

"Listen. Here are your instructions. Empty your trays carefully on the desk. Put all your exercise books back in your tray in size order, smallest on top. Put in your pencil, pen and ruler. Put in your reading book. You will be left with your papers' folder and other things that are yours. Sort the papers into subjects and put them neatly in your folder. Any you think you can throw, leave in a separate pile, and we'll come round and check."

This activity was always great fun because children would find treasures they had forgotten about buried at the bottom of their trays. They'd be reunited like long-lost friends, then placed back in their trays and forgotten about once more till the following end of term.

Alfie liked organising his papers best. He stacked his neatly in small piles and placed several pieces to one side that he deemed not worthy of his folder. Mrs Vearn was supervising his table, and it wasn't long till she was sifting the junk paper piles of the pupils in her charge.

"Don't you want this, Alfie?" she asked.

It was a picture he'd drawn of a museum brick.

"Nah, not really, Miss, it's not very good. I'm no good at drawing. I mean, what is that?"

He pointed to one of his pictures on the sheet.

"Well, I think I know what it's supposed to be, but the artist from the past did it in his style. It's not your fault, Alfie. Horses are difficult to carve on bricks. Anyway, if you're sure, then put it in the bin bag."

As the bag went round each table, it gradually filled with paper but also special treasures such as sycamore seeds, pieces of string, even a sticky window-crawler man covered in bits of fluff and the multitude of things that nine and ten-year-olds deem important for just a fleeting moment. Two children were then tasked with taking the bag out to the large bins at the front of the school near the boiler room. Trays were put away, and the half-term drew to an uneventful close.

It was on the way home that Alfie, who had again joined up with Charlie, saw the temple he'd made and was carrying home and asked about it.

"It was just Saima telling me what it was like while we were drawing that head."

"The head drawing Saima did was well good, but your one was a bit naff."

Sometimes Alfie hadn't quite got the idea of how to be tactful.

"What did you draw then?"

Charlie wanted to get away from discussing his drawing and the temple but was more polite.

"A brick. Not the one Miss showed us in class, another one."

Charlie let Alfie's words hang. He didn't want to invite more chat, and anyway, they were close to Alfie's road. He'd turn off any second.

"Oh nice," was all he added.

But Alfie just carried on regardless,

"Yeah, this one had a funny horse on it. I couldn't draw it properly, you know, the horse, but Mrs Vearn said that the artist would find it hard to carve a horse in brick, so if mine was a bit wonky it didn't matter."

Charlie stopped in his tracks. A horse on a brick at the temple. What for? The temple had nothing to do with horses.

"Alfie, tell me. What did it look like exactly?"

"Not like any horse I've ever seen, just a few lines."

Alfie lived in Poplar Close, which was across the road opposite the convenience store on Alder Close where Charlie lived. He was about to cross when Charlie hauled him back by his backpack.

"I want you to draw it for me and Saima. Look, her shop's just here. C'mon."

Alfie dithered, but seeing as he was Charlie's friend now and Charlie was his friend, he didn't want to ruin the new relationship so decided it best to go with him. They opened the door to the shop, and Mrs Noor was behind the counter.

"Hello, boys. In for more football stickers?"

"Not this time, Mrs Noor. We wondered if we could see Saima for a minute."

"No problem, she's upstairs. I'll call her and you can go up."

They found Saima waiting at the top of the stairs. Charlie left no time getting straight to the point.

"We need a pencil and some paper. Any old scrap will do."

"What's this all about?"

"Just wait and see. I'm not a hundred per cent sure myself but bear me out. Alfie is going to do a drawing."

Saima got some paper and pencil and the three gathered at the table. Alfie was told to sit, and the other two leaned over his shoulders.

"Right, draw," said Charlie.

"What?"

"The bloody horse, draw the horse!"

"Charlie, language," said Saima.

"Sorry," he said genuinely for once, "I think we might have a breakthrough."

Saima had no idea what Charlie meant but watched as Alfie made the few marks needed to draw the horse.

Saima held her breath then nearly exploded, "That's it. That's the horse."

"I know. Alfie drew it by copying a brick at the museum."

"But that means…"

"Exactly, Ruus has left us a clue, a message on the bricks."

Alfie hadn't finished drawing and was engaged in making more marks under the horse.

"Alfie, we've seen all we need to see, thanks."

Saima, however, was not so hasty. "Hold on, look what he's drawing now."

"It looks to me like a broken fence on a railway line," said Charlie.

"Well, that was on the other brick, which was with the horse brick. I told you, Charlie, didn't I?"

"It's got to be part of the clue then," said Saima.

"What clue?" said Alfie.

"A treasure clue," said Saima and Charlie, giving each other a major high-five. "Roman treasure."

CHAPTER LVIII

Saima and Charlie agreed to meet the following morning and invited Alfie to join them as it was he, after all, who had found the clues. What the clues meant, they would think on overnight, and then they could pool their ideas in the morning. Alfie couldn't believe his luck. It seemed that he was now making friends and he'd got two, and what's more, he'd been invited on a treasure hunt. He decided he liked half-terms if this is what they were going to be like in the future.

When they met outside Saima's shop the next morning, none of them had come up with an idea about the extra clue.

"It's just gone 10 o'clock, the museum will be open. We can go and look for ourselves. Perhaps when we see the bricks together, we'll work it out. Anyway, I've brought some paper and pencils so we can all have a go at drawing them," said Saima.

Off they walked down Hornbeam Lane, and where the road widened, they noticed two men unloading a lorry.

"What's that all about?" asked Alfie.

"Metal mesh fencing and concrete block feet. I expect they're starting to fence off the building site for the new houses."

Attached to one panel there was a large banner proclaiming,

LOOK WHAT THE WIND...

BLEWIN

and Co.

Another Development of Tomorrow's Houses, Today!

Saima had spoken with her dad when she got home that day after the temple and museum visit. He had explained about the choices he had, and he knew she would be upset, but he had to think of the welfare of the village, not have his own selfish view. That's why he had voted as he did. Saima sort of understood, and in her heart of hearts she realised he was right. It was just that she trusted him so deeply and he'd lied. Why wasn't everything ever straightforward? She could never stay angry with her father for long, but her disappointment was still there. All their library books were going to the large town five miles away and worse still, all those tiny bits of Wicton's history being swallowed up with a load of others in a large museum. Nobody'd know, see or care that this little village, her village, their village, had such an important past. A past she'd experienced first-hand.

CHAPTER LIX

They arrived at the doors and went through the library into the museum. A couple of people were looking at a case containing flint heads and stone axes. The children brushed past and found the case holding the marked bricks.

"That's the one," said Alfie.

"Yes, and the other one is there too. Let's get drawing."

Saima handed them paper and a pencil each from her bag and they started to draw.

"This is hopeless," said Charlie, trying to draw with the paper on his knee.

Alfie was just making holes in his paper as his sharp pencil poked through to his trousers and spiked his thigh. Saima was trying to draw with the paper on the floor, but even she was having problems. Her lines seemed to keep following the pattern of the wood grain rather than the one she intended.

"Nice to see some interest in old things."

The children jumped. Miss Dean, the soundless stalker, had crept up on them without notice.

"Having trouble? Go to a library table. I'll unlock the cabinet and bring the bricks. It'll be easier for you."

Saima stammered her thanks and they got up and went to the library.

"How did she know what we were drawing? Mine's barely recognisable."

"Charlie, there wasn't much else that we could have been drawing."

"I suppose so," he said but wasn't wholly convinced.

Miss Dean arrived promptly and laid the bricks on the table.

"Take as long as you like."

When she'd gone Charlie whispered, "Why's she being so nice? She's usually Miss Miseryguts."

"I expect she is happy that at least some people are interested in the museum and what it holds. She knows it won't be here much longer. It's so sad really."

Saima said no more but got down to drawing. Charlie looked across at Alfie and raised his eyebrows, which made Alfie break into a broad grin. Then they began to draw both bricks in earnest.

On the first brick was the rather crude carving of the horse. Although weathered and not a great piece of art, it couldn't have been clearer to Saima. This was the shape of the horse brooch on the stall that she couldn't afford. The other brick, however, made no sense at all.

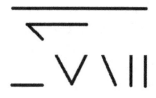

Saima stopped drawing and showed the boys her pictures. Charlie whistled through his teeth, then added, "Yep, that's definitely your horse; we're on the right track."

"The second I saw it, I knew. We've got to work this out. Have you guys finished?"

They nodded, so Saima stood up and picked up the bricks and started to walk back towards the museum. Isadora Dean met her halfway.

"Finished, dear," she said in a kindly fashion that unnerved Saima as she wasn't sure Miss Dean was that friendly and helpful, "I wonder what tales those bricks could tell?"

Saima thought for a moment and asked, "Where did you say they were found, Miss?"

"They were still in the temple wall, one above the other, but it was thought that they might become damaged or even stolen, so they were carefully extracted and donated to the museum to be looked after."

"But where exactly in the wall were they?"

"My goodness, how curious you are! Not a bad thing but most unusual in one so young. The horse, at least I assume it's a horse, was on the south-eastern corner of the temple. The other was directly underneath it."

"Thank you." Saima turned and started to walk away.

"Ahem!" Miss Dean made a coughing sound which pulled Saima up sharply. "The bricks, dear?"

Saima was still holding them. Her mind had not been focused on anything other than those strange symbols.

"Oh, sorry, I forgot," she said apologetically, coming back and tipping them gently into Miss Dean's cradling arms.

"Easily done with such absorbing objects."

She watched the children leave and then deposited the bricks back in their cabinet. The pair of adults who had been looking at the stone-age artefacts arrived at the brick cabinet.

"Ah," said one. "Excuse me, are these Roman? Where were they found?"

"Yes, they are," said Isadora. "They were found high up on the hill. We believe they were probably part of the ancient Roman fort walls to the north."

She lied a little. It wouldn't do for others to pry now. The couple looked back at the cabinet, and then a moment later the lady turned to ask another question, but Miss Isadora Dean had melted away.

CHAPTER LX

Saima explained what Miss Dean had said to her and suggested that they go and look where the bricks had come from. Perhaps that would help if they could look and imagine. They talked over the symbols, but none of the three could make sense of them, and eventually they arrived at the south-east corner of the temple. The river was low, so they were in little danger.

"That's moved," said Charlie, "it wasn't that close before."

"What's moved?"

"The river, it was at least two or perhaps three metres further away from the temple before."

Alfie laughed. "Great joke, Charlie, but it's not April Fool's Day."

"You're right," said Saima, "and in another two thousand years, this wall will have disappeared into the river if it keeps going."

"You two are mad."

"Just trust us," said Charlie.

"Yeah, right, okay; whatever you say." There was no chance of him trusting that kind of rubbish.

Saima told them once more about how the bricks were placed, "The horse was on top and the other brick below right on the corner."

The three friends took out their drawings and began to study the wall, but there were no clues as to what they meant. Saima put hers on the ground and held it down with a stone. Charlie thought he'd do the same, so he put his down and looked around to find one that would be suitable. This was not a clever move because a second after he laid it flat on the grass, a gust of wind blew it away. Alfie saw it fly off and, with a giant leap, placed his size five right foot on top of it. The problem was it had landed upside down on top of Saima's drawing, and Alfie's dewy-damp sole had squeezed them together. Saima was outraged; the drawings were ruined.

Then he shouted out, "I've got it!"

"Thanks, Alfie," said Charlie, not taking much notice of the wetness on the bottom of their drawings.

"No, you don't understand. I've got it."

"Yes," said Saima, "and a right mess you've made of it."

"Not that, this. Look!"

The paper was rather thin and not of the greatest quality. Alfie could see through Charlie's paper and make out Saima's underneath. He picked up both pieces and held them up to the sunlight. He shuffled them slightly and urged them to look. This is what he saw.

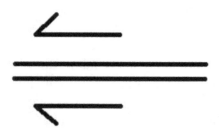

"It's like in class. That's a line of symmetry. Look, it's an arrow."

"Nearly," said Charlie. "Bring them closer together."

Sure enough, when they were matched as close as possible, the arrow was clear as day.

"So the line is a mirror," said Saima. "Oh Charlie, Ruus used the mirror from our temple plan. You know, what the lady sold us at her stall."

"Where would the arrow brick point to?"

"South-east across the river." Saima pointed, and they looked out over the water meadow beyond.

Alfie, meanwhile, hadn't taken any notice of their chat. He was far more interested in seeing if the other symbols meant anything. He hadn't got a mirror but decided he could draw the opposite halves.

"I don't think it can be symmetry," said Alfie, "I've just drawn the same halves, and it makes no sense."

"Hold on. Where did you put the mirror?" asked Saima turning to him.

"Above like before."

"OK, Alfie, if that doesn't make sense," said Saima, "try reflecting below the symbols; see what that does."

Alfie drew the symbols again.

"Eureka, Alfie. Eureka!" said Charlie.

"Is he saying I smell?"

"No, of course not; it means you've done it. You've found it. You've broken the code!" said Saima excitedly.

"Have I? Great. What's that all mean then?"

"They're Roman numbers, at least some are. X is ten and the C that's backwards for some reason; that's a hundred then two ones."

"Oh yeah, I see it now."

"So," said Charlie, "if you add them together, that makes?"

Charlie did a quick calculation. "One hundred and twelve."

"Not quite," said Alfie. "The X comes before the C, so that's ninety and two, which makes ninety-two."

"Clever. Do you think the *denarii* are ninety-two steps south-east?"

"Might be, but I'm worried about the first number and that backwards C. I think we're close, but not quite right. We need a mirror," said Saima. "And we're going to need a spade to dig, I reckon."

"We've got one in our shed," said Alfie.

"Right, it's nearly lunchtime. Let's go home, have lunch and meet back here with Alfie and his spade, and someone get a mirror. Let's say meet here at 2 o'clock."

All said and done, they agreed and scooted off home to find what they needed for further investigations that afternoon. All three wolfed down their lunch and arrived back at the temple within five minutes of each other at ten to two. Saima had redrawn her copy of the symbols and it was much cleaner, apart from the smudge of chutney from her sandwich on one corner. Alfie not only had the spade, but he had also brought a flat, plastic school mirror. Saima was horrified,

"How come you've got school property?" she asked as though it was a personal insult that he'd got it.

"Just forgot it from my maths homework, that's all," he said, feeling rather ashamed.

"Never mind where it's come from. Well done, Alfie, I couldn't find one. Did you, Saima?"

"Actually, no. My mum's is too precious and mine is attached to my dressing table."

"There you go then. Get started, Alfie. What can you make of those symbols we can't work out?"

Alfie tried the mirror vertically to left and right on the first symbol with the single line but no joy, so he moved to the second one and did the same thing.

"Yessssss," he hissed happily. "Got it. I'm smelly," he chuckled.

"Eu-reek-a, it's a V," said Charlie.

"So it's not a backward C," said Saima. "That makes a difference. So now we've got – XVII – that's seventeen. What about that first one, though?"

After several more unsuccessful attempts by Saima and Charlie, who each had a go, Alfie said, "I know, I'll move it bit by bit around in a circle and see what that does."

As he moved the mirror and they all watched, it slowly became obvious what the letter was. When the mirror reached a diagonal of forty-five degrees, there it was as plain as a pikestaff – the letter L.

"L is fifty but with X after it that makes sixty, and another seven is sixty-seven," announced Alfie.

"So, we need to walk sixty-seven paces south-east, 'cos that's the corner where the arrow was, but we've got a problem, Houston," said Charlie in an American accent.

"What is he talking about now?"

"Ignore him, Alfie. He's doing his Apollo 13 impression."

"The river is the problem," said Charlie. "We can't walk through that and count our steps, can we?"

"Simple," said Saima. "Count the steps from the wall to the river, then we count them crossing the bridge and add those on. Then we start again from the other side opposite the temple."

The plan was a good one, and the river was only three of their steps from the corner. They crossed over the bridge and then walked along the bank to the spot they reckoned was on the right track.

"Right, we've taken sixteen so far, so fifty-one to go."

They counted together as they went, like soldiers marching in time as they called out their numbers. Fifty... Fifty-one. This was it, the place, sixty-seven steps from the temple in line with the arrow.

"Well, we're here. Let's get digging."

They'd stopped about a metre from the hedge next to Temple Street at the top edge of the water meadow. Charlie asked Alfie if he could be the digger, and Alfie was happy to give him the spade. It wasn't too big, and the ground being damp it wasn't hard to push the spade into.

"Does this remind you of anything, Saima?" said Charlie when he was about half a metre down.

She shivered and said, "Don't remind me."

Charlie dug another spade depth and looked at the other two. The hole was pretty deep, and he'd found nothing, not a trace.

"I don't think it's here. All this soil is all the same. I don't think anyone's ever dug here. We've got something wrong, but I just can't think what. Everything we've done and worked out makes sense. It should be here."

Charlie started to fill the hole in but ran out of energy, and it was left to Alfie to finish it off.

"Oh, Charlie," said Saima putting her hand to her mouth, "I think I know what's wrong, but I'm going to need to work it out."

"Can't you tell us?" said Alfie.

"Not until tomorrow. I need to do some research first. Let's meet tomorrow outside my shop at 9 o'clock and I'll tell you then."

CHAPTER LXI

Saima's idea required some calculations, and she could have used her phone's internet app to find the information she needed to do them, but she preferred to work this through carefully. She didn't want to waste everyone's time, and so after her dinner she went to her room and looked up Roman steps. That was hopeless. She found something about a walking trail in Wales. However wonderful that surely was, it had nothing to do with what she was after. She changed the words of her search – Roman paces. This was much more like it, but the *Wikipedia* page was extremely complicated with all sorts of names and dates. She looked further down the results, and under Roman pace on the *Britannica* site she found what she was looking for precisely. Romans counted their steps each time the same foot hit the ground. So they didn't count left then right as two steps; that was only one. A Roman *passus*, pace or step, was left – right – left. She noted the distance that a double step like that would be. The site said 1.48 metres.

"So, I must multiply 1.48 by 67 and that will tell us where to dig," she said out loud in triumph, although the rest of the family were in the lounge and wouldn't have heard her even if she'd shouted. She did the calculation and wrote it down ready for the morning.

That's where they'd gone wrong, and now she had found the answer.

She met the boys as arranged the next morning and, without saying a word, took them to the spot on the pavement near to where they had been digging just over the hedge in the water meadow.

"So, will you tell us now?" said Charlie, quite exasperated that Saima hadn't told them anything straight away.

Saima could be quite superior sometimes, and Charlie thought she loved the drama of being the only one to know stuff.

"We should have thought of it before," she began, "it's obvious when you stop and think."

Charlie had had enough, "OK, smarty-pants, tell us poor idiots who are stupid in your eyes, what the heck it is."

Saima realised she was longing it out and decided she'd better tell them.

"Well, Romans and therefore Ruus would have…"

She explained all the ins and outs, ups and downs of her searches and calculations, "…which means we should be looking at between ninety-nine and a hundred metres from that corner on the temple, not sixty-seven."

They looked at her and then at the spot they'd been digging before.

"How far then from where we were digging to get to the treasure?" said Charlie.

"Easy," said Alfie, keen to show his mathematic prowess. "Thirty-two or thirty-three more."

"Well, I reckon we're about two metres from the first hole, so thirty or so more should do it."

They started to count as they crossed the road and onto the far pavement, then stopped. In front of them was a metre wide strip of grass and beyond that towering to a height of three metres stood the museum garden wall. Sixteen paces they'd taken and one for the grass in front of them made seventeen.

"Here we go again," said Charlie. "Only thirteen steps to go and a bloody wall gets in our way, talk about unlucky or what?"

This time Saima didn't tell him off for swearing. She was as frustrated as he was.

"Come on," said Alfie. "We can walk through the library and museum and get to the garden that way."

"Not with a spade, we can't," said Saima.

"Yeah, and we can't just go digging a hole where everyone will be able to see us. It's hopeless. Unless…"

The other two looked at him, waiting. "… we can sneak back when it's dark, when no one's about."

"What if we get caught?" said Alfie.

"Where's your sense of adventure? Anyway, once we're over the wall, nobody will see us."

"I'm afraid I can't do it tonight or tomorrow," said Saima. "We've got relatives coming for my parents' anniversary celebrations. I'll never get away, and I can't sneak past their put-u-up bed in the lounge, can I?"

"It's OK. I can't make tonight either. We'll leave it till Wednesday and decide our plan then."

As they agreed that Wednesday was good for them all, they noticed a removal van was parked in the space in front of the library. A man was carrying a stack up onto the back of the lorry.

"Oh," said Saima, "they're clearing the books already. I hadn't realised it would be so soon."

"With planning permission granted, I don't suppose they want to waste any time, which means we must get digging as soon as we can," said Charlie.

CHAPTER LXII

The days seemed to drag by. Saima had to stay in and be respectfully polite to the guests and help in the kitchen. Alfie and Charlie took it in turns to go in goal using their jumpers for posts, then home for the inevitable lunch or dinner, TV and bed, and so the days went by.

Wednesday dawned, and as breakfast was rushed down, clouds scudded across the sun and put a chill in the air, which seemed most unseasonal. Charlie hoped this wasn't another bad omen. The three met on the corner of Alder Close and excitedly walked down Willow Street and turned into Hornbeam Lane. The sight that met their eyes made them gasp. The museum garden wall was just rubble. A digger was piling it up and scooping it into the back of a large tipper truck. Where the wall had been, there was now metal mesh fencing planted in concrete block feet. The tops had been joined by bolted, metal clasps. The smart, grassy lawn was trampled flat, and men with a lens on a yellow tripod were taking measurements standing in their tan, steel toe-capped boots. It looked to all three like a war film set. They sprinted forwards and pressed their faces against the wire mesh. Signs warning of building site dangers were spaced at intervals, and in-between were faces with hats in blue circles telling us that safety hats must be worn on site. Everywhere was a bustle. Looking at the windows of the museum, they could see empty cabinets and Miss Dean in a chair, looking more forlorn as each artefact passed her by on its journey out and away forever.

"This isn't so bad," said Charlie. "At least, some of the trampling and churning will have loosened the ground, and this fence will be easier to climb than the wall."

"We don't need to," said Alfie, beckoning them over to a part of the fence where the short end wall had been, "I can reach that clasp. If I borrow my dad's socket set, we can undo it and squeeze in."

"You are a genius," said Charlie.

The plan was laid, Saima would bring a torch. Alfie would bring the socket set and spade. Charlie... Charlie would bring himself.

"Rendezvous at zero hundred hours," he said.

"Eh?"

"We'll meet here at midnight," said Saima. "See you then."

CHAPTER LXIII

Temple Street had no streetlamps past the zebra crossing near the library. The road was dark, and the very few house lights that could be seen at this hour had no impact on breaking the blackness of the night. There was no moon, and even if there had been, sombre clouds shrouded the heavens. Charlie had no problem getting out of his house. His mum's bedroom door was closed, and she was doing her deep sleep, mutter and snore. Nothing was going to wake her till next morning. Saima's mum had gone to bed before the 10 o'clock news. It was her turn to open up the shop early next morning. Her dad watched *Newsnight*, and she wondered if he'd ever go to bed, but she needn't have worried. He was well asleep before she left at ten to twelve. She came out of the door, and she had almost closed it behind her when she remembered just in time to take a key. She crept back upstairs and avoided the one tread that always creaked when she stepped on it, grabbed the key from the hook on the landing and came down and out onto the street. Charlie was just in front of her. She ran to catch him up and they walked in silence together to the museum fence. Alfie wasn't there. Charlie checked his watch, which had luminous dots and hands. They waited.

"It's nearly ten past," he said. "Perhaps he's not coming."

"Wait a bit longer, give him a chance. He might have had a problem or something."

Another minute, then two more went by before around the corner of the fence popped Alfie, out of breath.

"Where have you been? We've been here ages," said Charlie in a harsh voice.

"Oh, yeah, I know, but I couldn't find dad's socket set and then when I did, I dropped the spade on our front path. It made an awful noise. I picked it up and pressed myself against the house wall. When I looked up, I could see the curtains moving, so it must have woken them up. Anyway, I waited till I thought it would be all clear. That's why I'm late."

"No problem," said Saima, giving Charlie a look that meant 'told you so'. "Well done, that was scary, I bet."

"It was, very."

"Hurry up then."

Charlie was impatient to get started. Alfie got out a ratchet handle and then reached up to try different sockets on the nut that held the clamp. Saima shone her torch to help the process. He soon found the right one and attached it to the ratchet. As he pushed the handle up, the nut suddenly came loose, and after a few more pushes he took off the socket and undid it by hand the rest of the way. He caught the clasp and placed it on the socket box lid so as not to lose it. Together, all three of them pushed on the mesh fence, and the concrete foot moved enough for the fence panels to come apart. The gap, though narrow, was enough for them to squeeze through into the garden. Saima came through last after handing the spade through to Charlie.

"Great job, Alfie," he said in a much happier tone now he was in. "Let's find where to start from."

They found the spot near where they'd stopped on the pavement but inside the garden.

"Okay, let's pace this out together side by side. Remember, we've got twelve or thirteen steps to go."

As they strode out what they thought were metres, they counted.

"Thirteen," they said in unison.

"Before we dig, Saima, shine your torch on the ground ahead, behind and around us in case we're slightly wrong."

Saima liked Charlie's idea; he was thinking clearly, not just rushing anymore.

"Look," she said. "There, a couple of paces ahead of us."

In the torchlight, the earth had a different colour. Even though diggers had driven over the ground, it was obvious. The torchlight shadow showed it more clearly than it would ever have been in daylight.

"That's where we'll dig."

"Can I do it?" said Alfie. "It is my spade, after all."

"Go for it," said Charlie. "Just don't dig too hard, we don't want to destroy anything."

Alfie began to dig. Spits of softened soil from the spade were placed to the side of the hole he dug. He was hardly down a ruler's length when he hit something hard. The spade refused to be pushed in past it.

"It's no good," said Alfie. "I don't think if I even went at it hard I'd be able to get past it. I think it's some sort of stone."

Saima got down on her knees and with a finger traced the object's outline.

"It's not a stone, it's made of stone, but it's square."

She rubbed her hand over its surface and handed her torch to Charlie, asking him to shine it so she could see. Her fingers scraped away the mud on top to reveal a square brick, like those at the temple, and on top had been carved three diagonal lines.

"Charlie, Alfie, I think we've found it."

"Why?" said Alfie.

"See those diagonal lines. Where have we seen those before?"

"My eyebrows!" shouted Charlie. "My *Adidas* eyebrows. Ruus has carved the brick to show us where to dig."

All three children knelt beside the hole and soon, with a bit of effort, had cleared around the brick and lifted it out. Saima's torch played on something dark lying directly below it. She wiped her finger on her sleeve and licked it; then she rubbed it over the small, black surface. Spots of azure blue reflected the light. She repeated her actions, and the object gleamed.

Charlie nearly fell in the hole with excitement. "It's your horse! Ruus bought your horse."

Saima eased it out gently. She held it up in the light, and where her fingers had rubbed, the silver shone through.

"I'm confused," said Alfie. "First we see your eyebrows on one brick, now Saima's holding a horse that was carved on another in the museum."

"I know this makes no sense, Alfie, but you have to believe us. We've seen that horse before. Saima's held it."

"You can't have. It was buried deep in the ground."

"Do you remember we told you there was Roman treasure? Well, this is a tiny part of it. I'll try to explain the story to you soon, but we need to dig just a little bit more."

Once more, the three got to work. It was only a matter of a few centimetres further that Alfie found the first coin. He rubbed it as Saima had done with her brooch, and it shone in the torchlight. Other coins emerged, but they had all stuck together. The deeper they went, the more they could see. They sat back on their heels and gave each other high-fives.

"We found it," said Saima. "We found the temple treasure."

It was strange, for although the batteries in her torch were now fading, the light near them hadn't seemed to become dimmer.

"Stay just where you are."

Torchlight swept across their faces and blinded them for an instant.

"Which one of you is Alfie Madely?"

Alfie raised his arm slowly in the air.

"Your father called us to say you were missing," said one of the policemen standing over them. "Your parents are beside themselves with worry."

"And may I ask," said the other, "who are your friends, and what are you doing in the middle of a building site at 1 o'clock in the morning?"

The excuse when it came seemed so ridiculous.

"We're treasure hunting," he said. Then he showed them the coin and pointed into the hole they'd dug.

"How on earth did you know about this? Don't answer that. You're trespassing on private property.

You're minors who should be at home in bed but have put yourselves in great danger. You've broken in, and what's more, you've stolen tools to do it. The list goes on and on."

"All noted down, Sarge. Think we best get them home to their parents and then inform the owner he needs to secure his site."

"There will be consequences, mark my words," warned the sergeant. "I'm quite sure that charges will be brought against you, all three."

It was nearly two in the morning before the policemen had delivered the children back to their homes and explained where they had been and what they had been doing to their parents. Saima's parents were in disbelief that their beautifully behaved daughter had acted so recklessly. Her father was appalled when he realised the whole village would know and that he, the chair of the council, had a daughter who had brought shame on the family by committing such a crime. Alfie's mum and dad were just pleased to have him home and laid all the blame on Charlie for leading their son astray.

Charlie's mum opened the door to their house and just said, "Oh, what's he been up to now? He's nearly as bad as his father was before he was caught thieving," she carried on. "What do they say? Like father, like son. Chip off the old block. Oh, Charlie. He's started his career early."

She'd have no doubt carried on, and the policemen were glad to make the excuse that they had to get back to file a report and that she would hear in due course what the outcome of the evening's events would be.

CHAPTER LXIV

It was Saturday morning. The post contained three identically written, official white envelopes dropped onto three doormats. The letters were opened. The usual titles, Dear this and that, dates etc. were at the top and then just a short note read:

As parent of_____ you are urgently requested to attend a meeting with Sergeant Mace of the local constabulary, Mr Blewin, Proprietor of Blewin and Co. Property Developers and myself at 8.30am on Monday 7th June.

It was signed by the Headmaster of Wicton Primary and Nursery School.

That weekend none of the three children was allowed outside their home, and on Monday morning, they were left by their parents in the playground as the parents themselves assembled for their meeting in the headmaster's office. A quarter of an hour later, the whistle went and all the children were herded inside and off to their classrooms. Registers were taken and sent to the office. Then Miss Parton spoke:

"I expect that you are all aware by now, as it has made the front page of our local paper, that three members of this class were involved in an incident last Wednesday night. We will not discuss it further. Today's assembly will be at 9.30 as there is a very serious

313

meeting being held at this moment. I want you to read silently for the next half an hour until then. Mrs Vearn will be helping me. You will get on by yourselves. No interruptions."

Charlie, Saima and Alfie felt as if they were about to be hung out to dry. When it came time to line up for assembly, they were placed at the front. As they entered the hall, there were three chairs near the front where they were instructed to sit. The usual teachers' chairs were down the sides, but some extra ones had also been placed behind a desk facing the children. Next to these were some more chairs upon which sat Saima's, Alfie's and Charlie's parents. Their faces were like stone. As each class sat down, there was usually a hubbub of whispering and shoving, but today there was absolute and complete silence. The double doors of the 'airlock' parted, and in came the head, the sergeant and Mr Blewin.

The sergeant and Mr Blewin sat down next to each other, and the headmaster remained standing. Charlie couldn't look at them. He feared the worst. Perhaps they'd be expelled or, worse, sent to prison. Then he reasoned that might not happen because of how old they were but something similar perhaps. He looked out over the faces that sat before him. Saima and Alfie were both looking down at their knees. Little kids stared up at the headmaster, and way back there were the large Year 6s on benches, a privilege Charlie would probably never see. Then he spied a face in the corner near the back. At first, he couldn't place it because of a strange, greenish light that seemed to come from the window nearby. It couldn't be, could it? He nudged Saima, who was next to him. She ignored him, but he did it harder and nodded in the direction of the corner.

"Is that the lady from the jewellery stall?" he said in a low whisper.

Saima peered over the heads, squinted, then looked again. "No. Be quiet. It's Miss Dean."

"What's she doing here?"

"Hush, we're in enough trouble."

The headmaster cleared his throat. "Good morning, children."

The usual response echoed around the walls, "Good morning, everybody."

"I have some special guests today, and we will hear them speak in a moment. I expect you have heard about a very serious and worrying incident this past week. I think you are all sensible enough to know that you should never be out in the dark without a parent being with you. It is a shame that three of our pupils here decided that was a good thing to do."

The headmaster looked across at the three children sitting to his far right.

"So, I have invited Sergeant Mace to speak with you about staying safe. Please listen carefully. His message is extremely important."

Charlie had expected Sergeant Mace to explain that they were going to be arrested and taken to the police station, but instead he gave a short talk on holding hands with your parents in crowded places and always walking with a friend, never on your own and especially never to leave your house at night unless you are with your parents. He sat down. The headmaster stood for a second time.

"My next guest is Mr Blewin. It is his company who will build the new houses on the site of the old museum and library. His company have also agreed to build two new classrooms for the extra pupils we are likely to receive."

Mr Blewin stood in his dark suit and shoes so shiny they reflected the lights in the ceiling. He spread an arm to his right.

"These three children put themselves in great danger. Building sites are dangerous places during the day, let alone at night. I never want to hear of anyone trying to play or even having a look inside a building site. Stay away. However..."

Mr Blewin paused and indicated for Miss Dean to come to the front.

"However," he continued, "it seems that these three may have been trespassing for a good reason. Let me say, right now, that trespassing is wrong and they should have got permission, but it seems they had solved a puzzle that nobody had understood or worked out before. They followed their instincts, they used their initiative, they were clever, bold and daring. Businesses up and down the country would cry out for just such qualities in the people they wish to employ. Why did they do it? What did they find on my land? Why is that important to me?

"They did it because they believed they'd discover treasure. They solved the riddle of the bricks. What do I build with? Yes, of course, bricks and mortar. That's why I think this is a great story. Did they find anything? Yes, they certainly did, silver coins, Roman coins it seems. They've been sent to be verified, and we believe this treasure is extremely valuable. These three will not be prosecuted. I wish to see such extraordinary work rewarded. Miss Dean, can you step forward, please? I have an important announcement to make."

Isadora Dean came forward and stood beside Mr Blewin.

"Firstly, I have spoken with Sergeant Mace, the parents and your headmaster, children. I have three special awards. Alfie Madely, come here, please."

Alfie got up and stepped over to Mr Blewin. He wasn't at all comfortable; he didn't like being on show.

"For your brilliant mathematical work, I award you this as a token of your excellence. Miss Dean, could you do the honours, please?"

She pinned the shiniest Roman *denarius* to Alfie's jumper. It had been specially adapted from the treasure and had a pin on its back.

"To Charlie Hipkiss for his daring and suggesting the search, I award this token for his bravery and initiative."

A similar, shiny *denarius* was pinned to Charlie's sweatshirt. Miss Dean looked him in the eye and winked surreptitiously. Charlie smiled and sat down.

"And finally, to Miss Saima Noor for her outstanding knowledge and research into Roman culture. Miss Dean, please."

This time, however, it was not a shiny *denarius* she received but instead a shiny, sinuous, silver horse set with the brightest *lapis lazuli* stones. As she went back to her place, the adults at the front all stood and began to clap. Soon the whole school and all the teachers and TAs were joining in. Charlie, Saima and Alfie stood too and were mightily embarrassed to find their parents all had tears streaming down their faces.

"I have one last thing to say."

Mr Blewin paused till the room was still once more.

"Headmaster, Miss Dean. You are pillars of this society, and I personally wish to recognise your years of dedication and hard work. You stand for all that makes a real community, and we at Blewin and Co. applaud you. I wish to give you a gift also."

He opened his jacket with its red silk lining and produced a folded piece of paper from an inside pocket.

"Before I bought that land, I had no idea it was so important historically or so important to the community. I build houses. It's what I do. But that hoard of coins is worth a mint of money. I don't need it, but I think you do. Here, from my pocket, are some extra plans to use the money from the sale of the hoard. We intend to build a state-of-the-art community library and museum attached to the school as soon as our plans are agreed. Miss Dean, I would consider it an honour if you would continue as librarian and curator. In gratitude to our intrepid trio of historical detectives, it will be called the Hipkiss, Noor and Madely Suite. That is, of course, if you are happy to agree, Headmaster."

The headmaster stood. He looked at his pupils before him, the proud parents, the beaming Sergeant Mace, the staff and the three children to his right and with a tear in his own eye said, "I couldn't agree more!"

The school erupted. Children stood and jumped up and down, teachers hugged, the police sergeant thought he'd dance a jig with Miss Dean, but a stern look somewhat put him off. Soon the classes were trooping back to their classrooms. The mums and dads hugged their treasure-hunting children and told them to be good, then laughed. Miss Nina Parton waited to gather them up and take them under her wing.

As they left the hall, Miss Parton asked Charlie how he knew that the bricks would mean there would be buried treasure. So Charlie started to explain.

"Well, Miss, you see me and Saima, we went back in time like, and when we got there we met this Roman kid called Ruus, and we found out that—"

Miss Parton sighed and cut him short, "Oh Charlie. Charlie Hipkiss. I really look forward to the day when, just for once, you tell me the truth."

GLOSSARY

abeamus	let's go
ambulatory	the walkway round the cella
amphora/amphorae	large earthenware jars for wine or oil
animum attendite	pay attention
aureus/aurei	gold coin/s worth twenty-five *denarii*
aurora	dawn, goddess of the dawn or the East
ave	hail (a greeting)
bactria	a country in central Asia
bursa	purse
calends	beginning of the Roman month
cella	the inner building of the temple
consiste	halt
contubernium	a group of eight soldiers who live together
defixio	a curse tablet
denarius/denarii	silver Roman coin/s
deus	god
eboracum	York
et	and
et cetera	(literally) and the rest; we say it as – et set rah; etc.
festinate	hurry up/quickly/make haste

fossa/fossae	ditch/ditches
gladius/gladii	Roman soldier's sword/s
gradum servate	keep in step
hoc nihil ad me attinet	this is nothing to do with me
Ianus	Roman God (NB. I was used in instead of J)
jambiya	a curved Middle Eastern dagger
lapis lazuli	a blue gemstone
lorica segmentata	Roman metal armour resembling overlapping scales
lugh	an ancient Celtic god
maximus	greatest
mercurius	Roman god of thieves and tricksters
miles	ordinary soldier
omnibus	by, with or for all or everybody/one
optio	second in command of a century (80 men)
Parthia	ancient Persia or Iran
pes/pedes	measurement of a Roman foot/feet
pilum/pila	Roman spear/s with a pyramid point
plebs	common people (plebeians)
populus/populusque	people (the *que* on the end means – and)
porta decumana	one of four gates in a Roman fort
praedandum	prey, something hunted
praetorian guard	a soldier serving in personal service to the Emperor

praetorium	headquarters and residence of the fort commander
procedite	forward march
Publicanus	chief tax collector
pugio	a military dagger
quaestorium	a strongroom
romani	of Rome
salve	hello, good day to you
scutum/scuta	shield/s
senators	senators, Roman politicians and leaders
stultus/stulti	idiot/s, fool/s, stupid
stylus	a pointed device for scratching messages on wax tablets
Taranis	Celtic god of thunder
tegula/tegulae	curved rectangular roof tile
temenos	area surrounding the temple *cella*
triclinium/triclinia	couch/es for reclining at a meal
venator	hunter
via principia	main road in a fort
via principalis	main road in a fort crossing the *via principia*
vicus	houses, shops and workplaces outside a fort
vitis	centurion's vine stick which shows his status
votive	offering when making a pledge, oath or prayer

ACKNOWLEDGEMENTS

The greatest thanks must go to my wife Pam who has supported me wholeheartedly throughout the process of writing Charlie's Truth. She has boosted my confidence when I found myself at a low ebb. Without her, *Charlie's Truth* could not have been written. She's been truly wonderful.

I also want to thank Margaret K. Johnson, a published author many times over. Her knowledge and enthusiasm gave me the tools and inspiration needed to write this, my first novel, in her online courses. I also salute my Norfolk Adult Learners Writing Group whose friendliness and encouragement for each other is a joy. In thanking all those who have helped in production, Jenny Warren, my editor, provided the tweaks so necessary and made such lovely comments and Brian Jones did a great job with several changes I needed to realise a super cover design. Finally, thanks to all at Grosvenor House Publishing and especially Melanie Bartle who guided me through the whole process with great dexterity and friendliness.

The lock mentioned is depicted in the *The Roman Era in Britain by John Ward*.

ABOUT ALISTAIR RAINEY

A retired primary teacher who plays golf and enjoys a bar or two of chocolate while watching rugby on telly. Moving to Norfolk with his wife Pam three years ago, he now often finds himself acting as her sous-gardener. He retains his Christmas cracker sense of humour and will sing Gilbert and Sullivan patter songs for a dog biscuit. Still a kid at heart, Charlie is most definitely a part of him.

CPSIA information can be obtained
at www.ICGtesting.com
Printed in the USA
LVHW111810090622
720834LV00001B/1

9 781803 810928